Dreams Do
Come True
Christopher
Andrew
Burton

Copyright © 2011 Christopher Andrew Burton
All rights reserved.

ISBN: 1463627440
ISBN-13: 9781463627447

This book is for my family.
A special thanks to my editor Natalee De Vrientt
Cover Design by Kathy Cook
And all of my friends that I bounced idea's off of
And to those that departed way too early
This is for you

OROHUNTER

FIFTH
PENTACLE
Of the
SUN

CHAPTER 1

"I think I've found him!" Carrie yelled, throwing open the door and bursting into the room.

The office that Carrie barged into belonged to Llewellyn Skopector, Carries boss, who was investigating some documents. Llewellyn glared up from the papers to study the young woman with long-straight brown hair standing before her. "It is customary for a person to knock before entering a department supervisor's office," Llewellyn scolded, shuffling the papers concealing the one in which she had been most interested.

"I'm sorry, miss," Carrie apologized. However, the excitement on her face betrayed her words. "...but I think I've found him," she repeated, not registering the hostility in her supervisor's voice.

"What makes you believe that after three years of fruitless attempts you have actually found him?" Llewellyn glared up at Carrie.

With the light of excitement dancing in her eyes Carrie, hastened to explain. "Well, miss, there has been some unusual magic coming from a small town in the United States that has no confirmation of any sorcerer or sorceress inhabiting there." Carrie shuffled the documents in her hand as if showing them to someone who was looking over her shoulder.

"Listen Carrie, I understand your obsession in finding Garrett and if I were you I would be just as diligent in my investigations." She shook her head, stood up and walked around her desk to confront the girl.

"You are a critical component of this office. Your research is valuable to the investigations of threats to our magical society. I cannot have you running off every time you discover some child is just developing their craft."

"My findings have not all been wild goose chases," Carrie retorted as if slapped. She then took a deep breath, realizing the good faith she had earned had vanished. "Just last week, we caught an enchantress due to my work," she protested putting her hands on her hips.

"Are you talking about Enchantress Tracy just out of Leper?" Llewellyn asked. Carrie cocked her head as she thought back to the small village in between the city of Leper, Belgium and the French border. Enchantress Tracy had been bewitching children to perform nefarious deeds throughout the village. Some of these children had incorporated magic into their acts, which had registered on Carrie's desk. She had been tracking unregistered magic hoping to track her partner who has been missing for three years.

"Y-yes miss," Carrie stuttered. The realization that it had not occurred just last week, dawned on her like a sledgehammer to the gut.

"Well, the capture of the Enchantress transpired over ten months ago," Llewellyn Skopector barked putting a hand that was supposed to be comforting on Carrie's shoulder, instead sent chills down her spine. "I know you are being vigilant in your search for your old partner. But, it may be time to move on. I mean, we cannot permit you to tramp around the world every time you get a feeling."

Llewellyn picked up a beat up manila folder that struggled to hold its contents. "Last week it was London which turned out to be a cat that had a peculiar magical ability."

Carrie noticed Llewellyn rolling her eyes as she gazed at the ceiling for an answer to an unasked question.

"The week before was the Ukraine and France where hexed dogs with the ability to speak turned out to be just a practical joke by boys in a neighboring village. Shall I go on?" Llewellyn had only browsed the first three papers in the folder, but Carrie got the point.

"I understand," Carrie answered, "but I will not stop until I have found out what actually happened to Garrett." Carrie defiantly thrust the report she held toward her boss.

"Fine, let me take a look," Llewellyn mumbled, taking the parchment. She walked back over to her desk and fell back into the chair. After looking over the report Llewellyn sighed, setting the paper down with the other clutter. "Okay, I will permit you to investigate this lead. However, when it turns out to be another bogus one I want you to go help the Canadian Charter of Sorcery. It seems numerous species of fish are in danger of extinction."

"Fish?" Carrie queried, knowing this was an assignment for a rookie Orohunter.

"Yes, it has been difficult selecting someone for this assignment, and if you are determined to go to the Americas, you had better have another destination ready." Llewellyn tried to smile but smiling was not a feature her face was used to.

"And what if it is him?" Carrie asked more like a statement than a question.

Llewellyn looked up, almost giggled, but this too was something that seemed to be unfamiliar to her. With a sigh she said, "Well then, you will need to find out why he has spent three years avoiding *you*." Carrie noted her supervisor stressing the word 'you' and could taste the annoyance in her sarcasm.

"You can take Sheba and Reginald with you," Llewellyn continued picking up the papers she had been studying earlier. "They have just returned from their summit in Germany and can help you sort out the fish. Hopefully, that will keep the Canadians off of my back. You are dismissed." Carrie looked at the skinny bat-faced woman, wanting to say something, but instead bit her lower lip turned around and left.

A tall lanky young man stood in front of an open locker. An attractive brunette stood next to him at her locker putting her coat away and closing the door. Carrie walked in with a grim look on her face.

"I was hoping to find you two." Carrie quickly told them of their new assignment.

"That old cow," Reginald insulted Llewellyn, closing the file on fish. Carrie told him and Sheba that they were to accompany her to America to search for Garrett. Reginald, the lanky young man, was sorcerer who had just been promoted to the level of Orohunter. He thought being a Hunter was going to be exciting, tracking down evil sorcerers and preventing their nefarious deeds. "I don't believe we're going to follow some two bit lead to nowhere."

"I know this is not the most glamorous assignment." Carrie began considering all the past failures in her attempt to find Garrett.

Sheba a senior Orohunter had been teamed with Reginald a rookie Orohunter because she was a very cunning investigator. Carrie, Sheba, Reginald and Garrett had attended the hunter academy together and became close friends while there. While Sheba had climbed the ranks nearly as fast as Garrett, Reginald had taken nearly twice as long.

"Reggie, will you please think of someone other than yourself for once," Sheba chastised taking hold of Carrie's hand. "Reggie and I will be pleased to help you in your search for Garrett. Wouldn't we Reggie?"

"Oh Yeah," he said looking down at his feet. "You know Garrett was the reason I wanted to be a Hunter. What happened to him—well, it's not right and I would… well, when do we leave?"

Carrie smiled as Sheba gave her a hug and whispered, "This time we will find him. I know it." Carrie nodded fighting the fit of tears that were trying to escape.

"Well, when are we going to do this?" Reginald asked again.

"Right away," Carrie answered, pulling away and wiping a hand across her puffy eyes. "I think if we materialize just in front of the house in…" She paused as she searched for the proper word. "…well, you know what I mean." They nodded and with a sound like glass shattering they vanished.

A loud crack from outside, made Carl Alexander jump and he set his Michigan Indian tribes text book on the table and rush to the window. He peered out not seeing anything that may have caused the racket. His first thought was that there must have been a car accident in front of the house, but when he looked out the window there were no cars in sight. Pretty boring life he thought turning his attention back to the Huron tribes of Michigan. Friday night and the most exciting thing to happen to him was what sounded like a car crash in front of his house. A shiver crept over him as someone began knocking on his front door.

Carl opened the door without hesitating to peek through the peep hole to see who was outside. Carrie, Sheba and Reginald stood gaping at the soul poised before them. Carrie felt a lump swell in her throat preventing her from speaking. It felt like someone was pushing against the back of her knees as she recognized the welcoming eyes that opened the door. She remained there with her mouth gaping open trying to say something but the words would not form.

"Can I help you?" Carl asked peering at the three strangers on his stoop gawking back at him. He first noticed an attractive girl in her late teens or early twenties looking at him. She had curly brown hair and a deep tan as if she had spent every day smothered in tanning lotion at a tanning spa or camped out at a beach. She wore faded blue jeans and a blue t-shirt. Her mouth hung open as if playing a game of freeze tag.

Next to the girl with curly brown hair, stood a young man appearing to be about the same age as Carl. He had spiky blond hair highlighted with tints of brown. He squinted as if he had forgotten his glasses. Carl thought the young man would be more comfortable in a Hollywood scene instead of being perched on his door step in the middle of Michigan.

The other young woman was very attractive with long straight brown hair defining her lightly tanned face. Her mouth hung open as if she had knocked on the door of her favorite movie star. She appeared surprised to see him. Carl noticed the perfection of her pink lipstick that appeared to be painted on. Her brown eyes sparkled, as they seemed to be welling with the weight of water.

"Really ... is there something I can do for you?" he pleaded again, wanting to return to his studies.

"Blimey, it's him!" the man exclaimed now smiling. It was as if Carl's speaking had woken the young man from a trance. He stared at Carl as if he were a five year old looking at Santa Claus for the first time.

"Told you so didn't I?" the woman with curly hair said in a matter of fact tone. "I knew Carrie would find him."

"Can I help you?" Carl demanded again, wondering who these people were and what they were rambling about.

"Don't you recognize us?" the pretty woman the curly haired woman called Carrie asked as a lone tear escaped and began its lonely race down her cheek. There was something in her voice that made Carl do a double take like a dog hearing a strange noise for the first time.

"I'm sorry, I can't say that I do," he answered, feeling his stomach protest with a quick flutter as he gazed uncertainly into her eyes. Another tear stole away chasing after the first in a torrid pace. An uncomfortable feeling pulsed through him, hating to see her grief. "Are you all right?"

Silent tears began to spill. He had obviously upset her, but could not understand how such a simple question could cause that kind of reaction. Carl had a sinking feeling seize hold of his belly as he watched the young man put a hand on her shoulder. The girl pulled away from his touch determined to beat back the tears, brushing them away with the back of her hand.

"It's alright Carrie; we couldn't expect him to remember us," the other girl said as she stepped forward assuming the conversation. "Let me see if I can clear things up. Now Garrett..."

"Sorry, but my name is Carl, not Garrett," he corrected as the man took the other girl a couple steps away from the door. "You must have the wrong house." With that said, Carl began to close the door. The bushy haired girl whispered something and the door stopped. Carl fought to shut it, but the door would not budge.

"I know this sounds strange and I don't know how to begin." She licked her lips as she searched for away to continue.

"Why don't you start by telling me who you are and what you want?" Carl suggested.

"Oh sorry about that, my name is Sheba and these are my friends Reginald and Carrie." She paused looking back at her friends as she introduced them. "There is no easy way to tell you this so I guess I'll just come out and say it. You are not who you think you are. You are actually Garrett Montgomery and we've been searching for you for three years." Carl looked at her as if she were speaking a foreign language until he realized they were waiting for his response.

"Right!" Carl gave a half hearted laugh and slammed the door shut, amazed it moved. He shook his head and began to turn when the door shot open. Sheba stood with a polished piece of wood in her hand. She looked angry for a moment but took a deep breath as a wave of calm swept through her. The other two peered up waiting eagerly to see what would happen next.

"The polite thing to do would have been to invite us in," she suggested in a quintessential tone that gave Carl an uneasy feeling. "So let us assume you have invited us in so we can conduct our business in a more private manner."

Carl backed away as they entered, closing the door behind them. The change of scenery seemed to cheer Carrie up. "This isn't what I had imagined; your place to look like..." She said surveying the interior of the house. The first thing that caught her eye was the plush carpet which looked something like a mossy swamp. The walls were covered with maps of the world as a typical house would have photographs of family members. It was like he was searching for something. "I don't see Belgium... umm..." In one corner of the living room, a desk waited with a computer and the book he had been reading before his guests' arrival.

There was a light brown leather sofa in the center of the room facing a large screen television. Next to it rested a reclining chair that Carl used as a shield, distancing himself from the three strangers. Carrie and Reginald remained a step behind Sheba forming a triangle on the other side of the tan recliner.

"There's more that we need to explain," Sheba began, pausing to lick her lips. "You are not going to believe this either. We just ask that you keep an open mind at the possibilities and permit us to prove ourselves to you," she smiled. Sheba could barely believe the circumstances herself. "I don't understand totally how this happened. But, you are not what you think you are. You are or were at one time a sorcerer."

Carl laughed snatching hold of the back of the recliner. "Who put you up to this?" He kept examining Sheba and the others expecting them to break into a fit of laughter.

"No one," Reginald answered looking as confused as Carl.

"Okay, if I am sorcerer where's my broom stick?"

"What do you need a broom for?" Sheba asked looking at the ugly carpet.

"Don't sorcerers travel by flying brooms?" Carl joked.

The three guests began to laugh. "Hardly anyone travels by broomstick anymore," Carrie quickly interjected.

"There are only a few magical clans that still use broomsticks as transportation," Sheba added.

Carl shook his head looking to the door wondering if he could make it there. He gave a sarcastic laugh, thinking about being chased out of his own home by three strangers. He wondered what his neighbors would say, seeing him flee from his home. Would they call the police? Probably not, he didn't know their names and they didn't know his. Nobody seemed to know their neighbors anymore except in small towns.

Carrie put her hand on Carl's forearm. He had not even noticed her approaching him. Her touch sent goose bumps racing up his spine as if an icy firework had gone off inside him. He wondered if she suspected he was thinking about making a run.

"It's like what the Rubes would call the Onlist," Sheba said breaking Carl from the trance. 'What was she talking about Rubes and Onlist?' he wondered. "You know that Rube religious group that doesn't use electricity or any modern inventions."

Carl shook his head squeezing his eyes shut trying to figure out what she was talking about. He opened them, hoping they were gone but was disappointed to see them staring back at him. "Do you mean the Amish?"

"Oh yes, that's it," Sheba said as if she had not mispronounced the name. "Those silly people still choose to travel by horse and buggy while the automobile has been around for over a hundred years. It's the same thing in our culture with broomsticks."

"There are foolish magical societies that still travel by brooms, brew potion in cauldrons and believe in tarot cards," Carrie explained.

"Hey, I use tarot cards," Reginald objected.

"Exactly," Sheba added, giving him a stern look.

"I don't know what the lot of you are playing at but I have more studying to do before bed," Garrett interrupted with a snort. He wondered if they were on some type of drug. They might be dangerous.

"Why did you say that?" Carrie questioned beginning to take charge of the conversation.

"Say what?" Reginald asked still pondering his tarot cards.

"Say what are you playing at," Sheba explained. "It's not a normal American saying now is it?"

"It's just one of the things I say," Carl explained feeling like he was on the other side of reality. He felt the stares of the three strangers as if they were trying to read him from the inside out. "You know, just one of my figures of speech I picked up."

"I see," Carrie said as Sheba and Reginald sat down on the couch. "Garrett said that all the time," she said as if it were not important.

"I bet millions of people say it all the time, so maybe one of them is your Garrett. My name is Carl," he said in a determined tone.

"This is not getting us anywhere," Reginald said leaning forward. "... and I'm hungry."

"When aren't you hungry?" Sheba barked sarcastically shaking her head.

"I don't know what I'm thinking but let me see what I've got to eat." Carl offered thinking he would later regret the invitation.

"I'll give you a hand," Carrie offered, following him into the kitchen. She looked around impressed with the tidiness of the room. She marveled at how organized the place was; again getting the feeling it was not a guy's place but a girl's. "You don't believe in magic do you?"

He opened the refrigerator looking over his shoulder, pausing to take in her beauty. A part of him desperately wanted to believe anything she told him. "There are a lot of things out there in the world that people can't explain. I don't know if that's magic or what but there's something," he said trying to keep it logical.

"What do you mean?"

He sounded like an idiot, he thought. He wanted to come off being deep but felt more the fool instead. Why is it when he talked to a pretty girl he kept stepping on his tongue? "I don't know," he stammered stalling for time hoping something clever would come to mind but clever would not come for five minutes after the conversation was over. All he had now was the truth and that scared him. Her voice made his stomach feel light. "There are things that some people can do that are hard to explain. Some would call it magic others would call it something else."

"What would you call it?" She knew she was flustering him and he sensed she seemed to be enjoying it.

"I don't know what I'd call it. What would you call it when you can make a child laugh with a simple look or gesture?" Why was she drilling him with all these questions? It was like she knew how uncomfortable he felt being alone with her.

"Well, what would you call this?" She waved her wand, mumbling something he did not hear, then there was a little crack and a platter of lunch meat appeared on the kitchen table.

"How... How ... how did you do that?" he stuttered studying the platter on the table without daring to move his arms, standing as if paralyzed.

"It's just a little mysterious thing that we call magic," she gloated while prancing around him.

"What is that thing?" he asked looking at the thing in her hand.

"Oh, this is my wand," she said matter-of-factly. "Come on, you've seen enough movies and cartoons to know what they are."

"I thought they were out dated."

"That's broomsticks." She smiled. "We still have not been able to accomplish difficult spells without the help of a good wand."

"How do they work?"

"A simple thing I call magic." She flicked her wrist, mumbling something else he could not make out. There was another little crack and a tray of cheese appeared next to the meat.

Again Carl shook his head trying to wrap his brain around what he was seeing. He began wondering if he was losing his mind. Perhaps these people were not really here and he was just having a hallucination. He felt his forehead but it was not warm. He took a deep breath clinching his teeth trying to think of a logical explanation to what had just happened. His eyes bulged out and he felt as if he were beginning to hyperventilate. He closed his eyes trying to shake the eerie feeling that invaded his spine. He felt like he just woke up realizing he was in a movie or cartoon.

"What about something to drink?" he asked not knowing what else to say or do.

She smiled at him waving her wand. Carrie said something making a pitcher of lemonade appear beside the two trays. "How's that?" she asked, folding her arms across her chest.

"I'll get some glasses," he relented, fetching the glassware. He put four glasses on the tray next to the lemonade and prepared to take them into the next room. Carrie carried the tray of meat in front of him. He half expected to find it floating by itself in front of her but she carried it like a normal person. Again he shook his head wondering what a normal person actually was.

"Cold cuts?" Reginald cried out as Carrie return with the food. "Come on Carrie, you're almost as good of a cook as me mom."

"Reginald Xavier Dean, how dare you complain about food," Sheba barked at him, giving him a little slap on the shoulder.

"What did I say?" he protested.

Carl did not wait around to listen to the debate, heading back into the kitchen for the platter of cheese. When he returned, he placed the platter down on the coffee table and sat down in his recliner, hoping the argument had ceased. Once he sat down he realized that they had no plates on which to put the food. He started to get up but felt as if an invisible hand was pushing him back down.

"Don't worry, I got it," Carrie said. Carl felt more confused. He began to wonder if she was able to read his mind. She took her wand out, making four plates appear from nowhere. They were not of the same design he owned. These appeared fancier, as if china. He resisted the urge to flip it over to see if there was the familiar seal on the bottom. Another deep breath, he told himself trying to forget what was happening.

Thankfully, in Carl's opinion, they ate in silence. He tried to come up with explanations for what he had witnessed so far. Every idea he came up with was even more farfetched than that of what his guests wanted him to believe. He studied the strangers that believed they knew him as this Garrett person. They had to be crazy or he was going crazy. Maybe they were some type of hypnotists. He had read somewhere about how cult members had the ability of hypnotizing people so they all believed the same thing. That had to be it. He was hallucinating through some form of hypnotizing mumble jumbo. He took a swig of lemonade feeling confident with his deduction, even being able to smile at his guests.

"You are not hallucinating and we don't go around hypnotizing people," Carrie said. He thought her tone was asking him not to be silly.

"Did I say...?" he questioned looking at her suspiciously. Okay, they were able to read his thoughts.

"After what you witnessed in the kitchen and have seen in here, do you really think that you're seeing things?" Carrie questioned as she set her empty glass on the coffee table. Carl just sat looking at the three strangers sitting on his couch. "Sheba and I are sorceresses and Reginald is a sorcerer."

"Right." Carl gave a nod, wondering if they could actually hear what they were claiming. "So you study Wicca?"

"Naw, that's just a minor sect that follows an ancient religion," Reginald answered.

"I'm sorry but I am not who you think I am or want me to be. My name is Carl Alexander," he pleaded with them hoping they would leave him alone.

"You are only what you have forgotten," Carrie retorted as she stood up and began to pace around. She stopped in front of him to explain. "You are an Orohunter," she said with her hands flying violently. He began to worry that she may hit him.

"A what?"

"An Orohunter is a magical person that investigates magical crimes," Sheba answered. "There are three levels of Hunters. There is Copper Hunter, when you get accepted to the Hunter Academy."

"The second level is Argent Hunter which I just graduated from recently," Reginald added.

"So it's like being a member of a secret society that has three levels of something or other," Carl interrupted, not understanding anything they were trying to explain to him.

"Listen, all you need to know is that there are three levels of Hunters. The first is when you are learning what to do which is Copper level. The second is Argent Hunter when you begin to practice your trade and the third level is Orohunter which is when you are a senior member of investigators." Carrie held out her fingers as she counted off and explained each level. "We are all Orohunters. You were the most prominent of us all."

"This might be easier for you to understand," Reginald said. "Copper hunter is like being in school learning to be a police officer. Argent Hunters are detectives that specialize in specific types of crimes. While Orohunters are like what the Americans would call CIA." The girls looked at Reginald with surprise.

"I don't know anything about Oro Hunters, Copper Hunters or whatever, but I am not one. I've lived in Michigan all my life," he pleaded.

"That's what you now believe because you've lost your powers," Carrie answered shaking her head.

"My powers?" he questioned with a laugh shuffling in his seat.

"Yes, you were very powerful." She looked at him as if it would somehow open up some chamber of his brain.

"Okay, so what happened that caused me to not be a great magician?" he relented, being sucked in by his curiosity.

"We don't know exactly, but you were attacked by a Goblin," Sheba answered looking back and forth from Carrie to Carl.

"This sounds like something out of a cheesy horror movie, sorcerers versus the Goblin diabolist," Carl complained as he prepared to stand up but thought better of it. "I bet if we turn on the television there will be at least three shows close to what you're talking about. I'm going to regret this, but what is a Goblin?"

"Goblins think that sorcerers, would be better off to enslave non-magical people," Sheba said.

"We call non-magical people rubes," Reginald added.

"Goblins are evil sorcerers, one of which somehow, with some strange spell, was able to erase your memory and transformed you into this person."

Carrie seemed to ignore his comment about the television. "The name Goblin came from the first real evil sorcerer named Globin."

"Goblins? I'm not saying I believe any of this, but why did a Goblin attack me?" He hated feeling the weight of their stares, so he relented a little hoping his questions would convince them he was not Garrett.

"Do you know what alchemy is?" Sheba asked as she stood up, motioning for Carrie to sit.

"Never heard of it," he answered quickly looking at Carrie who stared at him so intently he couldn't help but feel a twinge of fear.

"Well you see it is a magical ability to process magical charms into adamant objects spells into metal," she explained sounding more like a teacher that just happened to be standing in his living room. "Sorcerers have been able to process magical abilities for ages into lesser dense objects such as wood. That's how we have magic wands." She pulled her wand out from its hiding place. "Non-magical alchemists used to try to change lead into Gold."

"You and your father were the only people to be able to combine magical abilities with metal," Sheba continued explaining, sending his head into a whirlwind of confusion. "You invented a ring that would repel the worse magic ever imagined."

"It's a killing curse, *Mordirian*," Reginald said in a small voice.

"Doing so eliminated the main tool the Goblins used to terrorize people," Carrie added looking up at him hopeful that they were getting through. "You were on the verge of another break through but disappeared."

"So how was I transformed? Why don't I remember anything you are saying?" Carl asked feeling like his head was going to explode.

"We don't understand it ourselves," Carrie said.

"It's a mystery which we are hoping to solve," Sheba added.

"Think back to three years ago," Carrie suggested.

"Did anything happen to you then that…," Reginald tried to join into the barrage.

"…was very traumatic maybe even life threatening?" Sheba finished glaring at Reginald then turning a smile to Carl.

At first nothing came to mind. Then he thought about something; but if he told them he'd only be adding fuel to their delusions. He looked at Carrie not helping but feeling it wouldn't be fair withholding anything.

"Well I was run over by a car." He recognized the shocked look on their faces even though he was sure the thin scars on his face had already betrayed him.

"You were run over by a car?" Carrie repeated, walking over to look out the window while nibbling her thumb.

"Yeah, I had two tires go rolling right over my head." He motioned with his left hand the path the tires took.

"Oh, my God!" Carrie screamed turning back to the others.

Carl was surprised by her reaction. It felt like she took it personally.

"That's it!" Sheba exclaimed with a sense of excitement of knowing something the others had not yet grasped. "Don't you see that's when you stopped being Garrett Montgomery and became Carl… um. I'm sorry; but what is your last name?"

"Alexander," he answered uncomfortably. "What do you mean I became Carl?"

"Do you remember anything about the accident?"

"Yeah, I remember it all." Carl searched her eyes for a clue to her madness.

"Tell us all about it, please," Sheba pleaded, pulling Carrie back to the couch.

CHAPTER 2

"It was two days after Christmas," he began. In his mind, he slipped back to the day his life changed.

The scars on his face were very faint now. He knew deep down no one could see them unless he pointed them out. Still, his stomach cringed when he thought about them. To him, they were large billboards screaming *look at me I'm an idiot*. "We were coming back from a skiing trip and anxious to get home. The trip hadn't been much fun. It'd rained most of the time, so the skiing sucked."

He broke off for a moment as his eyes glazed over, replaying it all over again in his mind. Snow was falling as Carl struggled to keep his brown Mustang GT on the slick road. The car fishtailed every time he slightly moved the steering wheel. His stomach cringed as his jaw muscles tensed. Already going twenty miles under the speed limit, he didn't want to spend any longer out on the road than he had to. No one else was foolish enough to be out he convinced himself and compensated for the conditions by driving in the middle of the road. The absence of traffic made the center even slicker.

"Damn rain made skiing suck!" he complained to his friend Walter who sat in the passenger seat.

"Your lack of skiing skill made it suck." Walter answered back.

Carl squeezed the stirring wheel with both hands.

"I remember you cussing the rain when you ate snow." He took a quick glance at his friend to read his face.

"I didn't eat half as much as you," he retorted, looking out the front window.

"Wish we stayed at the lodge."

"You won't think so when we're home in the morning. How's the road?"

"Better than the slopes."

"More like a rink, we should've played hockey."

Carl nodded as snow and ice pelted the windshield. The headlights made it seem like they were in a spaceship going light-speed rather than twenty five miles per hour. The light only allowed them a few feet of visibility. Through the snow, he never noticed the sign warning of the curve ahead. Even if he had been in the proper lane he didn't think he would have seen it. It would have been much, much worse if they had been going any faster.

The back end began to swing around as he tried to maneuver the curve. He turned into the curve but overcompensated losing control as the GT backend spun around to where the front should have been. He thought he had done everything correctly turning into the spin. He hadn't slammed on the brake like most people would have. Still, they had wound up off the road and slamming into a ditch.

The man standing there telling the tale could still feel the crush of the collision. Beams of pain shot up from his spine through his back and out each of his ribs. The air in his lungs exploded out in protest as the car violently came to a stop. His body screamed in rage. It wouldn't permit him to take a deep breath. He suffered taking short sucks of air that coursed fresh shock waves through his body. He sat there wanting to cry with his hands still clutching the steering wheel.

Walter moaned, clutching his knee. It had slammed into the dash board.

"How bad?" Carl asked fighting the pain as he released his seatbelt.

"Bad," Walter moaned.

Carl took out his cell phone from the center compartment. "No signal."

"Could use that automatic crap to indicate we had an accident."

"You ain't going to be any good pushing us out."

Walter shook his head.

"Can you drive?" Carl asked.

"Suppose." Walter opened his door. "You're gonna have to help me get around," he said, grunting in pain.

Carl swore looking back up at the road. It was a slight incline and should be no trouble getting out but to him right then it looked like a friggin' mountain. He stumbled through the snow, feeling sick each time the icy snow cracked on his way to reach Walter. Walter hopped, keeping his left leg straight, putting his weight on Carl. The guilt swelling in his throat.

"By the way, nice job." Walter smiled as he rolled down the automatic window.

Cold air slapped at Carl as he positioned himself at the rear of the Mustang.

He struggled to get the car rocking while fighting the pain that burnt inside him. Like a pendulum, he pushed, rocking the car back and forth. The Mustang spun its tires and then mercifully began to edge forward. Carl flung all the might he could muster, running along as the car began to move up the embankment. He stepped in a rut slipping, losing his balance and tumbled face first to the ground, where he watched the Mustang climb out of its trap. "Come on baby, make it. Make it," he pleaded, gazing up from the frozen earth.

His stomach quickly protested as ice and snow began melting against the warmth of his body. Still he laid there watching and pleading with the car to make its escape.

His head sank with disgust as the tires began to spin. He cursed as he slid into a push up position ready to get back to his feet and continue the pursuit to free the vehicle. For some reason, he just waited there watching the car back up, the white warning reverse lights warning that the car was coming toward him. Instead of getting to his feet, he collapsed as if someone was holding him down. It felt more like an invisible foot was pressed against his back. This must be what a deer feels like when it's caught in the beams of the headlights of an approaching vehicle he thought waiting to die. His mind screamed to move but he couldn't. He just laid there thinking that this could not be real, hoping to wake from a dream. This was not the way his life was supposed to end.

Not until the first tire rolled over his head, did his body obey his mind's command for action. He began to roll and tuck himself into the fetal position as the second heavier tire followed the same path as the first.

His head felt as if someone had just filled it with helium. He sat up blankly looking at the headlights shining on him like a spotlight in a weird circus. This could not be real he thought, now in front of the car. His brain silently screamed. Something was majorly wrong with what had just transpired. Is this what a balloon feels like when it's being filled to the limits before bursting he thought. He stood up on wobbly legs. More like being lifted off the ground by a puppet master. He made out the silhouette of Walter beginning to exit the car. He tried to scream, "Help me," but his mouth must have been too swollen. The voice, his voice he corrected, sounded more like a pitiful mouse. In his mind he heard himself screaming, but his ears only made out a tiny 'help' followed by the word 'me.'

'Where was the blood?' he thought, trying to stagger to the car. He was suddenly tired overcome with the urge to sleep.

"No!" a voice in his head warned against the darkness which tried to seduce him. Amazement sprang as he comprehended; he was standing after having two tires pass over his head. He marveled feeling like his head was now full of Novocain. There was no pain. That would come later. Walter tried to run to him but his broken knee cap slowed him. The desire to laugh filled him watching him hop straight legged through the brush and snow. That was the last day he remembered seeing Walter. They had just grown apart he told himself.

Everything slowed as sight vanished from his senses. His teeth felt slippery as if they were touching his nose. If he had a mirror, he would have seen that his upper lip had split all the way to his shattered nose. It felt like someone was pouring hot syrup over his head. He reached up feeling the tacky wetness spilling down him. It felt like he put his hand into a bucket of warm rubber cement. 'Oh God, I'm dying,' he thought fighting to see through the darkness that overtook him. His knees felt like they had been transformed to goo, no longer supporting his weight. He swallowed back the bile that wanted to erupt and collapsed to his knees still whimpering, "Help me," over and over again.

'I don't want to die,' he thought, battling in darkness. 'Not here, like this.' He swayed as gravity teased, would he fall forward on his face or backward. He couldn't move his arms to brace himself either way.

Finally he began to timber face first to the frozen blood covered ground. Walter caught him. Relief filled him, feeling the support of his friend.

"I gotcha buddy," were the sweetest words he had ever heard. His world had gone dark with a humming in his ears sounding as if he were having an annoying hearing test that wouldn't shut off.

Walter guided him back to the car laying him in the back seat. The urge to sleep seized hold again but he fought it, knowing he would never wake. Yet, his brain begged for peace.

He never found out how they got out of the ditch. Maybe the tires had more traction from rolling over his face. All he knew was he could not go to sleep. The next thing he knew, he was in the hospital with a policeman badgering him with a bunch of questions. Walter was in shock and unable to answer.

"Were you wearing your seat belt?" the man asked, scribbling on a black notebook that was flipped open.

He struggled to open up his right eye even a millimeter to try to make out the fool, wanting to see his face. It was the third time he had asked that same stupid question.

"Yeah, I had a special one put on the bottom of the car just for the person that wanted to ride underneath it." The man didn't even look up. "I'm done answering your questions."

Carl shook off the horror that had transported him back in time. He was home, safe in the living room with three people, their mouths gaped open, looking up at him. Carl leaned his head toward them, wanting one of them to say something; hoping they didn't realize he could still feel the ghost of the pain. They shifted on the couch too shocked to speak, or just letting it sink in. Carl guessed they realized their blunder. He couldn't be the person they were looking for and were trying to figure out how to bow out gracefully.

Sheba broke the silence. "When you saw this, what was your perspective?" she asked matter-of-factly, as if she already knew the answer. The others looked at her, as confused as Carl felt.

"I was in shock!" he exclaimed, insulted by the brutal question.

"No, I mean how did you witness it? Was it from above, the side or as if you felt the car?" She stammered, trying to clarify the question for him and the others. She looked surprised they didn't understand what she did.

"Well it's strange, but it was like I was witnessing everything from above until the car went over me. Then it was like I was being pulled into the body as I stood up." He thought it was like having an out of body experience, but didn't want to mention it feeling foolish enough already.

Sheba was excited. "I think I understand it now, Garrett." Carl looked to Carrie and Reginald for help but they wore the same blank expressions on their faces as he could well imagine was on his own. "When you were attacked, the Goblins somehow switched your spirit with Carl. There must be some kind of connection between the two of you. The Goblins, like us probably had no idea who they sent you to or they would have tracked you down and killed you by now."

"That means they're probably still searching for him," Carrie added understanding what Sheba knew. Carl shook his head. He was relieved Reginald was as lost as he was.

"Do you have a picture of yourself before the car accident?" Carrie asked, noticing Carl's confusion.

"Sure." He went to get the picture from his bedroom.

"I'll bet he looks just like Garrett did back in school," Sheba said excitedly as Carl listened from the bedroom.

"I don't understand," Reginald said.

"Reginald, you've heard that everyone has a twin before, haven't you?" Carrie asked.

"Yeah." He looked at the girls as if this had nothing to do with them finding Garrett.

"Well," Sheba sighed. "Carl was the twin to Garrett. Carl got in a car accident at the moment Garrett was to be murdered."

"But Garrett had his protection," Reginald said twisting the ring on his finger.

"Preciously," Carrie said. "When Garrett was attacked, Carl had died or would have. The spell the Goblins used to attack Garrett somehow transported him to Carl's body."

"How?" Reginald asked.

"Yeah, how?" Carl reiterated, handing a framed graduation photo to the girls. They weren't surprised to see the boy in the cap and gown looking exactly like their friend. "And how come it's not this Garrett guy that died and I am alive."

"Because Carrie would know," Reginald said.

"I don't understand," Carl said frustrated with the entire idea.

"It's not important that you understand what is going on right now," Carrie said rather quickly as if she were covering something up. She walked over to Carl. "What matters now is that we found you first and that we understand what happened."

"This is nuts." Carl or Garrett, he was so confused that he didn't know who he was anymore. Wait a second, he was Carl and they were crazy, not him.

"We'll try to help you understand it better," Sheba said trying to reassure him as she paced back and forth. "What kinds of changes have occurred since you were nearly killed?"

"What do you mean?" He began rubbing his face as if this would help him break out of this crazy dream.

"For example, have you been more interested in certain things than before?" Carrie asked.

"Well, I guess I've been more serious and have had a thirst for knowledge that didn't exist before. I can't seem to get enough of learning. It seems like I'm always reading or trying to learn something." He looked at Carrie who seemed to have something to say. "I was never a gifted student in school, but now it's like I have to know everything."

"That sounds like Garrett," Carrie said. "You and Sheba were always competing for the highest grades."

"How did you find me?" Carl asked, not aware that this sounded like he accepted their insinuation.

"Carrie has been searching for you every day for the past three years," Reginald answered as the others glared at him.

"Three years?" Carl questioned, looking at Carrie wondering how anyone could have such devotion. "I just don't believe I'm your Garrett."

Carrie walked up and took his hand so he would look at her. "You were our friend, we just want you back with us."

There was a kindness in her eyes which gave him a warm feeling in the pit of his stomach. He felt a strange attraction for her. "I wish I were the person you're looking for. I really do."

"You only think you aren't," Carrie retorted grasping his hand even tighter as if squeezing them would help him remember.

"I really do sympathize with your plight but I am not a sorcerer!" Carl pulled away pacing in front of the room and looking down at the floor. "I am just me. I am a simple guy. There is nothing you can say that will convince me."

"Okay, what about your ring?" Sheba asked, taking his challenge. She pointed at the gold ring on his left hand.

He looked at the lion head ring that resided on his ring finger. Normally this would be a wedding ring. Carl hated to shake hands with it on his right hand so he wore it on his left. It was bulky and fit better on his left which was a little plumper than his right. It was made out of gold with two rubies for eyes and a small white diamond mouth.

"What about it?"

"Where did you get it?" Sheba asked. "You can't remember can you?" she answered too quickly.

"A friend gave it to me," he answered smugly, pleased to recall receiving the gift from his teenage friend.

"Nope," Reginald contradicted. "You made it."

"I made it? This is getting better and better."

"See you gave me one too." Reginald stood up walking over to Carl holding out his hand. Carl saw the identical ring. Elegant curves carved into the gold made the mane and ears while diamonds shone in the open mouth with two fanged teeth surrounding it. Two rubies glistened in the place of eyes as if they had been forged with blood rather than stone.

Carl looked up into Reginald's smiling face which beamed as if this would finally convince him. He fought the urge to punch him in his smug face. "I suppose you two have rings also," Carl said to the girls.

"Of course we do," Sheba answered, extending her left hand showing a lioness rather than the lion which the boys wore. It was on the ring finger of her left hand also he noticed feeling ill. It was carved with the same detail with two blood red ruby eyes and a shinning white diamond in the open growling mouth. "You made them for us and somehow magically enchanted them against the *Mordirian* curse. It's an amazing bit of magic."

"It's the only known defense," Carrie added, displaying her lioness ring. It was as if they were all married or in some strange cult.

"Well it used to be known," Reginald argued. "With his memory gone, the spell isn't known anymore, is it?" He glanced at the others quickly as they glared at him. "It's more of a charm now. We can't duplicate it," he nervously explained.

"Reginald Xavier! Hush," Sheba barked. Reginald collapsed back into the couch taking refuge behind his lemonade.

Carrie shook her head turning back to Carl. "You see you're the only person that knows how to enchant them. That's why the Goblins got rid of you and one of the reasons why you are so valuable to us."

"So what you're saying is as long as this ring is on my finger...," He twirled it around his finger as if trying to take it off. "...I can't be killed?"

"Nope," Reginald stated, wondering if it was okay to speak again.

"You can't be killed by the *Mordirian curse*," Sheba answered.

"So what about hocus pocus or abracadabra, will they kill me?" Carl clowned, feeling more like a fool.

"Don't be silly," Carrie ordered, letting out a puff of air.

"Those aren't real spells," Sheba added. "You can still be assassinated in non-magical ways."

"You're also vulnerable to other forms of evil magic," Carrie said.

"I'm sorry but this is just a cheap piece of tin." He pulled the ring off, tossing it to Reginald on the couch. "You see, it leaves a green shadow on my skin if I wear it too long." He showed them the echo the ring left behind. "I only wear it because it's a nice conversation starter."

Carrie retrieved the ring, marched back to Carl and shoved it back on his finger. "Don't you ever take this off again!" she scolded like a mother correcting a child. "You are in danger. We've probably been followed or traced by whoever did this to you," she warned.

"We can't be sure of that Carrie," Reginald insisted.

"Wait a minute, this is crazy." Carl began rubbing his forehead. "I must be crazy. This is just a novelty piece of tin." He reached to take off the ring but thought better, catching the fury which raged in Carrie's eyes. "It probably cost a dollar at the most. There are probably billions of them. So the fact that you have one like mine means squat."

"Are you saying you don't believe we are sorcerers?" Reginald asked taking his wand out prepared for the challenge as if ready to duel.

"No," Carl said, standing nose to nose with Reginald. They had proved well enough. "What I am saying is that *I* am not a wizard, witch, warlock... and never was. *I am not* a warlock. I am not a sorcerer." He glared as they began to laugh.

"Forgive us," Sheba said fighting to suppress a fit of laughter. "It's that we don't call ourselves witches or wizards."

"Yeah, they're old. We wouldn't be considered a witch or wizard until we were at least a hundred years old," Reginald said.

Carl shook his head as Reginald bantered on. "Enough! Please. I don't want to play word association games. It's not the point. I am a normal person with no supernatural qualities."

"We understand this is difficult for you," Carrie said, braking off the discussion. "I just ask again that you try to keep an open mind and remember we are your friends."

"Now Garrett, there is a way to prove this," Sheba said.

"Please call me Carl." He shook his head not knowing if he would be able to do what they were requesting but somehow it seemed the most logical step to prove they were wrong. "This is all too weird."

"Oh I'm sorry; we just remember you as Garrett," Sheba apologized but looked like she could care less about his feelings.

Carrie took out her wand and with a wave of her wrist a small triangle thing that looked like a portable television appeared. It looked like a flat plasma computer screen. He wondered if they thought showing him some old photographs would convince him. He took a deep breath waiting for them to try to explain what was going to happen.

"This is what we in the magical world call a Chronicler Recital. It's a way of storing and viewing old memories," Sheba explained, waving at the thing Carrie had just made appear.

"So it's like a television that show memories," he said and they nodded. "I have a DVD player too, but it doesn't look as stupid."

"It is not a DVD player," Sheba answered shaking her head as if she were battling a younger brother that just wouldn't quit pestering her with foolishness. "Just watch Carrie and she'll show you how it works."

Carrie nodded to Sheba. She took her wand and put it up to the center of her head just between her eyes and began to concentrate. She squeezed her eyes closed and Carl waited expecting her to vanish or something. She took three deep breaths and lowered the wand. She plucked a single hair from the spot with a slight grimace of pain. The single strand of hair plucked appeared more red than brown. The root glowed blue like a butane flame. Carrie dropped it on the screen which soaked it up like a sponge. She placed her wand into the screen as if it were a pot and began stirring. Carl's eyes widened as the screen took on a whirlpool shape. It reminded him of the photos of a hurricane caught on radar systems with an eye in the middle. It kept dancing on the screen as if he were looking into a crazy video game.

"Now this is going to seem a little bizarre," Carrie warned, catching his eyes. "We'll go into the Chronicler together, able to communicate to each other but not with the other people in the memory. They won't even know we're there."

"That doesn't sound any crazier than any of the other stuff you've been saying." How was he going to be able to interact with a memory? The urge to turn and run returned but he figured they would only follow him. What would his neighbors think if they saw him being chased by a goofy looking guy and two pretty girls?

Perhaps, he had had a brain embolism and was now on the verge of a massive stroke. That would explain this hallucination. It would not be safe to drive himself to the hospital. It could burst on the way. Maybe it's a residual effect from the accident years ago. He should call for an ambulance.

"You are not having a stroke," Carrie said shaking her head again. "Remember, just open your mind and your heart will follow. Everything will be fine."

"Relax," Sheba suggested, taking Carrie's hands. "I'll go back to Brussels and do a little research. Reggie will stay and watch over the house, making sure we were not followed."

Reginald nodded, beginning to march back and forth like a sentry with his wand drawn to his nose. 'Some guard dog,' Carl thought.

There must have been something about the ability to read minds because Carrie gave him a smirk. "Don't tell anyone of our discovery yet," she said to Sheba. 'We don't know who we can trust."

"I won't. Good luck." Sheba hugged Carrie, whispering something in her ear that made tears well in her eyes again. A rogue tear made a run down her cheek as Sheba pulled away nodding to the two boys. There was a clatter of a broken glass and she vanished.

Carl thought back to the movie *The Wizard of Oz* when Dorothy said, "My how people come and go around here." He couldn't help but let a snicker slip out as he watched Carrie and Reginald. This was not a movie. This was real life, his life now gone extremely crazy. He nodded to Carrie who took his sweat covered hand.

"Why did it sound like broken glass when she vanished?" Carl asked.

Carrie wiped the tear away with the back of her hand giving a sort of laugh. "Oh that, well you see when we materialize or vanish we have to announce ourselves."

Carl didn't understand.

"The Goblins used to be able to sneak up on their victims you see," Reginald explained in a voice that sounded like he was telling a ghost story. "They could pop up right behind you when you came out of the shower and blamm! You're dead."

Carrie nodded. "So the elders passed a decree that anyone teleporting would be announced by the sound of broken glass."

"Yeah, anyone teleporting would announce themselves," Reginald reiterated. "It's the principle of the fifth pentacle of the sun."

"The fifth pentacle of the sun?" Carl asked, looking to Carrie to clarify.

"There's no time for that now," Carrie said, looking at the Chronicler Recital. "It's time."

CHAPTER 3

Carl took a deep breath trying to calm the butterflies that were dancing in his belly. He nodded to Carrie indicating he was ready. They led with their heads as if diving into a swimming pool holding hands. He recalled the cartoon circus clowns diving into a cup from the roof of a big top. He squeezed his eyes shut as his head met the cloudy whirlpool, expecting to hit something but instead was greeted by a falling sensation that seized his stomach. It felt like doing a summersault underwater. There was a tight feeling in the pit of his belly begging him to be ill. He clinched his teeth fighting the urge to spew. Then as quickly as the sick feeling began, it faded away. Surprised, he felt his feet hit the hard stable surface of the ground.

"You can open your eyes." Carrie stood shaking her head. "You get used to it and I don't think it was that bad either."

He exhaled, testing the solid ground with his feet. There was no way he was going to get used to this. It would be his first and last time going through it. "You wanna bet," he challenged, opening his eyes expecting to see his living room and the funny computer. Instead he was insulted with the bright sunshine and overwhelming scent of fresh salt air. He was near the ocean.

"Welcome back to the Palace of Sitnalta," Carrie greeted, smiling at his state of confusion. "It is a replica of an ancient palace where we came to learn our magical craft."

"It's amazing." He gazed star struck at the large stones which sparkled appearing carved out of silver. It was a huge magnificent structure poised on top of a hill, he guessed to be equivalent to the size of three football fields. It stood four stories tall and sparkled like a diamond. The old Beetles song popped in his head *Lucy in the Sky with Diamonds.*

"The limestone and gypsum have crystallized so they appear like silver. It is a vast royal patronage of magical learning with over 1300 rooms interconnected by miles of hallways and secret passages." She led him up the hill to one of the many doors that led inside. There were lit torches guiding them through the outer most hallway, but it became lighter the further they walked inside. His head and heart began to race.

Carl ran a hand over one of the redwood pillars that stood guard at each new corridor they passed. The wood felt as smooth as glass. Carl saw his reflection in it sparkling like a star. It was surprisingly warm. "How did we get here?" he asked, pulling her to a stop. She ignored his question trying to tug him on.

"We have to hurry; this is the day we met," she explained.

They could hear what sounded like a couple of young girls approaching. Carl raised his eyebrows, curiosity biting him softly. He spotted two young girls walking toward them chatting about boys. He guessed they were sixteen. One of the girls was a younger Carrie. He recognized those dark brown eyes, but she didn't have her dark hair. Instead, she had wavy flaming red hair. The other girl had straight red hair not as light as Carrie's. She spoke to the younger red haired Carrie about some boys from Kenosis. At least he thought she had said Kenosis.

"C'mon," the now Carrie instructed nudging him on. They followed the young Carrie and her friend. "That's me in my fourth level with my best friend Susan Medico. We were ... are fifteen," she added as if answering his question.

Carl made another mental note to try to figure out a way to protect his thoughts. Somehow she was pulling them out of his head as easily as she had snatched out the strand of hair. The older Carrie glanced over at him. She gave him a playful shove while motioning with a nudge of her head to pick up the pace.

They turned a corner leading to another long corridor, the walls covered with tapestries. There were smaller marble pillars with vases full of flowers framing each tapestry. Carl made out the faint sound of piano music sounding like it was coming out of the wall.

"Where's it coming from?" Susan asked, hearing it too.

"Don't know," the young Carrie answered, glancing around in search of the music. They walked back and forth in the hallway. The young Carrie pulled back a large tapestry showing two dolphins jumping out of the ocean on a full moonlit night. "Here it is…Sh…," she whispered, opening the door.

They crept inside as if entering a church in the middle of session, trying desperately not to disturb whoever was creating the beautiful harmony. Carl and the adult Carrie snuck in behind them. Even though they had no reason to sneak, they crept around reverently. Carl stood a little behind Carrie using her as an emotional shield.

Carl studied the room. In the center sat a white baby grand piano. It sparkled like fresh snow. A young man in a white toga sat playing. He had long light brown hair that came to the bottom of his neck. They could only see the back of his head as he made his fingers dance over the piano keys.

To the right of the player on the wall rested a mahogany bookcase filled with books and sheet music. In the front were two more marble pillars with the busts of two famous piano players. Carl thought he should know their names but could not recall. On the left rested another bookcase filled with more music and one shelf devoted to old fashioned metronomes. There were about twenty-five in different shapes and sizes.

The player continued his amazing performance. Carl thought there was something in the music that bewitched the air. His insides began to warm. He could feel a power growing in his solar plexus cascading outward like rays of sunshine. He felt the urge to lie down and just listen. He wondered if the music was what Carrie had wanted him to experience. It was beautiful even though he fought the urge to relax. He inhaled deeply tasting the sweet aroma of the music as if he had just entered a coffee house.

The two girls silently cooed at each other engulfed by the magic of the beautiful music. Carrie was mesmerized by the melody that danced in the air. She seemed to have forgotten about Carl. Her eyes danced to the player and the girls. A glow radiated from her soaking in the memory.

"What is it you are playing?" the youthful Carrie boldly asked.

"It's the *Rhapsody on a Theme of Paganinii by Sergei Rachmaninov*" the boy answered without missing a beat as if he expected the girls to be there. Once the boy finished the piece, he turned around to face his audience. Shock seized Carl as he gazed on his own younger face. He recognized the voice too but it hadn't registered. His knees buckled. How could this be? It was impossible. He did not know how to play the piano. This could not be him but had to be someone that looked and sounded like him.

"You didn't think you were a sorcerer either, but yes you can play the piano famously," Carrie answered, never taking her eyes from her younger self.

'Damn,' he thought. 'I've got to be more protective of my thoughts.'

'Yes, you do...' a voice not his retorted inside his head. He looked at her shocked. She smiled finally breaking her attention from the memory. '... only not with me, now pay attention,' she ordered in his thoughts once again.

They returned to the teenagers. "That was really beautiful," the young Carrie complimented, walking over to the bench and putting her hand on his shoulder while examining the sheet music. Carl watched the way the young pianist studied Carrie as if she were an alien to him, like the older one was to him.

"I was so amazed at the complexity of the music you played," the now Carrie whispered. He was grateful she spoke.

"You can understand this," the red haired Carrie asked, motioning to the sheet music in front of him.

"Yeah it's pretty easy once you get the hang of it. It's tough at first but it's like casting magic. Once you succeed in simple spells you progress into tougher more advanced ones. Until you can play this as if it were just a simple charm like *nemtosis!*" He waved his wand and a small white dove materialized.

"My name is Carrie Ann and this is my friend Susan," she introduced while waving her wand making the dove disappear.

"Hi," Susan said cautiously. Carl noticed she had not ventured any further into the room like Carrie but remained poised at the door.

"I know we're on the same floor. My name is Garrett Montgomery." He turned back to the piano coyly.

"You're a fifth level aren't you?" Carrie asked.

"Yeah, but this is my first year at the palace."

"You came from the America's didn't you?" Susan asked, sounding as if this were a bad thing.

Garrett slowly nodded his head. Carl noticed Susan retreat a couple of steps. Garrett appeared to have noticed this too but didn't seem as surprised by the reaction as Carl. Instead, he turned his attention to Carrie.

"I thought the palace didn't permit anyone from the Americans attending?" the younger Carrie asked as the older Carrie looked amazed at her younger boldness. She glared at herself, scolding for being rude.

"That's true," Garrett answered, beginning to poke the piano keys. "You see my great great-Grandfather was an Irish wizard. He was one of the first wizards to be sent to the Colonies to try to prevent them from defecting."

Susan looked at the boy like he was a predator and she the prey. She had managed to slide back to the door. Carl noticed she had her hand on the doorknob prepared to flee.

"So, how did you come to The Palace of Sitnalta?" the young Carrie asked, not noticing her friend.

"My parents passed away last summer. The only relative I have in the magical community lives in the nearby magical village of Neosis. He was kind enough to take me in." The tune the boy was now playing felt familiar to Carl but he could not register it. "He used to be a sage here at the Palace of Sitnalta and believes it to be the best place for me to further my education."

"Really." Carrie planted herself on the bench next to him. Garrett shyly backed away giving her more room, not missing a note as he did. "What's his name?"

Carl was stunned by her forwardness.

"I'm not to say." If the boy was uncomfortable with the questions he didn't show it. "He's worried it may influence the students and other Sages if they knew we're related."

"Rumor has it you are an Indian," Susan blurted from the door. The older Carrie's mouth sprang open.

Garrett glanced at her and gave a shy smile. "Yeah, my great great-Grandfather married an Indian maid who was a spiritual advisor. My great great-Grandfather taught her how to be a proper sorceress. Most witchcraft the Indians used was primitive. They experimented with making potions and divinations, mainly exploiting dreams through interpretations though." A smile crept across his face knowing Susan's uncomfortable state. "My great great-Grandmother was different though. She could talk to animals."

"Really?" Carrie asked excitedly.

"Yeah." He turned to face her forgetting to play. "There's a legend of an ancestor that used to live with bears."

Young Carrie looked at him in amazement. "Will you tell it to us?" she begged excitedly.

"Yeah," He said, smiling as he pulled his wand out again, conjuring a stool that appeared next to Susan. "You might as well be comfortable."

Carrie looked back, laughing. Susan cautiously sat, holding the stool as if expecting it would vanish before her butt hit the wood.

"There was once an Indian boy about five years old," he began, "whose parents had died leaving him alone in the world. The only person the boy had to take care of him was his uncle."

"Like you," Carrie added.

"The uncle, unlike mine, was not a kind man nor cared for the boy as he should. The uncle believed the boy to be too much trouble. He fed him scraps from the table and dressed him in tattered clothing and moccasins with soles nearly worn away." The boy smiled as the girls listened to the story.

The tribe banished the uncle and the boy forcing them to live outside the safety of the tribe. The tribe believed that the boy's parents to be unnatural spirits and if they allowed the boy refuge it would bring them bad luck. At night the boy slept outside his uncle's teepee far away from the warmth of the fire. He tried not to complain remembering his parents teaching him to respect the elders.

The uncle blamed the boy for all his misfortune. One day he decided to do away with the boy, thinking this would get him back into the tribe.

"Come, we are going to hunt today," the uncle commanded.

Happiness spilled over the boy. His uncle had never taken him hunting before. Normally, he was left alone on past hunts when his uncle would not come back for days. Today, he followed his uncle into the dark menacing woods. He marveled at the gigantic trees that reached to the clouds.

His uncle first killed a long eared rabbit. The boy gleefully picked it up ready to head back to their camp. His uncle shook his head calling the boy back. "We will go on. I am not done hunting," he ordered in a deep ravenous voice.

The boy was respectful. He knew the rabbit had more than enough meat for his uncle to eat. The boy envisioned the scraps of meat he would get when his uncle finished. Instead, they ventured further into the field. The boy chased out a red-necked pheasant that his uncle killed. The boy was very pleased. They now had more than enough meat from the rabbit and the pheasant to eat. Surely, his uncle would feed him proper tonight. His stomach danced anticipating the warm meat. He picked up the pheasant and with the rabbit slung over his back he turned toward camp.

"No," his uncle shouted, shaking his head again. He pointed away from camp. "We must go further."

The boy dare not protest even though he worried knowing they had more than enough meat to eat. They trudged further into the darkening forest. They went further than the boy had ever ventured before. They came to a cliff and at the base housed a cave. The opening of the cave was only large enough for a small person like him to be able to crawl inside.

"There are animals hiding in there," the uncle proclaimed. "You must crawl in and chase them out so I can shoot them with my arrows."

The boy became very scared. He opened his mouth to voice his fear but recalled his mother telling him never to question an older male. It could be a test of your manhood she had warned. He took comfort in this thought. Perhaps, if he passed his manhood test in the darkness alone his uncle would be more kind to him. He may even allow him to sleep near the fire inside the teepee.

Mustering his courage he slowly crawled into the cave. The waterlogged leaves were mushy under his fingers. The stench of decaying leaves in the moisture curled the boy's stomach. Tiny stones cut into his tender hands, but no animals met him in the darkness. He crawled deeper into the cave. His skin shivered as his hands sank into the muck of the cold damp earth. He bit back tears that begged to appear, proceeding on until he reached the very end of the cave. He turned back, shame washed over him realizing he had not chased out any animals, as the sting of tears burned his eyes. He feared his uncle's displeasure. Would he be banished rather than being invited to the tee pee?

He neared the entrance to the cave following the faint light that trickled from the end. Confusion slapped him as the light began to be gobbled up by shadows. He looked up fearing night must be closing in. Instead he watched his uncle rolling a large stone in front of the mouth of the cave.

Everything went dark and cold. The man had sealed him in this tomb alone and frightened. The boy struggled trying to move the stone, but it was no use. He was too little. He had not near enough the strength of a man that was needed to move it. He was trapped! Why had his uncle done this?

After an hour of crying a memory of his parents teaching him about the magic of music gave him strength. If you do well and have faith, good things will come to you. They called this magic Orenda. The memory made him happy. He began to sing. As he sang, his voice grew stronger and the song louder, until his fears vanished. He had his mother and father with him.

Then he heard a scratching noise outside and stopped singing. He thought his uncle had come back for him. The magic had worked.

"Don't stop singing boy," a loud voice beyond the great stone called. He began to sing again scared of the voice on the other side. It was not his uncle's voice calling to him. He listened closer hearing other voices from outside the cave. He knew this to be wrong. Fear began to swell in his belly.

"'We need to help this poor creature,' a little voice encouraged from the other side of the stone.

"Yes," said a very deep voice which sounded warm and loving. "He is so small and needs our help."

"There is no doubt that we should help him," another squeaky small voice said. "Yes, yes yes…"

"One of us will have to look after him," another voice ordered.

"We will all look after him," a stronger voice confirmed.

There were too many voices for the boy to keep track of. He thought they spoke in different languages but somehow he understood them. Still, they could understand each other and him. "Allow me," a strong burley voice offered. The great stone began to shift and light spilled into the cave blinding the boy. He cautiously crawled out shielding the glaring light with one hand. His body was very stiff and cold. He glanced around blinking his eyes into adjustment. He could not believe it. He was surrounded by animals.

"Come here child," an old bear-woman ordered, walking over and pulling him into a hug. Her rough fur was warm. "You will come with me and live as a bear."

"Yes," the boy answered. "I will come with you. You will be my family."

The boy lived in the woods with the bears for many years, learning from them and the other animals. He had two brother bears. One day in the forest seeking berries the bear-woman motioned them to silence.

"Listen," she said. "'here is a hunter." They listened and sure enough they heard the sounds of a man walking. The old bear-woman smiled. "We have nothing to fear from him," she said and they headed away from the hunter. "He is of too heavy of a step and the leaves and branches of the forest warned of him."

Another time as they walked along the old bear-woman again motioned them to silence. "Listen," she ordered. "Another hunter," they listened and soon they heard the sound of singing. The old bear woman smiled. "This one too is not dangerous except to himself. He is flapping his mouth. The one who talks as he hunts and does not remember everything in the forest has ears is nothing to fear. We bears can hear his light singing."

So they lived happily for years and the boy learned, talking to all the animals until one day when the old bear-woman motioned them to silence. A frightened look came over her face fear seeping into her eyes. "Listen," she warned. "It is the one who hunts on two legs with four legs. This one is very dangerous. We must hope he does not find us. Four legs who hunt with him can follow us no matter where we go."

Just then they heard the sound of a dog barking. "Run for your lives," screamed the mother bear. "Four legs has our scent." So they ran the boy and the three bears. They ran through streams and up a hill but still the sound of the barking dog followed closing on them. They ran through a swamp but the hunters still followed. They crossed a ravine forcing their way through thatches of thorns, but the sound of the barking dog kept closing in. Their hearts were ready to burst with exhaustion when they came to an old hollow log.

"It is our only hope," the mother bear called. "Get inside and stay quiet."

They crawled into the log waiting silently panting and afraid. There was no sound until the noise of the dog sniffing at the end of their log echoed in their ears. The mother bear growled fiercely. The dog did not dare come after them. Again silence, the boy began praying his family would be safe. However, his prayers were destroyed by the smell of smoke. Two legs piled brush at the end of the log attempting to smoke them out.

"Wait!" the boy cried out. "Don't hurt my family."

"Who is speaking?" shouted a confused voice from outside the log. "Is there a human inside there?" two legs asked more to himself than anyone else.

The boy heard the sound of the brush being kicked away from the mouth of the log and the smoke vanished. The boy crawled out looking into the face of the hunter.

"I have been cared for by the bears you hunt," the boy, now a man, said to the hunter. "They are my family and my friends. Please, do not harm them."

"Bring out your friends. I will not harm them if what you say is true." The hunter looked suspiciously at the boy as he snarled into the log. The old bear-woman and her two sons slowly crept out from the log but were still full of fear. The hunter dropped his bow and bowed at the boy's feet.

The old bear-woman hugged the boy, now a man. "We will always be your friend and your family," she cried.

"Remember what it is to be a bear and all that you have learned from the other animals. Pass it on to your children. My children will watch over your children." she pledged.

"I will never forget you." He realized that this was goodbye.

She looked at the feet of the hunter. "Now go, return to your kind." She sniffed and shuffled off into the forest with her two sons in tow.

The hunter led the boy to his tribe telling the clan the story. The boy became known as the one that lived with bears and he was accepted as a wise priest. He talked to the animals. The tribe only hunted what they needed to survive.

"What a bunch of rubbish?" Susan blurted getting up from the stool.

"As I said it is only a legend of my ancestry. I am sure there are some exaggerations. It is a rather good story though." He turned back to Carrie smiling. "I can talk to animals."

"Prove it," Susan barked.

"Okay, what do you suggest?"

"Let's go see the Crypto zoologist," Carrie offered. "He'll know how to prove or disprove this," she said looking back to Susan

"Okay but I'm going to go to lunch first, coming?" She opened the door.

"In a minute," Carrie said as Susan escaped out the door. "Play me something else please." She stared at him with those big brown eyes batting her lashes at him. Carl knew Garrett didn't stand a chance.

He nodded and waved his wand, "*Poctome* Metronome." Carl watched as one of the metronomes went floating into Garrett's hands. He started it leading into another song. Guitars and drums joined in with a wave of his wand. This song was more rock and roll. Both Carries bounced to the beat. Once Garrett finished, the fifteen year old Carrie put her head on Garrett's shoulder. "This is going to sound funny but will you escort me to the Winter Solace celebration." She looked up at him knowing it was customary for him to ask her. "We can tell everybody you asked me if you like. That is if you'll go with me?"

"Yeah," the boy looked stunned.

"I can't wait until you break out of your shyness and I think I have just the ticket." She jumped to her feet giving him a peck on the check before running after Susan.

Carl stood there admiring the boy who was rubbing the spot she had kissed.

"Okay Carl, I think it's time to return." The now Carrie grabbed his hand. They were floating back up as if coming up out of the water or sleep. He didn't want to leave. He opened his eyes finding they were back in his living room.

CHAPTER 4

"How did everything go?" Reginald asked, leaping from the couch and nearly crushing his leg against the coffee table. He spun away just before making contact, saving himself. He looked like he had been caught sleeping while on guard.

Carl staggered to the recliner collapsing into it. Carrie watched him with uneasy concern. He glanced up forcing a smile. She walked over, sat on the floor at his feet with her legs curled under her as if she were a cat.

"Are you okay?"

"I'm not sure," he answered truthfully. Confusion had seized hold of him. Everything he knew had been a lie. They had been telling him the truth but he didn't know what to do now. Who was he now? His life had been a charade orchestrated by some mad man. What did this mean for his future? Where was his future? What had he missed the last three years?

"That's okay. I'm alright. Don't worry about me," Reginald said, realizing the others had not noticed him being there. "Fine, I'll be going then." Reginald vanished.

"I know you must have a lot of questions." Carrie began to rub his hand hoping the act would help comfort the sorrow she saw in his eyes. "I'm going to send word to Sheba while you soak in what you witnessed." She stood up and began to walk out of the room, sending a concerned look back before leaving the room.

As soon as she left, Carl stood up on wobbly legs, pacing around. His mind raced through what had transpired in that *thing*. He glared at the memory returner... or whatever it was... as an uneasy feeling slithered in his gut like a snake. He had to make sense of what was happening, but how? There was no way to make sense of it. There was no logical way around it. There were no answers. He had been a sorcerer and now what was he? He felt the terror swelling inside him as he pondered the possibilities of trusting these people. Why couldn't he be having a stroke or this just be a hallucination?

He had no idea what the consequences would be, but decided to trust Carrie. He felt she was a good person. She seemed to care about him, having spent three years searching for him after all. That had to count for something he told himself.

"Okay, all set," Carrie announced, coming back in. "I'm sure you have a hundred questions but we need to eat first. I'm starving."

Food, wow, all of a sudden an aching feeling in the bottom of his belly announced its desire for food. He glanced at his watch seeing it was now past eight.

"I am famished," he announced. "I'll order a pizza if that's all right with you."

"Great. How about salad, too?" she suggested.

"Sounds good, what kind of dressing would you like?"

"Blue cheese, please."

"Got it." He went into the kitchen to make the call. Moments later, he returned carrying a tray of leftover cold cuts and cheese. "This should tide us over until the pizza gets here. It'll be about twenty minutes." He set the tray down on the glass coffee table and began nibbling on the scraps.

"I'm surprised Reginald didn't finish this off," Carrie said, snatching up a piece of cheese. "Where is he anyway?"

"I thought I saw him when we returned." They called out his name but there was no answer. "He must of left." Carl shrugged his shoulders.

"Strange. He didn't say goodbye," Carrie said, sitting on the couch and wondered if she should report him for leaving his post. "So, what do you want to know first?" she invited, trying to figure about her personal dilemma.

"Okay." He cleared his throat with a cough. "First of all, why were you all wearing togas?"

Carrie laughed. Carl liked the way she laughed. "Each year sixth level students vote on what would be the proper attire for the upcoming school year."

"Huh?'

"At Sitnalta, there are seven levels of education. The final semester of your sixth level you choose the attire for the school the next season. The seventh levels that year chose togas. It's more fun than wearing the same boring uniform year in and year out."

"Tell me more about the Palace at Sitnalta?" he asked, amazed at how hungry he found himself to be. He picked up a couple scraps of cold cuts nibbling on them as she talked.

"It's amazing when you come out of the chronicler, you are *so* hungry." she echoed his thoughts. "The Palace of Sitnalta is on a hidden island in the Mediterranean Sea."

"How can an island be hidden? Satellites must pick it up."

"The palace is protected by magic. You see anytime satellites or airplanes pass over it all they get are pictures of the sea. There may have been times new technology has accidently glimpsed the island but then it only appears to be a volcanic rock mass which they are unable to find again."

Carl nodded. "You said earlier that it was a replica of the original?"

"That's right. The original palace was uncovered by archeologist in the early 1900's and totally unearthed in 1966."

"What do you mean unearthed?" He gave a queer little cock of his head like a dog hearing an unfamiliar noise.

She took a deep breath. He could tell she was considering if she should actually go into this with him or not. "I was advised that when I found you that I should not give you too much information."

"By whom?" he asked innocently. She shook her head, silently answering his question.

"I can't say until you find that out for yourself." He could see she was struggling with doing what she thought was right versus keeping her promise.

"What can you tell me?" He asked a little perturbed.

"I can answer questions about what you saw today." She smiled at him pleased he understood or at least pretended to understand.

"Tell me about the original palace." he requested.

"Well, the original palace was hidden from normal people just as the replica is. It was much easier in the past. The island appeared to be uninhabitable covered by a volcanic eruption."

"How could a volcanic eruption hide the palace? It looked so beautiful," he interrupted.

"It only appeared to be hidden. It's hard to explain. So please listen." She sounded more like a school teacher begging the natives to remain calm.

She went on to explain that the original palace had been open to everyone, those with magical abilities and those without. It was an acropolis sitting on top of a great hill with crystallized stone of gypsum supported by large redwood pillars. It had been built around 2103 B.C. powered by a complex water system more suitable then than the water systems in most third world countries today. It was a society living a utopian experience in all facets of life.

The problems began within this peaceful community when a priest by the name of Globin Bailey also called Glob began to complain about non-magical people. The people were becoming so dependent on the world of magic, that they were turning very lazy, expecting sorcerers to provide them with everything they needed to survive. Glob began rallying supporters from the magical world, their goal, to enslave all non-magical beings. Glob labeled non-magical people as Rubes, a term we still use today. They formed a small group called Glob Bins which eventually became Goblins. The Goblins began torturing and killing all those opposing them magical and Rubes alike.

Carrie continued explaining about the revolution of 1600 B.C. The palace had become a stronghold for sorcerers most of whom did not wish to harm the Rubes. The Goblins were a different story. They developed a curse, the *Mordirian curse* which kills the person it's aimed at immediately. Carl recalled Reginald quivering from the name earlier.

The war between the Rubes and the Goblins raged on becoming very bloody. There were many incidents of innocent people being executed or tortured, inspiring the Rubes to vigilantly hunt witches in the future.

Carl sat there soaking the story in. He had not expected all this. He jumped when a knock came from the front door followed by the ringing of the door bell. "That'd be the pizza," he announced, hoping to conceal his jump with movement. He started for the door wondering why people knocked and had to ring the door bell, too. It seemed silly.

He reached for the door about to open it, when Carrie shot off the couch with a yell, "Don't open the door!" She yanked her wand out and rushed to the door. "Nooo…"

It reminded him of a funny movie. She seemed to be talking and moving in slow motion. Shock spilled through his mind. She moved more like a cartoon character being drawn frame by frame. Her words echoed and floated in the air as her leg rose up. They fell back to the ground as her arms pumping like a slow moving piston of a train beginning its struggle to life. He expected to find a bubble over her head announcing her thoughts. She waved her wand rushing toward him.

"What?" he asked as concern shot through him. She shoved him away from the door with surprising strength. Time compensated for its earlier slowness by speeding up.

Carl fell to the floor with a crunch.

Carrie positioned herself between him and the door.

He expected a Goblin to burst in.

There was another crack of a knock on the steel door.

Pain seized Carl's arm, his elbow had hit the wall after bouncing off the floor.

"Is everything all right in there?" a young concerned voice called from the other side of the door. Carl figured the boy was confused hearing the commotion. His mind raced for an explanation.

Time slowed, returning to normal. "What the..?" he whispered, looking stunned at Carrie.

"We have to use caution. Now that I've found you, they could have followed me." He shook his arm, loosening the electrical twinge of pain which possessed it. "Whoever attacked you three years ago could easily know that we've found you. They'll want to ensure you do not return. They went to great risk to attack you the first time."

She slid the sidelight window curtain aside to peer outside. She spotted a teenage boy fidgeting on the stoop holding the pizza in a warmer and a brown paper bag containing the salad. "Just a second," she called through the closed door. She put the chain on the door cracking it cautiously open.

The delivery boy gazed through the gap cocking his head curiously. Carl guessed he was trying to figure out how the pizza and salad were supposed to fit through the narrow gap. "Sorry." Carl jumped up. He pushed the door closed taking off his t-shirt, throwing off the chain and messing up his brown hair. He tried to put on an innocent face before reopening the door.

"Sorry again, but she's not decent," Carl apologized with a laugh as he stood bare-chested in front of the boy, making sure to keep Carrie from his sight.

The boy laughed uncomfortably handing the food over. Carrie's mouth sprang open with surprise. Her wand still clutched in her hand aiming at the boy through the tiny crack of the door and jamb.

Carl dug in his pocket fishing out his wallet. He fumbled with it nervously, noticing that Carrie had turned the wand away from the boy and now aimed it at him. She teasingly taunted him with it. He smiled. "You know how women are. When they get... Well... You know they can't control themselves," Carl teased, feeling the temperature of his face grow warmer.

Carrie shot a spell at Carl. He leapt back feeling a warmness fill him as if he had just swallowed warm medicine. He stumbled shifting his posture to hide his chest where the faint hairs began to blossom. They began growing so quickly Carl now resembled a bear. "Keep the change!" he hollered, shoving the food to Carrie and two twenties at the guy.

"Gee thanks," the boy said as the door slammed in his face. "Some people! Why'd they even order food in the first place?" He turned heading back to his car thinking how lucky he was to get a seventeen dollar tip.

Carrie turned away from the window once she was sure the boy had entered his car in the gravel driveway.

"Very funny." His chest hairs were now reaching the floor. "Please put it right."

"Oh, it will return to normal in about a week." She giggled.

"A week!" He tried to chase her but couldn't move with the enormous amount of hair. She waved her wand removing the extra hair in the blink of an eye.

"You'll watch what you say from now on then, aye," she said, taunting with a wave of her wand.

They laughed their way into the kitchen. "That wasn't fair," he said still laughing. He put his shirt back on while grabbing a bottle of wine from the refrigerator. "Seeing as I have no way of defending myself."

"You'd best remember that then," she said, laughing behind her hand.

They sat and ate not really talking. Carl thought of it as the calm before the storm knowing that after dinner they returned to the living room and his real identity. Carrie curled up at one end of the couch, Carl at the other. She ran her finger over a glass of wine she held studying Carl over it. It felt like she was burning a hole in him with her eyes.

"So what happened to your hair?" he asked, breaking the silence as if she willed him to speak first. He took a sip of his wine worried about the possibility of hitting upon sore subject. He felt clumsy being alone with her now hoping not to say the wrong thing sending her back into tears. He was unfamiliar with talking to beautiful a woman and lacked confidence talking to one as pretty as Carrie.

"I changed it when we realized what happened to you." He was surprised she spoke so freely. He noticed her eyes beginning to puff and she appeared to choke back tears. She took a nervous sip of wine trying to muster her own courage. "This is rather good for being a non-magical drink."

"It's all right if you don't want to talk about it. I'm sorry." He felt bad saying the wrong thing.

She took a big drink setting the empty glass on the coffee table. He started to get up to fetch some more when she halted him. She gave him a coy smile and his stomach leapt noticing the vulnerability in her eyes. She seemed younger than the girl in the chronicler now. Suddenly, he regretted bringing up the subject.

"Don't be silly." She gave a false laugh still fighting the urge to cry. "Actually, I changed my hair the moment you disappeared." She stood up beginning to pace the floor. She put her arms around herself as if giving herself a hug. "You see you were my partner and my responsibility."

"How's that?" He pulled his head back as if being slapped.

"I should have been with you when you were attacked but wasn't." She collapsed back into couch. He slid next to her innocently putting a hand on her knee trying to sooth her pain.

"I'm sure there was nothing you could have done." He didn't know why he said this but it felt right.

"That's easy for you to say. You don't remember." She turned staring into his eyes. He saw she had lost the battle with the tears as a couple slid down her cheek. "We were supposed to stay with each other no matter what. Your work was… is vital. We knew that there were… are those that would want it for themselves and others who don't want it discovered at all."

"It wasn't your fault." He couldn't bear watching her cry. Her silent tears were stampeding down her checks now. "I'm sure it wasn't. I know me and I am very pig headed. I probably was then, too. It had to be more my fault than anyone else's."

She pulled away from him wiping the tears away with the back of her hand. He grabbed a tissue from the box on the end table. "Thanks, you're right you were always very pig headed. But it still was my responsibility to keep you safe. So after you disappeared I changed the color of my hair and swore it would remain this way until I found you."

"So let's get back to the palace," he requested, desperately wanting to change the subject.

"Well, the battles took on more deadly consequences." She began slipping back to the history easily. "The magical world had the advantage of spells and charms but the Rubes had numbers. Glob couldn't overcome the sorcerers and sorceresses that joined the Rubes. He became desperate. You see the Palace is located near the tectonic plates of Europe and Africa. There were always earthquakes. Glob used this predicting a fierce earthquake that would destroy the island and all that lived there."

"Sorta like the prediction that California will one day fall into the ocean?" he asked.

"We don't know if it was meant to scare people or a true prophecy. Goblins love to use fear to repress their victims."

Carl could almost envision it. He closed his eyes feeling like he was back on the Mediterranean island. A foul faced man with a long dirty beard carrying a long staff stood on a beach right before the break of volcanic rocks. There was a large nasty mole on his left cheek giving him a more sinister appearance. "When the earthquake didn't destroy the island as predicted, Glob took matters into his own hands." Her voice seemed like an echo.

Carrie did not have to tell him anymore. He saw it behind his closed eyes inhaling as if it allowed him to witness it more clearly. The man took a boat which was magically gliding over the sea to the base of a volcano. It had been a place of worship for many magical and non-magical people in the community. Bailey now stood at the mouth of the volcano calling upon his magic. Carl felt the weird sensation like he was standing next to Glob as the evil man chanted over and over. Then with a mighty blow, he slammed his staff into the ground. The volcano heeded his call erupting, spilling ash, mud and magma. For four days the volcano spilled ash polluting the air until the palace was completely covered with lava.

Many Rubes were killed. The magical community had cast spells of protection from the lava and other toxins that the volcano dispelled.

Some Rubes survived thanks to the magic of good sorcerers. They fled to Egypt and Greece in hopes to find allies there. In Egypt, they became slaves to the pharaoh. It wasn't much better for those that chose to flee to Greece. The waters of the Mediterranean were not kind and the Greek army was mighty. The refuges were enslaved there as well.

The Rubes blamed their plight upon magic community declaring all magic as evil. They sought to hunt down and kill all that they believed to yield magic. Years later those that managed to free themselves returned to the island searching for their sworn enemies. They began telling stories about the evils of magic. The prejudices of the survivors grew over Africa and Europe. It wasn't long until both continents sought to rid their lands of all magic users.

Thus, the palace remained underneath the rubble until it was discovered in the early 1900's. Through sorcery, the magical society had been able to live in peace for nearly 3000 years until their buried world was unearthed.

Through the centuries some magic users ventured away from the safety of the palace. It didn't matter where they went rubes eventually hunted them down. Even in America which had been founded on the rights of individuals to have the freedom of religion, they were hunted for practicing magic.

"Sit-nal-ta," Carl said slowly. "The name makes me think of Atlanta, a city in Georgia, a southern state. They names sound alike," he informed her not knowing if she had ever heard of the city.

Carrie didn't say anything just smiled at him. He thought he could see a secret behind her brown eyes.

He repeated the name a couple more times trying to scramble the syllables. "You know... It can't be, can it?"

"What?" she asked, eagerness spreading over her face.

"Sitnalta couldn't be Atlantis, could it?" he asked, feeling the warmth of excitement in the heart of his belly.

"Well done," Carrie beamed at him. "The Rubes that were enslaved in Greece told the story of their plight to many. One who heard it was Plato. He retold the story many times. However, whoever copied it wrote the name backwards."

"I thought Atlantis sank off the coast of Florida?"

"That's just a rumor we help spread to keep people from searching for the proper sight." She smiled at his discovery and proud he was still so clever.

"How was the Palace discovered?" Carl asked, joining Carrie on the couch again.

"We aren't exactly sure." She covered her mouth from a yawn that surprised her. She suddenly realized she felt extremely tired. It was six hours ahead at her home. It would be five in the morning there. She set the empty glass down on the table taking out her wand. *"Poctome Shoughtwes,"* she said conjuring a small vile of amber liquid.

"What is that?" Carl asked, sitting up.

"It's a potion that'll help me remain awake." She pulled off the vile's cork sniffing the brown liquid. Carl saw her mouth wrinkle and knew the smell was unpleasant.

"How long do you plan on staying awake?"

"Until someone else comes back to watch over us," she answered, standing up and walking over to the window once more. "I'm sure the people that attacked you know I've found you. So it wouldn't be wise to let our guard down. I shall take a post outside."

"You don't have to stay outside," he said, getting up from the couch and following her to the window.

"I was hoping you'd say that," she said relieved not to have to spend the night outdoors.

"I'm sure you'll be more comfortable inside. You can sleep on the couch." Her smile faded as his grew. "Just kidding; there's a spare bed right over here." He showed her to the bedroom and gave her a quick tour of the rest of the house.

"Thanks." She let out another big yawn. "It looks really comfortable," she said, eyeing the bed. "I'll cast some protective spells and put the potion away." She re-corked and made it vanish.

"Well, make yourself at home and let me know if you need anything."

Another big yawn escaped and he waited as she tried to shake it out to talk. "I'm sure everything will be great. Good night."

"Good night," he returned, heading to the room next to hers. He closed the door changing into his night cloths. He turned off the light and blindly made his way into bed.

He was startled by a light knock on the door. "Come in," he called as Carrie opened the door. She was wearing a long pink teddy t-shirt with a picture of a lion and a bear. Her hair was back to red like the younger her in the chronicler. Carl was struck dumb admiring how her hair fell against her.

"If it's okay with you, I'd like to keep the doors open," she requested. He noticed a slight blush creep across her cheeks.

"No worries, pleasant dreams," he said, trying to sound cool but not too cool. She smiled turning to go. "Right then, have pleasant dreams."

"Oh, by the way…" he said. She stopped turning back to face him as he lay under the covers. "You look much lovelier with your hair that way. It looked nice the other way but this is outstanding."

Her face brightened as she inhaled the compliment. She smiled her mysterious smile. "See you in the morning," she called from the hallway.

Fifteen minutes later Carl heard faint snores coming from the spare bed. He laid there thinking for about another twenty minutes. Sleep would not welcome him so easily. He thought of the chronicler and the memory they had visited. He laughed thinking about his chest hair. Then he thought of the girl lying in the other room.

He tiptoed out of his room, glancing through the open door that led to the room in which she slept. He walked over to the doorway peering in, feeling uncomfortable, afraid she may wake. The covers were pulled up to her chin reminding him of a sleeping child. He turned back heading to the living room. He sat on the couch grabbing the remote control for the television. He turned it on careful that the volume would not wake his guest.

From the spare bedroom, Carrie smiled, rolling over and falling back to sleep.

Somewhere across the ocean in a dark room, the silhouettes of two black caped figures kneeling before a figure in an orange cape sitting in a chair as if it were a throne. A male voice came from one of the two kneeling figures. "It is true. Montgomery has been found."

The orange caped person rose from its seat. "I was informed that this would never happen." A whinny female voice came from underneath the cape.

"We shall find him and eliminate him," the man answered, keeping his face to the ground.

There was a loud crack and the two kneeling figures' heads jerked up slightly and lowered just as quickly. A man appeared still wearing his bed cloths. "Session, I have just found out that Garrett Montgomery lives. How can that be?"

"Master, I do not understand," the man stuttered obviously just being awakened.

"Mordirian!" the orange figure cursed the man, who fell dead at her feet. The two kneeling figures trembled. "Bring me Montgomery's head," she said, sitting back down and waving the away.

CHAPTER 5

The next morning Carl woke with a stiff neck, a pillow resting behind his neck and a comforter covering his body. It took a moment before he realized Carrie must have covered him, but when? He stood up taking a deep breath. His stomach then noticed the sweet aroma of bacon filling the house. He staggered into the kitchen following the beacon his stomach had honed onto. There was no better way to wake up he thought than to someone else cooking bacon.

"Good morning," Carrie greeted, standing at the stove preparing breakfast. "We have a lot to accomplish today."

Carl sat down at the table which was covered with food. There were hotcakes, waffles, eggs, sausage, biscuits and gravy, and the bacon was on its way. "Are we expecting an army?" Carl asked, overwhelmed by all the food.

"Oh that," she said, shoveling the bacon out of the frying pan and onto a plate to drain. "Well, I never learned to cook for just a couple of people. I grew up in a big family and being the eldest daughter I was in charge of most of the household chores. Besides we may have some visitors."

She joined him at the table as he poured them both some orange juice. "Well, it all looks and smells amazing," Carl complimented, beginning to fill his plate.

"Right about that," a voice from behind them called. They turned spying Reginald dressed in jeans and a t-shirt standing in the doorway. "It smells like we arrived right on time." He rushed in and quickly took up one of the vacant seats. Sheba followed him dressed in a very smart business suit as if ready for the board room.

"Happy birthday, Carrie," Sheba greeted with a kiss on the cheek. She turned and glared at Reginald who already had his mouth filled with a piece of toast and marmalade. He grunted what might have been happy birthday, shrugging his shoulders as if saying what did you expect?

"Thanks," Carrie laughed smiling at Carl. They ate enjoying the great food and not speaking much. Carl sat wondering what events were planned for him today. There was a part of him that did not want to know. Yet, he wondered if this was what it was like to have a family. The feeling of belonging grew inside him. He just realized how lonely he had been over the past three years. These people had known him and treated him with a surprising comfort of familiarity that gave him a warm feeling inside.

It did not take long for his comfort to vanish. "Right then," Reginald said, breaking the silence while sliding his chair back. "I have something for you Garrett." He gave his wand a wave and a long thin box appeared on the table in front of Carl.

Carl looked at the girls. They nodded looking so excited at the prospect of him opening the package you would think it was Christmas. He had his doubts. All of a sudden, he was shocked he hadn't been surprised when Reginald called him Garrett. Biting his top lip he knew he could not stall any longer, taking a deep inhale he lifted the top of the box. Inside resting on blue velvet pillow sat a wand of about four inches in length. His stomach cramped as mixed emotions spilled through him. This could be fun he thought thinking back to the chest hair. Fear also lurked in the shadows of what it stood for.

"It's your old wand," Reginald announced as if Carl didn't know what it was. "It's made out of a white beech tree and contains the magical hair of a Dolphin."

"A what?" he asked, gingerly taking the wand out of the case. "Dolphins don't have hairs."

"Yes, they do." Sheba corrected matter-of-factly.

Carl looked at her as if she were crazy. All the doubts from the previous day sprung back to life.

"Carl," Carrie began, "Dolphins do have hairs but they are very fine. You have to pet one to know."

"Yeah," Reginald added. "You let me pet one once."

"I let you pet a dolphin?" He ran a hand through his messy brown morning hair.

"Yeah, but petting the lion was much cooler."

"You pet a lion?" Carl asked.

"Thanks to you I did," Reginald answered.

Carl swore. If yesterday was strange, this was downright mad.

"Carl," Sheba began holding up a finger. "Dolphins are the most magical creatures on the planet. I know you've read that dragons and unicorns are but their entire species are no match with the magical ability that resides in a single dolphin."

"But," Carl began to argue but could not think of anything to say. Luckily Reginald seized the opportunity to add to the conversation.

"Dragons were so weak in magical ability they had to evolve into small lizards to avoid extinction to survive."

"I don't think I would call a creature that can magically transform itself from one of the world's largest creatures to one of the smallest weak," Carrie warned.

Reginald half laughed half coughed and escaped into the living room. Carrie and Sheba followed leaving Carl alone with the wand, his wand. He sat there a moment alone wondering if he should follow but for some reason understood he was to wait for them. He guessed they were plotting their next course of action. He waved the wand as Carrie had done the night before and was surprised to feel music coming from it. It reminded him of something soothing like a lullaby. Confusion fogged his brain, trying to figure out how he was feeling but not hearing the music.

He waved it again more vigorously. The window over the kitchen sink shot open so fast it shattered the upper panel. Carrie burst into the kitchen followed closely by the others. They each had their wands poised for battle. Carl gazed at the floor embarrassed. "What happened?" Carrie demanded after doing a quick search to ensure they were all safe.

"I waved the wand and the window shot open," Carl tried to explain as tremors of shock still echoed in his veins.

Reginald began to laugh. Carrie tried to conceal her smile by looking sternly at him. Sheba walked over to the window and surveyed the area. Carl guessed she was making sure no one was watching before repairing the damage, *"parieren."* The window sprang back to normal minus the dirt that had once been covering it. Carl could not help but shake his head surprised. He laughed to himself realizing he would need to clean the other panel now so it matched.

"All right then why don't we all go into the other room?" Carrie suggested, leading the way into the living room. They took the same positions they had taken the night before. Carl sat in the recliner his three guests on the couch.

"Okay, today what we are going to do is take turns going into the Chronicler Recital," Sheba began, getting up from the couch. Carl had the suspicion Sheba felt more comfortable giving orders rather than receiving them. He noticed the day before that Carrie was not as assertive as Sheba and Reginald appeared to be happier coming along for the ride.

"I have some errands to see to back in Brussels," Carrie announced. Catching his feeling of being abandoned, she reassured him by saying, "I will have to clear up my schedule to make sure I can stay with you until it's safe for you to return home."

"I'm returning to Brussels?" Carl asked.

"Once we have rehabilitated you to your previous magical state first," Sheba answered while walking over to the Chronicler Recital. "Reginald will take you in first while Carrie and I return to Brussels. Carl, I cannot stress enough the importance of you remaining focused and having a strict intent when you go into the Chronicler Recital."

Carl looked around wondering how he was going to have strict intent. Confusion spilled over him like someone cracked an egg of it over his head. Last night when he'd laid on the couch he had decided he would do what these people asked. He was curious and eager to learn more about Garrett Montgomery. He thought it strange that Sheba had not given these instructions the previous night. Had he and Carrie done something wrong?

"Good luck," Carrie said to Reginald. She looked at Carl with an approving smile. He felt she was trying to read his thoughts but he was resisting. "Trust your feelings and remember that the magic is still inside you. You just need to be reacquainted with it."

Carl nodded. He wasn't sure there was any magic in him but he would give it a try. What did he have to lose? If he was going crazy, then going with it seemed to be the most logical thing to do. If what they said was true, then there was an entire world out there he once knew and had been taken from him.

"Very good then, I'll see you later tonight," Carrie said.

"Oh, by the way, happy birthday," Carl smiled, just remembering.

"Thanks," she smiled, nodding at him and then disappearing.

"Right then," Sheba began, ordering them about. "Reginald will take you through the first part of the Chronicler Recital, I the second and Carrie will finish up tonight. Our intent is to strengthen your belief that you are a sorcerer and for you to begin learning some magic."

She looked at Reginald who nodded, understanding her instructions. She smiled at Carl. He gave a look saying he understood the directions too. "Well then, I will be going, bye for now." She mumbled something and disappeared.

"Blimey, I thought she'd never leave." Reginald walked over to the Chronicler Recital putting his wand to his temple and concentrating. He pulled out a red and silver thread that looked like a thick hair. He began stirring it into the cloudy inside of the Chronicler Recital. "I have always wanted to do this but this is going to be my first time. I hear it's a little strange at first. What do you think?"

"Well, I didn't like it at first, but it's cool seeing what someone has remembered."

"Yeah, cool huh? Well, I suppose it's ready." He turned around tipping his head back as if he were a scuba diver slipping into the ocean. Carl watched as he disappeared then walked over to the screen and peered inside as tall lanky boy with red hair appeared through the hurricane like image. Did they all have red hair back then? It was Reginald but much younger about fourteen or fifteen. "Are you coming or not?" Reginald of today called from somewhere underneath the mist.

Carl leaned forward as he had done the night before, tumbling face first into the eye of the storm. He felt the tingling twist of doing a somersault under water hit his gut. This time he noticed his nose felt like cotton swabs had been shoved up it. He closed his eyes trying to wish away the eerie feeling.

"This is cool. I look so goofy," Reginald greeted as Carl landed next to him. Again he expected to see his living room instead he was greeted by bright sunshine and sea air.

Today he was further down the hill away from the palace on the opposite side of what he saw the night before. Reginald of today was walking around the younger Reginald. He had to agree the boy looked goofy in a white toga and flaming red hair. Carl studied the rest of the scenery. The salt air invaded his senses as the realization they were back at the Palace of Sitnalta overtook his expectation of being back in Michigan. Quickly a warm feeling washed over him, like a comforting hug. He wondered if it was the warmth of the Mediterranean air or being back at the palace. Either way it felt like returning home. He and the older Reginald were hidden behind large boulders that lay behind a small palace that reminded Carl of the Kremlin. It had large redwood pillars like Sitnalta but on the top of the Pillars were onion shaped orbs. Trembles whisked through Garrett/Carl realizing this was Atlantis.

He heard chattering, looked left and saw young Carrie, Susan Medico and Garrett running down a hill to the small palace. Reginald crouched further behind the boulder afraid to be seen, as did the younger one. Carrie pounded on the door which was answered by a bald black man with a thin mustache. Carl could hear the echoing calls of a dog from inside the smaller palace.

"That's Sage Byterian; he's harmless. Let's get a closer look," the Reginald of today suggested. They crept up to the door. Reginald seemed not to be as trusting that he would not be detected. He crept closer prepared to dart out of sight if anyone turned in his direction. Carl studied Sage Byterian; a muscular man shaped more like a bull.

"Quiet Fuss! Now, what can I do for you three? Are you here to see the skionts? It's not normal for fourth and fifth levels to be together you know?"

"Not precisely Byterian, we are here for an experiment." Carrie explained how Garrett claimed he could talk to animals. She actually went over every detail about their encounter as though very impressed. The young Reginald seemed to be impressed too.

"Holy shark's teeth," Byterian said. Carl thought he almost said another word instead of shark. "I have heard of such things but never met anyone that actually could," Byterian said, rubbing his stony chin. The more Carl looked at him the more he thought he resembled a statue. He stood about five foot eight with the shoulders of a prize fighter.

"Do you mean there are actually people that can talk to animals?" Susan asked.

"Why of course," Byterian boomed with a hearty laugh. "Mostly they can only talk to snakes though."

"I can't talk to snakes," Garrett said as if it were a bad thing. "I tried once but it seemed to upset the snake and I nearly got bit."

"I bet you did." Byterian looked at him amazed. "You are the Indian lad ain't cha'?"

Garrett looked down at the ground nodding his head.

"You don't have to do that," Carrie said, glaring at Garrett.

"Do what?" he asked, glancing up but keeping his chin lowered.

"Looking away froms people when's speaks that is," Byterian croaked and a shy smile sprang to the boy's face when he looked up. "Yous cans keep yas head up and should boy, you study at the greatest learning facility there is, Sitnalta." Carl had a feeling Garrett was not the only person from the United States. As much as Byterian tried to disguise it, the hint of a charming southern American drawl slipped through.

Carl looked at today Reginald seeing he stood taller with his chest out a little more. "It is the best school in the world," he said, smiling at Carl.

"It's just... most people don't treat me well when they find out. In fact, other than my uncle no one has talked to me too much until today." The smile vanished from his face.

Now, it was the others turn to look at the ground unable to meet Garrett's eyes. "I suspect that true," Byterian finally said with a sniffle in his voice. "I've known sorcerers to be very mean to newcomers. You just need not pay them no charm though. Use your voice boy and let them see who you are. They will come around they will. You'll see. Just looks at these lasses here."

Garrett smiled as the girls smiled back at him. Carrie began to glow at him and Susan looked ashamed to have felt scared of him before. "I'm sorry Garrett," Susan apologized. "It's just I've never met anyone that was an American Indian and I've heard horrible stories about them." Garrett nodded he had heard the stories all of his life. He knew too often of Indians who rejected their own heritage and succumbed to another nationality to be accepted.

"I understand...," Garrett started.

"It's just you've been lonely by yourself," Carrie said, finishing his thought. "I am excellent at Leer Poma, an ability to delve into the minds of people and interpret their feelings," she explained as if she were teaching him rather than explaining her talent. "I can usually guess what they are thinking by what they're feeling."

"Brauchen is when you are able to shut down feelings and memories so they can't be detected," Garrett answered. Carrie looked surprisingly at him. "I'm sorry I was just lazy a moment ago. Normally, I protect my thoughts better by having them locked away in a safe."

"So, that's it!" Carl said, turning to Reginald. "I just need to shut down my feelings and memories?"

Reginald gained his courage and ventured closer now standing next to Carl. "That's one way but I think there are others."

"What do you mean?"

"Don't know. I was just told to tell you that there was another way."

"By whom?"

"Sorry bud I can't tell you that yet. You'll just have to figure it out for yourself or ask someone else." Carl glared at Reginald wishing he could use Leer Poma on him. Perhaps a slap up side his goofy head would make him feel like telling him.

"Thanks you're a lot of help, you know." Reginald nudged his head toward the memory. It seemed Reginald worried something important might slip past.

"Oh I see," Garrett said, looking a little confused. "Well, Susan how do you purpose I should prove I can actually talk to animals?"

"I was hoping Sage Byterian would come up with something. He is the Crypto-zoologist," she answered, looking to Byterian. He stroked his strong chin with his massive black finger a moment.

"All right then, Susan, you and Carrie take Fuss into my home. I'll walk with young Garrett here making sure he can't hear what you tell Fuss." He smiled at the girls who looked like they understood the plan. "Be sures that it's something no one already knows so Garrett can't guess though."

They disappeared inside the small palace. Byterian clasped one of his huge hands on Garrett's shoulder. Garrett stumbled but did not fall. "Excellent, well Garrett I's wish you'd let me know in class that you could talk to animals. We could have saves somes of the skionts we could."

"Sorry sir but I don't understand them." He looked up at Byterian. "They're not the friendliest creatures I've come across. I think I have heard them laughing at us though."

"They be all right if you know how to treat them. They is just likes us need a bit of love and they are good little creatures." Carl wondered if Byterian heard what Garrett had said.

"If you say so sir, you are the expert." Garrett gave Byterian a doubting look.

Byterian enjoyed Garrett's response. He rolled back howling with laughter. "An expert is I?" He slapped Garrett on the back sending him into a run three paces forward. "Your uncle was right you are a good lad."

"You know my uncle?"

"Sh…" He held a huge finger up to his mouth. "We is discussing that at another time. Comes down to see the skionts alone, we's discuss it then. My sister and I were born in South Carolina but none here know that."

The door to the hut flew open. Fuss a female German Sheppard came bounding out as if she had been locked up for days, finally freed to relieve herself. She did not take care of natures business though. She ran straight to Garrett almost knocking him over with excitement. Garrett regained his balance bowing a little to pet the excited pooch.

It was nothing like what Carl had expected. Byterian, Carrie, and Susan watched as Fuss did something that sounded like humming. Garrett nodded continuing to pet the large dog. Everyone looked expectedly at Garrett once the dog stopped humming. Fuss sat panting at Garrett's feet looking eagerly at the other three.

"Well first of all, Fuss says Reginald Dean is hiding behind a boulder." Garrett pointed to where the red haired boy hid.

"Reginald Xavier Dean, you comes over here now," Byterian bellowed.

"What are you doing spying on us?" Carrie demand.

"I was not spying." He looked around swallowing heavily, his face almost as red as his hair.

"What were you doing then?" Susan demanded, hands on her hips.

"I was just going for walk and saw you. I tried to avoid you but kinda got stuck there." He looked very scared and kind of sad. "I saw Garrett and wanted to see what was going on."

"That would be spying!" Susan yelled, waving her finger at Reginald scolding him.

"Honestly, I was trying to avoid everyone." He looked at everyone his eyes finally resting on Carrie who was studying him intensively.

"He's telling the truth," Carrie blurted. "He just asked a girl to the Winter Solace dance and was rejected."

"Thanks," he said, looking glum. It was obvious he didn't want anyone knowing this.

"Never mind that," Garrett said, feeling sorry for Reginald and wanting to draw the attention away from him. "Fuss said Susan told her she got your aunt a new beautiful blue bonnet for Christmas and wished she could see her expression, but would not dare miss the Winter Solace celebration."

Susan's mouth hung open as she looked over at Carrie. "It's word for word."

"Fuss also says that, Byterian, you over cook the steaks. Steaks are supposed to be medium. The way you make them you might as well grind them up and call them a hamburger. She doesn't mind the sweet beer to wash them down with though."

"Does she now?" Byterian bent down rubbing the head of the Sheppard.

"She also says she doesn't like being called a coward. She wishes you would stop or she'll tell me something you wouldn't want us to know."

"Enough of that then, I won't be blackmailed by my dog." Byterian looked cross at Fuss then smiled to show he was just playing and not really upset.

"Blimey," Reginald blurted. "Did she really say all that?" The red haired boy looked at Byterian, Fuss and back to Garrett.

"I made up the blackmail part." Fuss wagged her tail jumping up on Garrett, giving him a sloppy dog kiss.

"All right Fuss." Byterian pulled the dog off Garrett and Fuss began to hum some more.

"What's she saying?" Carrie asked, excited.

"She wants me to come back so she can talk to Byterian. She likes me and wants me to help Byterian." Garrett felt happier than he had ever been.

"Help Byterian do what?" Reginald asked. Everyone looked at Fuss and back to Byterian.

"Don't know." Garrett rubbed Fuss' head but she didn't say anymore. "By the sounds of Fuss I would guess cooking." They all roared with laughter.

"All right now that will be enough of you lot," Byterian laughed. Fuss began barking and running around them excitedly.

"Well, I think that's all for us," today's Reginald said grabbing hold of Carl's elbow. "I think we'd better return. I'm not sure how you're supposed to learn to speak to animals."

Carl had gleaned some other useful information he suspected Reginald had not picked up on. Carrie had been able to sense his feelings. It was a reminder that he needed to guard his feelings and memories. He would think about how best to defend his thoughts. Being able to talk to animals might be a cool party game, but he would keep a note of it just in case it was *useful*. Who knew, he might get a pet.

"Okay now," Reginald said as they returned to the living room. Carl collapsed onto the couch. Reginald stared at him. "Are you all right?"

Carl wasn't sure. He felt as if he'd just left his strength in the Chronicler Recital. His mind felt fine, racing with excitement. His body however, felt worn out as if he had just run ten miles.

"Yeah, I just need to catch my legs," he panted, rubbing his eyes with the palm of his hands.

Reginald studied him as if he didn't believe Carl's explanation. After about ten minutes Carl stood up and walked to the kitchen. "I think I could do with a spot of food," Carl announced with Reginald following him.

"I bet Carrie's left some treats in the kitchen for us."

Sure enough, they walked into a kitchen full of snacks waiting for them. "When did she make these?" Carl asked.

"Don't know," Reginald answered as he tore into the sandwich, stuffing it in his mouth. Carl stood gawking as Reginald woofed down the sandwich in three bites. "Aren't you hungry?" Reginald asked, grabbing another sandwich. Carl nodded joining in.

When they finished eating, Reginald pulled out his wand. "Er- I'm going to teach you a couple spells while we wait. They aren't much but the girls told me I could if they weren't back when we finished."

Reginald was surprised at how quickly Carl picked up the new spells. He first learned *hiscentolt* which was a spell to open locked items. It did not open all doors though. Reginald explained that some doors were charmed to repel the spell. The second spell that Carl learned was *parieren* which Carl had witnessed Sheba use earlier on the window he had broken.

"That's very good Garrett," Reginald congratulated, clearing his throat again. "Don't tell the girls but I'm going to teach you another set of spells. The first is a spell to instantly paralyze someone. It can be helpful if you are being attacked. You just wave your wand like before and say *Todavia*. The counter-curse to *Todavia* is *Locotvia*."

Carl learned the spells with ease. It felt like he had been using them for years. This magic stuff could be pretty cool he thought while practicing. He jinxed a fly with *Todavia,* watched it fall to the ground and released it just before impact with *Locotvia*. He smirked trying to think what the fly thought being so far off course.

"Excellent," Reginald laughed, looking like he wanted to join in the sport.

"What is a Crypto-zoologist?" Carl asked.

"A Crypto-zoologist is a keeper for creatures that Rubes don't think exist."

"Like skoints?"

"Yeah," Reginald frowned.

"What is a skiont?" Carl asked, letting the fly escape.

"They're evil water creatures that like to come on land at night. They are part lobster and part stingray."

They jumped as something broke in the other room.

CHAPTER 6

"Well, how did it go?" Sheba asked as Reginald and Carl returned to the living room to see what had made the noise.

"It was bloody wicked!" Reginald stated, beaming. Carl noticed some mayonnaise remained on the corner of his mouth.

"I was asking Carl, or would you now prefer Garrett?" Sheba asked, appearing annoyed with Reginald; perhaps the traces of food around his mouth were the cause. Carl recalled how alarming it had been watching Reginald eat.

"Carl, if you please." He felt grateful she asked. "I am really impressed with the details of the memories. I mean, there was no way Reginald could have overheard everything we heard or had seen everything we saw. Still, he managed to show me the *entire* memory without gaps."

"Welcome to the magical world!" Reginald said, still smiling. Carl noticed Sheba taking great effort in ignoring Reginald.

"Good, well now I have something special to show you," Sheba announced as she preformed the same ritual of plucking a hair like substance from her head and placing it into the Chronicler Recital. She began stirring it with her wand as the others had done earlier. She studied Carl not watching the Chronicler at all but forcing a smile. "It takes place after Reginald's and before the one Carrie will show you later."

The first time he entered the Chronicler, he had felt eager to see what would happen. Even this morning, he had looked forward to revisiting another memory. He had not originally anticipated going in with Reginald but it had been interesting, just not as exciting as it had been with Carrie. Now, he felt uncomfortable going into it with Sheba. Something stung his brain about Sheba. He just couldn't pinpoint what it was though. It might have been that he'd hoped to be going into the thing with Carrie again. He felt a connection with her. The fact she had spent the past three years looking for him had him in awe and he admired her for it. He could not imagine the guilt or devotion she must have felt compelling her to spend so much time searching for him. The devotion she displayed was astonishing. He wished she were with him now. He felt calmer with her around.

"Okay, I think it's ready," Sheba said, breaking him from his trance. She looked up at Carl and Reginald forcing a smile again. "We shouldn't be too long," she told Reginald who nodded. Carl suspected Reginald expected to go with them or maybe planning on watching from above. Whichever it was, Sheba obviously did not want either to happen. She glared at him until he understood her cue. It was time for him to leave.

"Right then, I'll see you back in London." He nodded and disappeared.

"London, I thought you were from Belgium?" Carl asked.

"Reginald and I live in London but work in Belgium." she answered, looking bored.

"So, you and Reginald are…"

"Married?" she finished his questions. "Yes, we are."

"Where did I live?" Carl asked, worried the last question might be a sore spot at the moment.

"Belgium, I guess. You were so busy at the embassy that it would make sense for it to have been your home."

He wanted to ask where Carrie lived but thought better of it. It might seem too forward.

"Carrie lived in Canterbury, England," Sheba answered, guessing his desire. Carl knew she hadn't used *Leer Poma* because he had carefully guarded his thoughts and emotions.

"Are you ready Carl?" Sheba asked, signaling the end of the polite questioning.

"Guess so," he said, shuffling his feet.

"NO!" she exclaimed, holding up a hand in protest. "You cannot guess. You have to know. There is no guessing. We either know what we are doing or we do not. We do not guess."

He stood back a moment dazed realizing how serious she was. "I understand and I am ready." He was determined to find the real him, the one from three years ago. He wanted to make his past and present whole somehow.

She nodded, realizing he understood her meaning. "Okay, what we need to do is state our intent."

He looked puzzled. Her expression appeared as if she had swallowed a spoonful of a nasty tasting medicine. "Okay, what memory am I visiting this time?" He quickly adjusted fearing the wrath that danced in her eyes.

"Well first thing, I think it would be best if I gave you some background." She looked down her nose at him as if she were a mother lecturing her child. "You and I had alchemy together. You were a year ahead of me but I had three classes a level ahead of my own, Alchemy, Rube Studies and Lost Worlds. I was the only one from my level to do so. So, when you came to Palace of Sitnalta we had those three classes together. I'm going to show one of the lessons from Alchemy after the winter holidays." She looked back into the Chronicler Recital and Carl felt a sense of loathing coming from her.

"What is Alchemy?" he asked, recalling the term from one of their prior discussions but still not sure exactly what it was.

"It's not important right now." She threw her hair back over her shoulder. Carl didn't like the way she tried brushing him off.

"Why's that?" It might help he thought.

"Because it is not important, what is important is that we focus on remembering everything we see." She shook her head glaring at him hoping he wouldn't push the matter any further.

He could sense her aggravation at his prodding about the meaning of Alchemy. A part of him wanted to continue until he got his way. Another part of him argued that it would not be a wise thing to do. He recalled the chest hair incident from the night before. Carrie had been in a playful mood. There might be a different outcome if the sorceress were upset with him as Sheba clearly was.

"Okay then, what is our next step?" he asked, proceeding with extreme caution in order to not upset her any further.

"We need to form our intent and don't ask why. You'll see soon enough." He could feel the hostility seeping through her and wanted to return it. This was not a memory she wanted to relive. He could feel she was doing this under some kind of protest.

"So, what is our intent?" he questioned cautiously. This *Leer Poma* thing was cool. He realized the more he aggravated Sheba, the easier he could understand her feelings. It might not be the wisest time to experiment though, he warned himself.

"Our intent will be to reestablish your mental cognition of three years ago with the you of today." She pronounced the words slowly as if this were obvious. He just needed to listen to her.

That's a stretch, he thought. He did not have experience with statements of intent up until yesterday but this one felt lame. He thought about the words mental and cognition. They really meant the same thing, cognition and mental cognition. But he repeated the intent anyway just to satisfy her. However, the urge to point out the blunder in word choice burned inside. He could feel her eyes glaring at him as she waited for him to finish. When he looked up indicating he'd finished they dove into the Chronicler Recital together head first as if diving into a swimming pool.

"Oh, how I loved this class. Sage Skopector was one of my favorite instructors. His wife is the head of our department back in Brussels," Sheba announced as Carl surveyed the classroom. Her mood had changed quickly but the ghost of anger still hung on him.

It was different style classroom than Carl remembered from his youth... well what he had believed to be his youth up until yesterday. There were seven great oak tables, each about eight feet long. They shone so bright Carl could see the cathedral ceiling reflecting in the polish. The first six tables were aligned in the form of a lazy "V" with a gap in the middle to allow students or the teacher to walk past each table. The seventh table rested across the back of the last set in the "V". Four chairs sat around each of the first seven tables allowing for twenty-eight students. The first six tables' seats were filled with students but Carl noticed Garrett sat alone at the last one. The table appeared larger with the vacant seats around him.

In the front of the class sat an eighth smaller table with different types of metals resting on it. A tall lanky dark haired teacher paced back and forth in front of this table. "Okay can anyone tell me what Lord Overton attends for Sorcerers to incorporate while producing Katapok?" The teacher didn't look at his class but looked at the floor. "Miss Marinilli."

Carl saw Sheba was the only student with her hand raised. She was so eager to answer the question he thought she was going to jump out of her seat. "Katapok is when an alchemist combines potions and charms to metal to magically transform the object. Lord Overton however found that said objects cannot be used to fend off evil spells." There was a huge satisfied grin on her face.

"Very good." The sage turned away, his back to the class as if getting an unseen object.

Carl noticed Garrett shaking his head in disagreement, his hand reluctantly extended in the air. He cleared his throat to get the teacher's attention.

"Yes, you back there in the back, Mister Montgomery," Sage Skopector said without looking at Garrett. "Do you wish to add something to your classmate's correct answer?"

Garrett stood up, sliding the chair back under the table before standing at attention behind it. His hands clasped behind his back with his chin held high. "Yes sir, I wanted to actually make a correction to Miss Marinilli's answer."

Sheba's head snapped around, glaring at Garrett who took no notice. The rest of the class broke out in low murmurs. Carl guessed that either no one had corrected Sheba before or they had not expected him to question a sage somehow he felt it was both. The class was stunned. This might be the reason she had been reluctant to revisit this memory, he thought. Sheba was not a person that would like to be reminded of being wrong.

"Don't be a fool young man; Miss Marinilli is one hundred percent correct," Skopector barked populously. Carl did not care for the way the man sneered while he spoke even if Sheba had liked him.

"What are you playing at?" the then Sheba whispered from the table in front of Garrett.

"I'm sorry to have to disagree, sir." Garrett nervously shuffled his feet, glancing quickly at Sheba then at the floor seeking support before continuing, "As Miss Marinilli is correct that early in his career Lord Overton did believe that evil magic could not be defended with alchemic formulation. However, he later found that with a strong intent this could be accomplished. Lord Overton published those findings in the Salem Witches Gazette."

"We are not interested in theories from an obscure paper from a country that has no formal magic foundation Mister Montgomery," spit flew from Skopector's mouth as he made this proclamation, dismissing the argument and turning away once more.

Carl was proud to see that Garrett did not back down. Instead he took out his wand and waved it intensively. Two magazines appeared on Garrett's table and two more appeared on Skopector's tables.

"Sage Skopector, if you would take a look at page thirty- eight of the Sorcery Review which you yourself are a member of the editorial staff, is that not correct, sir?" Garrett instructed a little more firmly than before.

Sage Skopector glared at Garrett. He was stunned to be contradicted in his own classroom. The fact that Garrett chose to use the Sage's own review fueled his fury. "Okay Mister Montgomery, I will allow you to try to make your point but you are treading on fire."

"Thank you, sir." The look in Garrett's eyes burned with determination. The way he said sir sounded like he was saying a dirty word. "Sage, as you will see on page thirty-eight of the Sorcery Review there is an article by our own Dean Belarus stating that the Salem Witches Gazette is the most accurate foreign literature, equal to any in the magical world. He also points out that it rivals the Sorcery Review and if it were published in Britain, as is the Review, it would possibly be considered the reining literary authority of all magical society."

Sage Skopector flipped through the pages of the review stopping at a picture of Headmaster Belarus. Underneath the photo of Belarus sat a picture of Skopector also giving an endorsement of the Salem Witches Gazette. Skopector was relieved Garrett had not read that headline. Garrett nodded at the sage as he registered Skopector had seen his article as well.

"Secondly, if you would please take the copy of the Salem Witches Gazette and examine it." Garrett had seized complete control of the class now. He waited for Sage Skopector to sit the Sorcery Review down and pick up the Gazette. The man looked like a child might after being slapped for being in the cookie jar.

"You will see on this page," Garrett waved his wand too impatient to wait for the sage to turn to the desired page and the magazine magically turned to the desired page. "You will notice on this page a picture of Lord Overton with Chancellor Sean Kennedy and Mister Shane Bourne of the Department of New Spells and Sciences."

Skopector glanced down at the article and then glared back at Garrett as though he saw a ghost. "YOU!"

"Yes Sage," Garrett interrupted quickly, "Mister Bourne and Chancellor Kennedy are congratulating Lord Overton on his discovery. Lord Overton also won the rubes' Nobel Peace Prize with that discovery." Carl thought he heard a hint of contempt in Garrett's voice as he said that last bit about the Noble Peace Prize.

"That is why the Department of New Spells was forced to confer the title of Lord upon Overton. They were afraid America would take credit for a British citizen's finding. He would have never been made a Lord otherwise."

"This picture...," Sage Skopector began but Garrett cut him off again. Garrett wanted to make sure Skopector did not say what he was thinking.

"I know sir." Garrett tossed the sage a warning glance. "That picture was taken last year; one month before Lord Overton and his wife Mary Francis Overton were killed in an awful automobile explosion in West Virginia. However, that is a discussion for another time. I believe it is almost time for us to leave."

Garrett waved his wand and the periodicals returned to him. Sage Skopector stared at Garrett as if he had just been slapped. The rest of the class sat in silence looking back and forth at each as if watching a tennis match. Sage Skopector looked as if he wanted to speak but Garrett beat him to the punch once more.

"You will understand these copies are important to me sir." He nodded at Skopector.

"Yes, of course." Skopector seemed to slip from his stupor and returned his attention to the entire class. "Class is dismissed." Skopector shot out of the classroom before any of the students stood up.

"Come on," the now Sheba ordered with a sour face not liking the way Garrett had treated her favorite teacher. They followed Garrett out of the classroom along with the other students. Garrett was pounded on the back with fervent congratulations by his classmates. Carl acknowledged how students stuck together especially when a teacher is put back in their place. He felt Sage Skopector had been a little arrogant and not much liked by the students.

In the hallway Carl was happy to see young Carrie standing there waiting for him or Garrett as it was. "What is that all about?" she asked Garrett as students were still patting him as they passed by.

"Oh still a little hero worship from the Winter Solstice I guess," Garrett lied trying to deflect what really happened in the class.

"Excuse me Carrie," the then Sheba interrupted. "Could I speak to you for a moment?" she asked Garrett.

Anger shot into Carrie's face as she took offense to another girl wanting to talk to him. Garrett quickly clasped Carrie's hand soothing her temper. "Sure what is it?"

"I was just wondering if I could see the article in the Salem Witches Gazette?" she asked.

Garrett looked at Carrie and back to Sheba. Carl could see the boy didn't want to but felt trapped. "Under one condition," the two girls looked at him wonderingly, "you can't make a big deal of it or tell anyone else."

They nodded. Garrett unsaddled his book bag fishing out the magazine. Garrett tried to distract Carrie but she was too interested in learning what it was Sheba wanted to see.

"This is you," Sheba exclaimed, holding out the journal showing the picture of Bourne, Kennedy, Overton and Garrett.

"Yes, Lord Overton was my father." Carrie and Sheba gawked at him in disbelief. "He wanted to stand out from the Montgomery name."

"Why?" Carrie asked, looking at the boy in the photograph.

"He was always compared to my uncle and wanted to make a name of his own. That's why he took the fellowship in America, to get away from my uncle's celebrity."

"Who is your uncle?" Sheba asked, looking at Garrett with more interest for the first time.

"That is none of your business," Carrie said, clasping Garrett's arm. "We need to hurry or we'll be late for music. Shame you don't take music too Sheba or you could walk with us."

Carl bit back the laugh that wanted to surface at watching Carrie marking her territory.

The now Sheba tugged on Carl's elbow. Carl wanted to follow Garrett and Carrie, eager to learn more and see the young couple together. He wanted to hear more about his father. Sheba, however, was determined to pull him back. "Wait!"

"It's time to go now." We've seen all that there is to see." Carl nodded as a fog faded away the image of his younger self walking away.

CHAPTER 7

Carl and Sheba were greeted by Carrie when they returned. Carrie studied Carl with a worried eye as he stumbled to the recliner blindly clutching it for support. Carl felt his legs wanting to give out but he fought to remain standing. He didn't want to alarm Carrie. He clinched his teeth and concentrated on protecting his thoughts.

"Great, Carrie's here. I'll take my leave." Sheba glanced at Carl, smiling briefly, unaware of Carl's struggle and then turned her attention to Carrie. "Everything went well?" Sheba asked referring to Carrie's other errands.

"Splendid," Carrie answered, watching Carl as if spotting his discomfort.

"Excellent, I won't keep you. Bye Carl and again happy birthday dear friend." She gave Carrie a hug and kissed her cheek. Sheba offered a false smile to Carl and then mumbled something. Carl heard breaking glass as Sheba disappeared.

"I don't think she was too thrilled with having to recall that memory," Carl explained to Carrie who still looked worried.

Carrie laughed walking over to him. "I fixed some lunch for us. When were done eating we'll use the Chronicler, then you'll be done with it for today." She led him into the kitchen where he was greeted with a huge feast. "Sheba was the brightest student in my class. She had to know everything. You were a year older than us but she still considered you her peer."

"Because we had the three classes together?" Carl asked, recalling Sheba's earlier insight.

"Partly," Carrie motioned for him to take one of the seats. "I think she was smitten with you. She and I were really never friends until the Academy."

He sat down hard. Carrie looked at him again with concern. Carl was happy to see she dismissed it for clumsiness. "I don't believe all this food," he said, changing the subject and eating some fried chicken. "When did you leave the snacks for Reginald and me?"

"I revanesced back right after you went into the Chronicler Recital." She laughed at his enthusiasm as he shoveled food into his mouth. "The benefits of magic are that cooking is easy and clean up is a breeze." She motioned toward the sink. He saw that the dishes were washing themselves.

"What is revanesce?" he asked, trying to disguise the fatigue he still felt from his trip into the Chronicler.

"It's how we appear and vanerize is how we disappear. It's just one of the ways we travel."

"Why don't you just use appear and vanish?" he asked between bites.

She choked down a swallow. She had never given the idea a thought before. "I really don't know. I guess it has to do with language and the elders."

"This is still a marvelous spread. You can cook for me anytime," he said, changing the subject.

"Oh really," she teased snidely. "Does the man think I should be cooking for him all the time?"

"No," he said, eyeing her cautiously. He thought she was teasing but he hadn't forgotten the lesson she taught him the night before. "I just thought that you're supposed to be protecting me and that my cooking would definitely have to be classified as dangerous."

"Perhaps I'll teach you how to cook. We can't have you being a danger to yourself. But what do I get in return?"

"I think I'm doing a fair job already at giving you what every woman wants," he bartered back.

"Oh, you think you're such a prize," she responded, setting down her spoon.

"No, that's not what I meant."

"What did you mean then?" She put her elbows on the table while folding her hands in front of her face then rested her chin on her fingers.

"What every woman wants is man that does everything he's told to do," he answered with a laugh.

She flicked her wand and a napkin appeared hiding her own laugh behind it. "It hasn't been that bad?"

"No, I enjoy finding out I've been living a lie. I can talk to animals but have no idea how. My father, who I don't remember being my father, is a famous alchemist, whatever that is, and is dead."

"I guess this has been a little trying." She gave a little smile. "It's not easy for us either. Tell me what's bothering you and I'll try to help. But first, let's finish eating," she said.

He grabbed a barbeque rib and stuffed it into his mouth. He looked at her smiling with his eyes. She laughed as he spat out the meatless bone. There was sauce on his face which gave birth to a new wave of giggles from Carrie. He guessed that she had few laughs like this in the past three years while also wondering if he looked as alarming as Reginald when he ate.

"You are doing really well," she complimented.

"What?" he asked surprised having no idea what she was talking about.

"I've been trying to figure out what you are thinking or feeling, but haven't been able to," she said with a hint of disappointment in her voice.

He smiled blushing slightly. "You mean you have to ask me like a normal person."

She smiled back still wanting to know what he was thinking, frustrated at not being able to tap in to him. "I didn't think you'd be able to master the skill so quickly." She took a sip of her water. "Sheba expected you'd catch on quickly, but I didn't think it to be quite this easy for you."

"I've had good teachers," he said, thinking about the memory he had visited with Reginald. "Reginald was surprised I learned the spells so quickly, too."

"All we did was introduce you to shared memories. You did the rest," Carrie said. "You mastered the skills."

"Yeah, but you also believed in me which is saying a lot. I can't recall the last friend I had that did," he said, taking a deep breath.

She looked ready to cry again. Now it was her turn to change the subject. "Are you finished?" She motioned to the food. He nodded fighting the tightness that seized his throat. Carrie took her wand and with a flick the table cleared itself. "Well it's on to the next adventure." She pushed back her seat getting up. Carl followed her into the living room. She put her wand up to her temple and closed her eyes. It was a strange ritual Carl thought. She breathed in deeply and with her other hand she plucked the memory out by its root.

Placing the long hair into the cloudy surface of the Chronicler, she began stirring it as if preparing a pot of soup. She glanced at Carl with a smile. He wished he could tell what she was thinking. He shuffled his feet trying not to feel so nervous, listening to his heart race still hating the feeling of going into the Chronicler while at the same time acknowledging his enjoyment at reliving the memories. It made him feel torn inside, this conflict of emotion.

"Well, that should be good." She tucked her wand away, clasping Carl's hand. Her fingers slid comfortably between his. "Just relax and take a deep breath."

"Are you sensing my apprehension?"

"Just an educated guess," she nodded. "I don't like going into the Chronicler myself."

"Thanks." She looked at him in puzzlement. "It's nice to know I'm not the only one. Reginald wanted to go in with Sheba and me."

"Reggie is a little off sometimes. On three, okay." She began to count, "One... two... three."

He was relieved she hadn't made a big production of intent like Sheba had done earlier. They were pulled into the memory head first while the same somersault underwater feeling attacked his stomach as his nose expanded as if someone was stuffing cotton in it. He opened his eyes, finding himself in a strange large room. "We're in the Banquet Hall of the Palace of Sitnalta. It's December 22 and we're celebrating the Winter Solstice." The room was decorated with ice sculptors that kept changing shapes. A swan turned into a dolphin and then into Santa Claus. Even though he knew they were on an island in the Mediterranean Sea, he watched snow drift from the ceiling magically melting before reaching anyone's head. It reminded Carl of confetti.

"What's so special about the Winter Solstice?" He asked.

She realized there were many things she and others took for granted that needed to be explained.

"We celebrate the change of autumn to winter. The Winter Solstice is a key time for magic. All the seasonal changes are important, but winter is the most magical. All ancient societies celebrate a holiday in the end of

December. Deep down they feel the magic too." Carrie tugged his hand leading him through the crowd. "Tonight is also your unofficial coming out party."

"My coming out party?"

"Yeah, you stopped being so uptight and started making friends," she said, giggling at seeing some of her old school mates.

Carl glanced around noticing the boys were wearing garments that appeared more like dresses. He thought about the medieval times and pictures of Henry the VIII during his reign. Other than people's attire and the palace's décor, it could have been any high school dance in the USA. Well, the fact that sages were dancing might be another difference. He couldn't recall a teacher dancing at his Rube school, especially not like the man with the bald head and long goatee. He was dancing so enthusiastically with a large lady that Carl couldn't help but watch. Just then, the man seemed to notice Carl. Carl thought he smiled at him for a moment. But, he remembered Carrie telling him the first time they were in the Chronicler that they couldn't interact with the people in the memories. However, he was sure the man looked right at him. Carl glanced around but noticed nothing that would have drawn the man's attention.

"That's Dean Belarus," Carrie said, noticing who Carl was watching. "He's dancing with Madame Archie. She's Byterian's twin sister." She laughed watching them dance. "It's is no wonder you were drawn to them."

"He looks familiar, kind of a déjà vu thing you know. It's like I've dreamed of him." He'd swear Belarus just winked at him. "Did you see that?"

Carrie looked back at Dean Belarus and Madame Archie getting the feeling that Belarus had been watching Carl too. She shook her head knowing people in the Chronicler had no idea they were there. "Come on, I can't believe I get to surprise you, again." She tugged urging him to the stage.

They marched to the front of the large stage. There was a long hair band playing. Carl thought the band could've been any band he'd seen before except for the fact that some of the instruments were floating in the air playing by themselves. "I can't believe I get to do this twice," Carrie repeated, pulling him as close to the stage as she could get as the band finished their song.

"Do what again?" Carl asked her but her attention was locked on the stage. Her face infused with color as a huge smile possessed it. He thought of the television pictures of girls going nuts for rock groups. Carl felt a twinge of jealousy.

"Well, welcome to the Winter Solstice Celebration," the singer announced as the dancers began vacating the dance floor. "We have a little treat for you. We received a message from a student here at the Palace."

He paused to take a breath letting his statement hang. "She sent us a song written by a student here and *we liked it*." He stressed the words *we liked it* for the crowd, encouraging them to display their excitement.

The students began cheering recognizing their cue. One of their classmates was going to have their song preformed by the band. "Now, we were requested to play the song but we aren't going to do that."

The students began to murmur lowly in disapproval. "Nope," the guitar player said, walking up to a mike that appeared from nowhere. "What we are going to do is have the student come up here and sing it with us."

There was an explosion of sound again as the students began clapping wildly and cheering. "That's right," the lead singer added. "Although, I think we might need your help getting him up here because we hear he might be a little shy."

The room boomed with excitement as the students went nuts. "Yeah," the guitar player hollered, "We need your help gettin' 'em up here."

"Who is he?" a boy's voice hollered as the auditorium grew nearly silent.

"Do you want to know who he is?" the guitar boomed, playing with the audience.

The crowd roared a resounding, "YES."

"Do you really want to know?" the singer screamed as he paced around the stage waving his arms to egg on the students. Again the crowd screamed. The sound was deafening. Carl wanted to talk to Carrie but he couldn't hear himself when he spoke. How was she going to hear him?

"His name is Garrett Montgomery!" the singer screamed. They were doing such a great job rousing the crowed into a frenzy that the hall continued screaming when Garrett's name was announced. "Come on, Garrett."

Carl swung his head around trying to find Garrett but not being able to locate him. He checked the other direction but still Garrett was nowhere in sight. Carrie tugged on his arm pointing to the back of the hall. Carl spotted the younger Carrie in a lovely pink knee high gown with a boy wearing a suede tuxedo that reminded Carl of a traditional Indian outfit.

Garrett looked to be attempting to leave the room but young Carrie stood in his way. Dean Belarus strolled over to help Carrie keep Garrett from escaping. Carl couldn't hear what was being said even though the hall was quieting down, searching for Garrett.

"Dean Belarus is telling you that it would be rude to leave without going up on stage. I think you would have left if it weren't for him," Carrie said.

"There he is," the guitar player yelled. A magical spot light captured the trio in the back of the room.

"I'm pleading with you while Belarus is saying he would enjoy hearing you sing. When Belarus said this you bowed your head agreeing to do as he wished. I was shocked just about to cry. You were very respectful when it came to Belarus. I was sure you were going to never talk to me again." She smiled at the young couple as if she were proud parents.

Carl could see the poor kid had no other choice as a sinking feeling grabbed his stomach. He watched as Garrett paced to the stage his head intensively focusing on his feet as if hoping a hole would magically appear sucking him away. He did not even look up as he marched up the stairs leading to the stage.

The singer took his wand and whispered a spell as Garrett walked to the front of the stage. The three of them, the singer, guitar player, and Garrett huddled in a circle together. After a nod from Garrett the guitar player motioned for the keyboard player to join the conference. The group nodded in agreement as the huddle broke. The guitar player walked to the front of the stage as the singer and keyboard player walked off the stage joining the students in the crowd. Garrett crept over to the keyboard taking his post.

"Okay students of Kenosis and Sitnalta," the guitar player began. "Are you ready for your own Garrett Montgomery to sing with us, The Phoenix?" The room erupted again with cheers. The guitar player strolled over to Garrett put his wand up to Garrett's throat and performed a spell to amplify his voice. "Okay kid, it's all you."

The guitar player began playing, the drummer joined in. They played the music but Garrett stood silent looking at the piano keys. The students began murmuring to each other. The guitar player and drummer stopped at the same time as if it were planned. Young Carrie made her way to the front of the stage feet from Carl and her older self, disappointment sprang to her face. The guitar player began heading over to Garrett.

"Sorry," Garrett began before he reached him. The crowd fell silent. Carl felt the sympathy seeping through the crowd for the boy who froze on stage. A couple of boys, however, began to jeer and heckle clearly thrilled with Garrett's panic. Carl noticed Dean Belarus walk up to console the young Carrie. Another sage joined Belarus but Carl had not seen her before.

"That's Sage Nancy Harding," Carrie told him as if answering his unasked question. Carl realized that he'd let his protection down, but rationalized it would be beneficial to communicate if he let Carrie inside his head. The noise had been so loud and he had no other way to get her attention. This way he would have another avenue available in which to communicate with her.

Carl watched Garrett feeling sorry for his younger self. The boy had not asked to go up and sing. It must be very scary getting up in front of the entire school. He didn't blame the boy for freezing up. He showed bravery just by going up there. Carl couldn't help wondering how this was going to help him break out of his shell, as Carrie had put it.

Older Carrie glanced over at Carl smiling as if saying I've still got a secret.

Carl looked back up to the stage. He could see a tear hanging in the corner of Garrett's eye then watched as Garrett stopped the guitar player with his hand. The boy didn't want him to come any closer. The guitar player stopped as requested. Carl had a feeling that the boy didn't want to hear what the guitar player had to say and expected to watch Garrett walk off the stage. Then Garrett blinked away the tears swelling up inside him.

"I wrote this song for my uncle as a Christmas present. So, I'd like to dedicate to him. I just thought you all should know that before we begin."

The guitar player turned around, a huge grin plastered on his face, and began playing again. He went through one verse of the song then the drummer joined in. Together they went through another verse. This is as far as they got the first time and Carl half expected them to stop again but on the third verse Garrett began to sing, *"Hold on tightly to your innocence and don't you let go of your dreams."*

Carl shook his head in surprise. The crowd of students and sages not swarming to the dance floor were pushing their way to the stage feeling the magic in the music pulsing in the air. Carl watched the young Carrie now beaming with tears of joy in her eyes. Her legs buckled and she nearly collapsed as Garrett burst out with the next line, "*Until you know it's gonna to be alright.*"

The guitar player and drummer played another versus. Garrett kept his eyes closed smiling as he sang, not yet playing the keyboard waiting in front of him. "*Watch the caldron in the fire, there's a potion that runs through us, so take a drink don't be afraid*". Carl found himself bouncing to the beat entranced.

Garrett fingers began to dance over the keys. Carl could hear students whistling, expressing their enthusiasm. The older Carrie was so overcome with emotion he worried she might faint. "*Sailing into the air It's something in the atmosphere Every star above reflecting in your sea of love, Is it just a dream Or are things as they really seem, Somebody help me make the scene*". The word "*scene*" lingered in the air and echoed with a magical reverb.

Carl saw that young Carrie's eyes were locked on Garrett. She had a huge smile on her face while bouncing to the beat. Sage Harding and Dean Belarus began dancing with a group of students. Young Carrie danced too but alone watching her Garrett as if he was singing just for her. There were two more verses of drums, keyboard and guitar with no vocals.

"*You are the light, that shines so bright, you show me the way to go, and if it's so.*" Garrett paused taking a breath and then burst out, "*I won't be surprised*". Another verse of music gave Garrett time to regain his breath. "*Just give yourself a chance and take a glance around to see the glow brewing in my eyessss.*" "Eyes" seemed to hang in the air and pierce the audience just has the word "scene" had done just moments before. It felt like lightning was striking at will in the auditorium. Carl wondered if this was magic too or just Garrett's stage presence.

Garrett paused preparing for the chorus again. "*Sorrowing into the air There's something in the atmosphere every star above reflecting in the sea of love This is not a dream It's a magic I've never seen rising to rise above it all.*" All the words were now hanging in the air dancing with electrical waves.

"*Somewhere on my broom we followed we'll be singing with everything I know as soon as tomorrow I could be flying.*" "Flying" now danced on the air. The band played alone for about thirty seconds as Garrett caught his breath once more. Then he plucked a keyboard solo as the rest of the band rested.

"Somewhere on the broom I borrowed. I'll be singing with everything I know as soon as tomorrow I'll be soaring higher and in my dreams I'm there by your side learning to love again." The music stopped and Garrett began playing the keyboard which now sounded like bells ringing in the background.

"The world we see," Garrett sang softly and the guitar player followed with (World we see and hear) in the background. *"It's a mystery* (Mystery but we) *But at Sitnalta we hold the key* (Hold the key to the door) *If we have the faith to love* (Have the faith anymore) *and believe."*

Believe hung in the air for a second and then was followed by silence. The lights went out for what Carl guessed was five seconds and then blazed back to life as the band began playing. Garrett began dancing as he played. The audience danced. The singer and keyboard player for The Phoenix were dancing with some girls as the rest of their band played the verse and chorus without singing again.

"Somewhere on the broom taking me higher what happens to the soul trapped in this emotion," Garrett bellowed, *"We'll be free to sing."* His eyes were clinched tight as he sang danced and played. *"I know as soon as tomorrow we are only surviving and in my dreams I'm there by your side."* The word "side" seemed to sink from the stage into the crowd. *"Learning to love aaaagain."* The last line hung in the air for everyone to absorb. Guitar. Drums. Guitar. Drums. *"Again."*

Silence as the room went dark again. The lights came up. Garrett was panting at the keyboard, spent, exhausted from his efforts. The guitar player took the spell off Garrett's voice and clapped him on the back. The room exploded with applause as he staggered up stage away from the keyboards. The lead singer and keyboard player jumped up on stage rushing to greet him.

"You can sing with us anytime, mate," the singer said. "Just don't make it a habit or I'll be looking for a new gig."

"Excellent," the keyboard player said, clasping Garrett on the shoulder.

Young Carrie ran on stage jumping and throwing her arms around his neck leaving her feet hanging inches from the ground. She squeezed him tight. He pulled his head back and kissed her deeply. They were still locked in the kiss when Sage Harding, Dean Belarus, and Madame Archie came up on stage. Belarus cleared his throat announcing their presence. The teenagers reluctantly broke free from their first kiss, looking to see who was with them but watching the other as well.

"A wonderful song like that is sure to ignite the passions in the young and the old;" Belarus complimented. "Only let's be sure we don't get too carried away," he warned with a smile in his steel grey eyes.

"Control yourself Miss Stephens," Sage Harding warned, playing the part of chaperone. "That was an excellent song Mister Montgomery. I'm sure your uncle will be very pleased."

"This boy should be in my class where we can expand a talent such as this," Madame Archie commented firmly.

Music is a very powerful magic indeed. Alas, young Garrett has more talents than music." Belarus saw the beginnings of a scowl on Madam Archie's face. "I will see to it that next semester he is enrolled in your advanced music class. It was wonderful performance and I am sure that your uncle would be proud. Yes, most proud. I shall send him word letting him know how you honored him here tonight. Only next time I suggest you look out at the crowd to witness how you have touched your audience." Garrett nodded in response.

It didn't take long for the students to rush the stage looking for Garrett. Carl smiled as Garrett was overwhelmed with congratulations. Carl felt warm inside. Strange how happy a song can stir people's emotions, he thought. Carl looked up again and was sure that Belarus was smiling back at him again not watching the young boy. Garrett took Carrie's hand struggling to lead her through the crowd of congratulating students.

The band began playing a slow song. Garrett stopped in the middle of the dance floor. Pride rose in Carl as he noticed that the dance floor wasn't as crowded as when Garrett had been singing.

"I could really use a drink but I'd rather be with you," Garrett said, "thank you very much for believing in me. I could feel it on stage."

She gave him a brief squeeze before pulling back a little to look into his brown eyes. "We could be together while getting a drink." She pulled to break free but he tugged her closer.

"After the song, I much rather enjoy holding you right now."

Carl could see the tears beginning to stream down the now Carrie's cheek. The kids kissed again then broke for air, danced a little more and locked into a kiss again. They continued in this vein until the song ended.

"Thank you," Garrett said, walking up to get a glass a punch.

"For what this time?" she was trying to recompose herself. She could feel the blue flame of desires burning inside her. It felt as if she was growling in her want to kiss Garrett more.

"For sending them word that got them to hear my song." He led her to the table with drinks. "How did you do it?"

She took a sip of her drink which turned ultimately into a gulp. Carl believed singing might not be the only thing that made someone thirsty. "My dad knows the singer and helped me get in touch."

"How'd you do that?"

"I can't reveal all my secrets to you," she said, taking another gulp. "Not yet anyway."

"Okay," the old Carrie said. "It's time to go back."

Again Carl didn't want to leave. This was a good memory leaving him with a good feeling. Carrie tugged on his elbow and they were somersaulting back into his living room. The sinking feeling punched him as he realized they were back in Michigan.

CHAPTER 8

Carl was unable to conceal the effects the Chronicler had on him this time. His skin had gone ghostly white and he was covered in sweat. Carrie rushed to get him some water as he hunched over hyperventilating. Carl felt dizzy, struggling to fall onto the couch. He lay on his side panting and clutching his gut. His eyes were clinched tight as he fought the cramps that tore at him.

Carrie returned with the water. She was half excited, half fearful. She hadn't expected this response, but she hoped it was a sign that he may be recovering his memory. The fit could go on for minutes, hours, or days. She worried not knowing what to do. If he was recovering his memories, what would it be like when twenty some years of memories came rushing back? Terror seized hold of her as she watched him suffer with so much pain. What if he wasn't recovering his memories? The doubt snuck in on her. What could be causing this reaction? Could it be going into the Chronicler so many times in such a short period causing this, or was there something more sinister at play here? Could it be that whoever erased his memory in the first place was attacking him from some unforeseen place?

Carl reached up with a shaking hand searching for Carrie's. She could feel his blood throbbing, rushing through his veins with every beat of his heart. Confused, she had no idea what to do. There were only a handful of people she could trust but dared not leave him. She set the water down on the coffee table. Helpless, she pulled his head into her lap, running her hand through his hair and gently massaging his forehead. She used her wand to conjure a moist towel, softly placing it on his head. She sat there massaging his scalp until he finally fell into a fitful sleep.

She held his sleeping head in her lap for about a half hour. She wondered what the twitches meant unable to resist the empty feeling of helplessness that surrounded her. She needed to help him but had no idea who to contact. She took her wand out thinking of Sheba. She could feel her forehead compress as she desperately willed Sheba to hear her plea while clinching her jaw tight. She had only tried to contact Garrett this way and was never successful.

She heard the breaking glass announcing someone had just arrived. Hope bloomed in her knowing Sheba had heard her plea.

"What's up?" Sheba asked, startled at seeing Carl unconscious on the couch.

"He had some type of reaction when we came out of the Chronicler. I don't know if it's because he's remembering or if we over did it or if someone..." She began to cry.

"I'll do some poking around when I get back to the embassy," Sheba said, rubbing Carrie's shoulder. "I bet he's just recalling memories and they're colliding or something. I'll see what I can find out."

"Thanks," Carrie said, trying to push the tears back. She was ashamed that she was crying so much.

"I'll send word back to you as soon as I can." Carrie nodded as Sheba disappeared.

Carl awoke three hours later. Carrie sat in the recliner dosing, waiting for him to wake. "What time is it?" Carl asked, making Carrie jump from her half sleep.

She shot out of the recliner looking around, exhaling when she realized where she was. "Oh dear," she said, ashamed she fell asleep. "It's... it's about seven o'clock."

"Wow." He sat up as she sat down beside him. "That was different."

"How do you feel?" she asked, wringing her hands.

"Like I just did five hundred sit ups. My stomach muscles ache." He smiled.

She kept wringing her hands wondering if she had somehow been responsible for the reaction. "Do you feel anything else?"

"Like what?"

"Well, I don't know... do you remember anything about who you are?"

"Oh, not really... only that my father was not my father. My real father was an alchemist. I am or was a sorcerer and could sing. I went to a school I don't remember at all except for what you showed me and I can or could talk to animals. Other than that I'm fine."

She laughed politely. "Okay mister, can you explain what happened when we came out of the Chronicler Recital. You really had me scared." She realized he was okay if he could joke about what he's learned over the last two days.

"You... I thought I was having a heart attack in my stomach." She looked more confused. "Well at first I felt really dizzy. I leaned forward to catch my breath. That's when it felt like my stomach was shaking like jell-o."

"Do you remember any of what you dreamed?" He shook his head. She half smiled and he saw a tear slide from her eye.

"I'm all right. Please don't cry." He hated seeing her cry. The memory had shown him that they once had something special. He wondered if they still did. It had been three years since they had seen each other. She had probably moved on with that part of her life.

"I was so worried." She fell into his arms sobbing in relief that he was okay and at the same time releasing three years worth of pent up sorrow. He gently rubbed her back. "You must be hungry," she said, fighting through tears.

"Starved," he answered. She pulled away wiping her face with the back of her hand.

"Well I'll fix something for us and we can talk about what we've learned today."

"I have a better idea," he said, standing up. His legs felt a little wobbly as if he had spent the entire time sitting Indian style. The tingling of blood finding areas in which it had been deprived teased him as he took steps he could barely feel. "Seeing it's your birthday, let's go out to eat."

"I don't think that's a good idea," she protested.

"Well I do." He went to the bedroom. "I don't know what it's like in the magical world but I am feeling trapped and could use a night out."

"You don't understand. Your life may be in danger," she warned, following him.

"I understand, but I'll be in danger here or out there. So we might as well go out and have a little fun."

She stood shaking her head. He walked back taking both her hands and gazed into her eyes. "Listen, one thing I learned in the Chronicler is the importance of having fun." Her look told him that she hoped he had learned more than just that. "You taught me to enjoy life by using my gifts. I saw the pleasure in Garrett's face as he was up on that stage playing. He loved it. I want to experiment with something and we can't do it here."

"What do you mean experiment?" She studied him but wasn't able to find the secret she was searching for.

It was difficult for her to hear him speak of Garrett in the third person. He was Garrett.

"You'll see. Now, let's get ready to go out. I am going to go. So, the only way you can stop me is by using your wand."

She shook her head. "Okay, I know that stubbornness too well." She turned away not wanting to see his excitement, as if she had lost a game. This was not a great idea she told herself but he was right about having fun. He had had really good intuition when she knew him before and it was her birthday. She deserved a good time. It was a day of celebration she told herself ignoring the aching voice that warned her it was a mistake. She had found him and they deserved to have some fun. What could happen in a small town like this? She smiled trying to convince herself that they were safe.

He began humming the song he heard Garrett singing in the Chronicler Recital. She glanced back smiling at how happy he appeared. He looked like a kid full of energy, excited about finding a new gift. Her fear was lost to Carl's excitement at wanting to do an experiment. It had to be a good sign. Something Garrett would want to do.

* * *

He zoomed into his bedroom. She could hear him still humming enthusiastically. It was a rather catchy tune and just think, he wrote it. He hoped what he was planning would help. He tried not to concentrate on his feelings or memories, wanting to keep it a secret. He could feel something vital in his wanting to get out like something or someone was calling to him. He couldn't tell for sure, but he felt as if it was Dean Belarus.

"All ready," he asked, walking out of the bedroom feeling energized. His jaw dropped when she walked out of the bathroom.

Carrie glided into the living room wearing a long black skirt that nestled an inch above her ankles, highlighted with three inch black high heels and buckles that appeared to be made of diamonds. A stunning hot baby girl pick blouse that matched her lipstick clung to her smartly. Carl blinked twice hoping she had not noticed his gaping dry mouth. There was no other way to describe her. "Beautiful," he mumbled.

"Sorry," she asked not hearing him or just wanting to hear it again.

"You are beautiful." He blinked his brain going dumb.

"Thanks," she smiled again. He noticed she began to blush. "You look very dapper yourself."

"Shall we go then?" He offered his arm hoping not looking as foolish as he felt.

"I just want you to know, I'm still not convinced this is a good idea," she said, taking his arm but feeling excited too.

"Yeah it is." He smirked, escorting her out to the car. She waited for him to open the door for her, noticing how his eyes examined her. She smiled again appreciating the attention and slid into the passenger seat taking note of his new found confidence. He ran around the car and jumped in. "By the way, where is your wand? It sure couldn't fit into that dress."

She opened her pink pocket book that was sitting in her lap. "I shrunk it so it would fit in here." She showed him a miniature version of her wand about three inches long. "It'll be easier to keep hidden while were out with non-magical folks."

Carl noticed, contrary to what she said that she was excited to get out and see the area. She kept asking him about things non-magical people took for granted. "What is that?"

"A water tower," Carl answered, smiling.

"What's its purpose?"

Carl had to think about that for a while. He knew they were once a source of water for the town but now with the water plants there was no practical use for them. "That's a good question. I guess it's just a reminder of our past." She looked at him questioningly as if not satisfied. Carl thought about it, it really didn't make sense. Carrie dismissed it continuing her investigation of nearly everything they passed.

They drove around for fifteen minutes before Carl found the place he was looking for. It was a little road side bar-restaurant that Carl had overheard some people from work talking about. He hoped they weren't there tonight. He didn't get along with them. He would've preferred a classier place to take Carrie. She looked way too elegant for a place like this. Carl had never been inside before and had no clue what to expect. He hoped the inside was better than the rickety outside with its white cinder block walls with peeling paint that showed pink underneath. Carl shook his head disgusted by the fast food wrappers taking refuge along the deteriorating long yellow parking blocks. He wondered what Carrie must be thinking. The owner or manager really didn't care too much how the place looked. Carl prayed it was better on the inside.

Carrie looked at Carl unsure if this was the correct place because she thought they'd passed it before. He nodded. She smiled, watching him rush around to open her door. He took her hand helping to ease her out of the car. She found this quite satisfying. She liked being treated with such respect.

"I know it isn't much. I mean you're way overdressed for here. But, it's the only place in town that has what I'm looking for."

"What are you looking for?" The suspense was killing her. She was surprised he was using Brauchen this well this quickly.

He put his finger to his lips leaning in to whisper, "Shh, it's a secret." Chills danced down her spine as his breath skipped across her neck. He led her to the door holding it open for her to enter. He followed taking a large breath and exhaling as he entered. The perfume she wore invaded his senses stirring the fire in his belly.

Surprisingly it was much nicer inside than outside. The floors were hard oak wood which at one time probably made a good dance floor but now were in need of polishing and years of neglect had left them pulling apart. There were two pool tables on the left hand side of the bar. Carl was happy to see neither in use. On the right side of the bar had ten bar stools filled with patrons looking at them. After a few moments, they turned back to what they were doing. Six feet behind the bar stools were two rows of four black tables housing four chairs around them. The tables could be easily moved to accommodate large parties.

On the far end of the wall was a large screen television. Thankfully, it was turned off for the time being. To the right of the television stood a stage a small band would find very cramped. It was nothing like the stage in the memory. To the left of the television another cluster of nine tables rested mostly unused. Three of the tables were close to the pool tables and were angled differently than the other six. On the other side of the pool tables were the doors to the bathrooms.

Carl led Carrie to one of the tables in the corner furthest from the bar and door. Carrie was glad for this enabled her to keep an eye on who came in and out. By sitting here, there would be no way of anyone sneaking up on them. Well, at least he was being cautious about that. But, she wasn't thrilled with the window behind their table. She had to concede that although it did give a spectacular, soothing, romantic scene of the sun setting over a placid lake someone out there would be able to see them.

She was thankful there were no people sitting by the tables closest to them also. That would allow them to talk freely without fear of being overheard. Perhaps, inside this place he will divulge his little experiment.

A young girl came over giving them menus. Carl ordered a bottle of wine. There were only two choices, red or white. He settled on white. They each had a simple tossed salad with ranch dressing to start with. For their entrée, Carrie ordered the peel and eat shrimp while Carl ordered the walleye dinner. The menu housed mainly seafood. Again, he worried that she wouldn't be pleased with his choice of where to celebrate her birthday.

"So are you going to tell me about this experiment of yours?" she asked, casually pushing her empty plate away.

"Not yet." The waitress came over asking how things were. They waited for her to leave before continuing.

"I don't like not knowing," she warned, crossing her fingers of both hands in front of her.

"Yeah, I can relate to that," he said, picking up his glass and looking around the bar. The place hadn't picked up much which was surprising with it being after nine on a Saturday night. "Let's discuss what happened today," he suggested trying to buy some time.

"Okay, what do you want to talk about?"

"Us," he said boldly. Perhaps the cheap wine had helped him relax and find his courage.

"What would you like to know?" The look on her face saying she'd expected this.

"We were boyfriend and girlfriend at school," he said.

She leaned forward. "Yes, we were."

"What happened between us?" he asked, swallowing hard.

"The United Magical World Federation," she answered, sliding back. "We went to work for the UMWF and things changed."

He looked down sadly feeling a black hole eating his insides. He'd hoped things hadn't changed. They always did though and not always for the better. "I'm sorry for that," he said, taking a sip of his wine, leaning back and wishing for something a bit stronger.

She leaned over taking his hands. "We remained important to each other though." She did not need *Leer Poma* to know he was disappointed.

He felt like someone had taken one of his lungs. It burned deeper than when he returned from the chronicler. The air he breathed with his good lung felt hot and bitter hurting as he swallowed. He struggled to take a deep breath trying to fight the sting in his belly.

"So what's next?" That wasn't what he wanted to know but he needed to change the subject. "I mean what's the next step in your plan for what you want with me."

She sat back, releasing his hands. "Well we need to find out what happened to you today for starters." She surveyed the room. There didn't seem to be a threat so she returned her attention back to him. "Your reaction when we came out of the Chronicler Recital is alarming."

"Alarming," he nodded in agreement, fighting the anger burning inside him. He felt foolish for hoping there was something more between them and she was worried about the damn Chronicler.

"We think it might not be wise to use the Chronicler for a while."

"I see," he said mechanically. The feeling of being used joined the anger and disappointment. He couldn't explain why the feelings possessed him. He just felt anger building inside him faster and faster. He had been fine a couple minutes ago but now he felt betrayed. "So what do we do if not the Chronicler?"

"Well we hope being around me will help sprout some memories." She gave him a polite smile. "Before you disappeared we were still the closest of friends and partners. We shared a lot of memories."

"Wouldn't it be wiser for me to go back to the places I've lived, visited...?" he pointed out fighting the rage back down. Someone had stolen three years from him and Carrie. They were once boyfriend and girlfriend and if it weren't for those people they might still have been together. "I mean it sounds like what I have is amnesia. One way of treating amnesia is having the patient go back to places that are familiar."

"That's very good thinking, I guess. I'm not too familiar with amnesia though." She took a sip of wine scanning the bar again. "We'd like to return you to Brussels but don't believe it would be safe just yet."

"I..." Carl stopped as three men stumbled up to the table.

"Well, well, well..." an overweight man stumbled to the table interrupting them. Carl looked up recognizing the man he worked with. "Look boys Carl actually made it out of his shack and see here with a girl. Didn't think you liked girls?"

The drunken man clapped Carl on the shoulder. "How's it going Danny?" Rage grew fiercer and now had a target. The urge to strike Danny square in his pompous face overtook his other frustrations.

"I'll be better when I get another beer," he barked, staring drunkenly at Carrie as if she were the beer he sought.

Carl did not like Danny sober or drunk. In his opinion, Danny was lazy and did just enough not to get fired at work. He was almost always grumpy to work with except when he flirted with one of the girls. His grey hair had flakes of black in them, as tall as Carl but about a foot wider probably weighing a hundred more pounds more and twice his age.

"How many you had all ready?" Carl asked.

"Not darn enough," he belched, moving away. Carl was relieved and surprised that he swayed away to the bar.

"Who was that?" Carrie asked. Carl saw her putting her miniature wand back into her purse.

"That's Danny. He works with me." Carl looked around watching a man walk up to the television and begin moving the speakers strategically around the bar.

"What's going on?" Carrie asked, noticing him and too uncomfortable not knowing what was going on. The feeling that this was not a good idea returned.

"A little surprise," Carl said coyly. He glanced around the room following Carrie's gaze. She watched a cute girl with long straight brown hair pass out large black books to people at the bar to people at the tables. Carrie knew that this was what he had come here for but had no idea what it was.

"I don't know if I like this," she reiterated.

"Me too, but you'd better wait before passing judgment," Carl said, sliding his chair away from the table.

"Wait for what," she asked.

"Patience," he smiled as the girl sat a book on their table with a pencil and scraps of paper.

"I'm no good with patience," she warned, folding her arms.

She watched him scramble through the book quickly finding what he was looking for. She stretched her neck trying to see what he was doing. He scribbled his name, the word *Patience* and a number on the piece of paper. Confused she crinkled her nose having no idea what this meant. He was enjoying playing with her and she didn't like that either.

Carl got a spark playing with Carrie. She and her friends had not been forthright with him, he realized. They were holding things back, important things. He might as well enjoy getting a little playful revenge. He let her see the paper knowing she wouldn't be able to decipher the meaning. He didn't know how he knew but he was sure that the magical community did not have karaoke.

"Excuse me a moment, will you please?" Carl said, fully enjoying being in control. He got up walking over to the man at the television.

Carrie glared at him as he walked over to the big white thing. Carl gave the man the paper who nodded his head and shook Carl's hand. She did not like this at all. Having a go at her was one thing but involving this guy was downright spiteful. She was about to get up and demand they leave when Danny returned to the table. The spell she cast must have worn off because of the alcohol.

"Left you, did he?" Danny stammered, taking a sip of his fresh beer. "Well honey, you sure are fine. I wouldn't leave you alone with the likes of these guys." He glanced around the room. She turned her head quickly surveying the room to see who he was talking about.

"I think I can handle this lot," she said, starting to get up.

Danny sat in Carl's empty seat managing to gently force Carrie back down with his free hand. He looked over at Carl. "I don't see what you see in that boy. He's nothing more than a line person at the shop with no future. I'm the one with the money and I can take care of you if you take care of me."

She laughed looking away from Carl to give Danny her full attention now. "Listen here, slug." She fought to keep from raising her voice. She didn't want to draw attention to herself. "Carl is a great man. He's done great things and will do even better things once he gets away from the likes of you."

"Now listen here little girl. I don't know what you lies that boys telling you or what you heard."

"I haven't heard a thing and apparently neither have you." She fumbled for her purse but it slipped through her hands falling to the floor. Danny kicked it out of reach as if saying if you want it back you had better listen to him.

Music began to play. Carrie looked up at Carl. The man he'd been talking to started singing as the music came from some gadget by the white thing. She saw Carl had been cornered by the guys Danny had been with earlier. Danny probably put them up to running interference to keep Carl from returning.

"What are you saying?" Danny asked, taking another swig of beer trying to look through her.

"I'm saying I don't enjoy your company and wish you would leave." She nodded her head annoyed and wanting her wand.

"How do you know you don't like my company?" he belched, scratching his head.

"Because I feel sick just looking at you."

He sat back in his seat drinking as if he hadn't understood the insult. She wanted to hex him but couldn't get to her wand. He could do with a good hex.

"I don't think that was a nice thing to say," Danny said, putting his beer down.

"Okay, I'm not a nice person. Now will you please leave?" she more ordered than asked.

"Nope." He took another swig of his drink leaning on the corner of the table. "I'll tell you what I am going to do. I'm going to sit right here with you until your date comes back."

She looked at him wondering if he even knew Carl's name. Rage began to grow in her now. She could feel Danny wanting to do harm to Carl. She was going to have to intervene but didn't know exactly how?

The man Carl had been talking to finished singing. He was now talking into the black shiny thing in his hand. "Good evening everyone, my name is John Flight and this is *Hole-in-One Karaoke*. Just look in those books, find a song and fill out one of the slips Karen's been so nice to hand out. We'll get you up here to sing just like our first singer of the night, Carl."

Carrie turned in her chair trying to recall what had been said. She hadn't caught everything because of the overgrown buffalo in front of her. The books were full of songs. Carl was going to sing. It had been so long since she had really heard him sing. Yes she heard him in Chronicler earlier and she had other memories of his performances but to see him sing live again. She really wanted to enjoy this but with the slug here...

Carl walked up to the white thing taking the black shiny thing from the man. "I hope this goes well. I haven't done it for a long time. I'd just like to say that this is for a special person on her birthday."

Carrie began to melt. It was the greatest birthday present she could imagine. The last time he sang to her had been a year before he disappeared. That would be four years ago, she quickly did the math. Tears began to build in the corner of her eyes again. This was becoming a habit. She had to find away to get rid of this pest before she began to cry and she was sure she would once Garrett began to sing. He was Garrett when he sang; she wouldn't think of him as Carl when he sang. They would not take away from her that it was Garrett singing to her.

"Isn't that sweet? Is he dedicating the song to you?" Danny looked at her with a snide grin. "I bet he's going to be awful. Hey waitress, we need some ear plugs. This clown's going to make the dogs cry." He began laughing.

"Listen here you slug. If you want to see your teeth again I would shut up if I were you. You are about to witness something special so you had better sit back, shut up and enjoy." She stood up thinking about smacking him but sat back down and took a deep breath instead.

Carl began to sing, *"I've been locked inside, empty space in my heart."* The karaoke host shot a confused look at the machine. That wasn't *Patience*. Carl held up his hand signaling that everything was okay. There was something strange going on Carl thought. This was not the song he selected. He had never even heard it before but somehow he knew it... or Garrett did.

Carrie couldn't hold the flood of tears back now. It had been so long since she'd been able to really enjoy his singing. He was singing again and she was taken back to before all the madness; they were together and nothing stood in their way. He was singing straight to her and making her melt.

Danny sat at the table getting even madder. The damn snot was actually good. Danny glared around seeing that everyone was touched by the brat's singing. The girl was crying and he could feel the urge to cry himself but men don't cry so he got even madder. But as the song continued, the urge he had to hit Carl lessened. He turned, looking around and wondering why he had never heard the song before. He saw the back of a very attractive blonde. He would go over to her after the song, but he wouldn't leave here until Carl came back.

Carl heard the song coming out of his mouth and could not believe the feeling that bloomed within him. *"Can you read my mind take a good look at my face? Can you change time and bring us back to paradise?"* He didn't need the words appearing on television monitor in front of him. He closed his eyes and sang with his heart as he'd witnessed Garrett do earlier. A single tear escaped down his cheek. He could feel his chest rise as he inhaled to sing. He couldn't remember ever hearing the song before but somehow he knew the words by heart. So, he just concentrated on his breathing, kept his eyes shut and let the words dance out of his mouth.

When the song was over, he opened his eyes as if coming out of a trance. The karaoke host stood next to him with his hand out. They shook hands again. "That was awesome," he said to Carl. Carl nodded, in shock. He never could have sung like that before tonight. It seemed natural though, like living a dream.

"All right, let's hear it for Carl who had told me that he's never sung before."

The bar cheered and strangers gave him high fives as he stepped off the little stage. The karaoke host inspected the machine shaking his head trying to find where the song had come from. He wanted to try singing that song sometime.

Carl struggled, making his way through the crowd of people that mysteriously gathered around him. He wanted to get back to Carrie and share the experience with her. All at once, over all the fanfare he heard a bottle break and a table being overturned then Carrie screamed making Carl's blood turn cold.

CHAPTER 9

"*Mordirian!*" The word echoed in Carl's ears. Someone had yelled the curse that had changed his life. He fought through the crowd spotting a flash of red light followed by a thud. It sounded like someone had thrown a side of beef off a twenty story building. Carl pushed his way through the crowd of people having no idea what he would find. The curse had come from somewhere near the area at which he and Carrie had been sitting. A horrible thought crept into his mind.

What happened? Did Carrie use the curse on Danny? Carl noticed Danny had cornered her and had thought it was funny. He should have gone to her rescue instead. Sure he had been cornered by Danny's goons at first, but he could've easily gotten away from them. He had chosen not to even try because he had enjoyed watching her squirm for once. He knew she'd been playing with him and had thought it only right to return the favor. His thought now was could his actions have caused her to do something so horrible?

He broke through the crowd stopping behind a figure in a black robe standing in front of his table. The robed figure loomed over its victims while pointing a wand at two people lying on the ground. Danny was curled up in a ball, dead. Carrie lay next to him, an overturned chair resting behind her. He saw that she was defenseless. Her purse had fallen near Danny. It was lying open exposing her wand. But, Carrie was staring at the tip of the wand being held by the robed figured as if looking up at a mugger who was pointing a gun at her.

Carl did the only thing he could think of. He rushed forward. The attacker let out a grunt of surprise as Carl slammed into him sending him flying to the floor and the wand bouncing out of his hand devoured somewhere in the darkness. Carl skidded to the right; the attacker to the left. Carl stared at the figure while cringing from his now aching shoulder. The robed figure wore a white mask that concealed all but his eyes. It seemed below were rib bones pieced together giving it an altogether barbaric look. Suddenly, the eyes of Danny's murder bugged out as he recognized Carl and realized that he had been the one to send him sprawling to the ground.

Meanwhile Carrie had crawled over to her purse pulled out her wand and was now pointing it at their assailant; but before she could curse the Goblin she spotted another hooded figure pushing through the crowd toward them. Unsure of what to do she ran over to Carl and grabbed him while whispering a spell. They vanished. The broken glass sound wasn't as loud when you were the one vanishing he realized. The next thing he knew everything went black and pressure squeezed in on him from every direction as if he were under water reaching the depths of implosion. He couldn't breathe, feeling like his eyeballs were being forced back into his head and his eardrums were exchanging sides.

All at once everything was normal and he was able to breathe again. Looking around he was surprised at their new environment. They were standing outside of his house. "We just reanesced," she told him, making sure he was all right. "It takes getting used to. There are a lot of sorcerers that prefer traveling by other non-magical means of travel; but when in a hurry reanesce is the quickest way."

"I'll stick to the car thank you." Carl said, taking a gingerly step toward the front door. His legs were supporting him but they felt heavy as if they'd been asleep.

"We need to hurry. There's no telling how long we have." She rushed into the house leaving him standing in the yard. "Come on!" she yelled from inside the house.

Carl glanced up and down the street then followed her into his house. He wasn't sure what had actually happened and he was worried about his car. By leaving it at the bar the police could easily find out who he was and he hadn't paid the bill either. He had never run out without paying before. The karaoke host had his name, too.

Danny was dead. The police would think he had something to do with it. He had fled the scene of a crime. He would be the prime suspect.

"We don't have time to worry about things like that right now," Carrie urged from the open door. "We've gotta get out of here." She had a satchel bag in one of her hands and waving her wand with the other. Another satchel appeared in Carl's hands. "Grab only what you need." She shoved the Chronicler into her satchel heading to the room she had slept in the night before.

He had no clue what he needed. The bag wasn't large enough for any clothes. Carrie could just do magic to get them whatever they might need. He went into the bathroom and picked up his toothbrush and toothpaste and placing them in the satchel. He hated the feeling of a new toothbrush. Going into his bedroom, he snatched one of the two pillows off the bed wishing he could take both. He knew there was no way they'd both fit. By the looks of things, he'd be lucky to force this one in. To his surprise though, the pillow slid all the way in. So, he took the other pillow and tried putting it in. It slipped right in. He felt around the outside of the satchel, it felt as if it were still empty. He shook his head, thinking magic, and returned to the living room.

Carrie was already waiting with her satchel which also appeared empty. He wondered what else besides the Chronicler she had put into hers. He suspected he could've put a ladder in there if he needed one and it would fit. He thought of the circus and all of the clowns coming out of a tiny car. He knew there was a hole in the floor at the circus but what was up with the satchels? There was no secret passage.

"Don't even try to understand it or you'll go mad," Carrie warned. "We need to get out of here. You were right before, it won't be long before the non-magical police come searching for us."

"We didn't do anything wrong," he said, trying to reassure himself that he was still a good person.

"Remember we fled. They'll think we're hiding something and hold us responsible for killing Danny." He already knew this but coming from her reaffirmed the situation. "Those were Goblins?"

"Yeah, they thought Danny was you or else you'd be dead."

He didn't know what they were doing but he figured that being with Carrie was safer than not although he did acknowledge that no one had been trying to kill him up until she had entered his life. Well at least the past three years of his life had been normal. The last forty-eight hours, however, had been something extraordinary.

"All right then," Carrie began. "We need to get out of here. I think normal magical ways of travel will be a bit risky. Only a few people know I've finally found you."

"Then how are we going anywhere?" he asked. "My car is back at the bar?" He wondered if she had forgotten.

Carrie waved her wand which she had already returned to its normal length. "I think this will be a good start." She looked at Carl shaking her head. "That won't do though." She waved her wand pointing it at Carl. His clothes changed from the tan khakis and white polo shirt he had been wearing to blue jeans, a white t-shirt and a brown leather jacket.

"It looks like we're going back to the fifties," he said, examining the new jacket he wore.

"Not quite," Carrie answered, turning the wand on herself. The attractive outfit she wore was immediately replaced with tight blue jeans, a t-shirt and a black leather jacket. "Yes, excellent. Well we'd better be off."

"How are we going to do that? My car is probably being searched by the police right now."

"No need to worry." She was already out the door before Carl began walking. When he reached the door he turned to look back at the house he had called home. It wasn't much but it was his. He didn't like running from it. He gave a halfhearted smile and turned closing the door and wondering if it would be for the last time.

Carrie stood in the drive way next to a candy apple red Harley-Davidson motorcycle. The chrome on it was shining as if it had just left the showroom. "Wow, this is sweet."

"It'll do." Carrie wasn't as impressed as Carl, but she seemed satisfied none the less. "You do know how to drive one of these, don't you?

"Sure, we'll need helmets," Carl suggested, walking around and admiring the bike.

Carrie waved her wand and two candy apple red helmets matching the bike materialized. "Anything else?" she asked. She handed one of the helmets to Carl who put it on. He couldn't lose the grin, excited to fire up the Harley.

"We'll never need to go shopping again," he said, finishing putting on his helmet. He straddled the motorcycle straining his leg as he lifted it over. He grasped the handle bars admiring the feel in his hands. There was something about being on a motorcycle that made a person feel free, almost like reliving your childhood. Carl felt the emotion stir in him. "It'd be nice to have some riding boots," Carl said, looking down at his brown loafers.

"As you wish," Carrie answered, smiling at him on the bike. She waved her wand and the loafers were replaced by ankle high brown leather boots complimenting the jacket.

"Sorry," he hadn't realized he'd actually said that out loud. "I didn't mean to sound rude. It's just that, I realized that it would be uncomfortable with the loafers." He admired the way she coordinated the boots to match the jacket though.

"No worries." She watched him jump firing the bike to life. "Anything else we need?"

"Well, now that you mention it," he hollered over the roar of the Harley. "I think we'll both be more comfortable with gloves."

She nodded and gloves that matched their jackets appeared on their hands. He nodded putting the face guard of his helmet down. She put down her face shield as well and slid on the bike behind him snuggling her arms around his waist. He thought he felt her quiver as she clutched hold of him. He felt the rush of excitement explode through him as they headed out of the driveway rolling away into the night.

He had no idea where they were going, just enjoyed the feeling of the wind beating against him as they rode. He wished he could take off the helmet but knew Carrie wouldn't permit it. No one would guess it was him on the bike with a beautiful girl clutching him. He thought back to the bar. The people had really enjoyed his song. Unfortunately, he hadn't had the opportunity to find out what Carrie thought of it. Two people he'd never met before had tried to kill him and had killed Danny instead thinking he was Garrett. Even though, he didn't like Danny he couldn't help but feel pity. It wasn't right to die in a drunken daze just because they thought he was Garrett.

He tried keeping his feelings open hoping to open himself up to communicating with Carrie as they went along. At the same time, he worried that she would think he was a wimp for feeling sorrow over Danny. He tried distracting himself from the guilt wondering if he was going the right way. He sensed the turns she wanted him to take. She hadn't voiced where they were going but he knew to get on the expressway. He imagined he could feel her heart pounding as they stole away down the highway.

Carrie tried to understand the feelings pulsing through her as she clutched Garrett. Why was her heart beating so fast? He was Garrett now after singing that song because there was no way Carl could have known it. She had only heard him sing it once before years ago. It was a song from a magical band whose name she could not recall, but once Garrett sang a song it was his. She couldn't understand how the music thing had been able to play it though. She sighed, resting her head against his back pondering this curious new development.

She needed to think and the ride would give her time for that. She purposely had not told him where to go. She willed him to head in the right direction careful not to give him too much of an idea where they were heading. She didn't want to argue with him over where she was taking him. The lump in her throat made it difficult to swallow as she attempted to calm the storm of butterflies raging in her stomach. The ride was uncomfortable on her back but the excitement she felt more than compensated for it. After riding for about two and a half hours she signaled for him to pull over.

"Where are we now?" she asked as they pulled into an all-night café.

"I believe we're just outside of Cleveland, Ohio," he answered, checking the gas. He took off his helmet inhaling the fresh night air. "I think there's something wrong with the gas gauge. It says we have a full tank but we should need some by now."

"Nope, I've bewitched the tank to refill itself." She took off her helmet and her lovely red hair danced out looking like she had just left a salon instead of having just taken off a helmet she had worn for over two hours.

"Wish you had done that with my car tank." Carl gazed at her in wonder. "Do you want a cup of coffee?" he asked, trying to figure out what to do next.

"I'd prefer tea," she said, shaking her head and rolling the kinks out of her neck.

"I'm sure they'll have tea." He gave a sheepish smile. "If we're lucky they'll have pie, too."

"Sounds good," Carrie said. She decided to let Carl believe it was his idea to stop and not her planting the idea in his head. She felt a little guilty but only tad. It was a women's right to lead a man as much as possible especially if he was not aware of it and even better is letting him believe it was his idea. She couldn't help feeling a little pleased, too. Garrett was such a powerful sorcerer. She had been amazed when she had taught him *Brauchen*. He had learned it so quickly, too quickly actually, and almost without any effort and *leer poma* had come even easier.

Carl pulled the café's door open and they were welcomed by the clanging cow bell announcing their presence. Carl walked in and held the door as Carrie followed behind him. "Howdy," a cute waitress greeted without looking up. "Just have a seat anywhere and I'll be right over." The waitress flirted with the only other customers, two men at the front counter.

Carl and Carrie sat down in the booth furthest from the door. The place was nearly empty. Carl guessed a cook was in the back but they didn't see him. Once they sat down the waitress came over carrying two caramel glasses of ice water with two grease covered menus.

"How are you doing folks?" she said mechanically, snapping the gum she chewed. She placed the menus and waters on the table taking out her order pad as if they had already had enough time to know what they wanted.

"Hi." Carl offered a flirting smile. Carrie shot him a disapproving look. "Do you have any pie?"

"Sure sweetie," she flashed her own smile finally making eye contact with him. "We have lemon meringue, coconut cream and chocolate."

"Well HONEY, I think they all sound delicious," Carrie said, annoyed with the waitress for not acknowledging her.

Carl glanced over at Carrie a little confused while saying, "Yes, they do don't they, dear." Seeing the look on her face, he turned his head away from the blonde haired girl and giving Carrie his full attention. "By the way do you have any tea?" Carl gave Carrie a big smile making sure not to look at the waitress.

"Yeah, but we don't get much call for it. Usually just old ladies order it and they don't make it in this late." He wasn't quick enough to stop a chuckle. So, he quickly started coughing. He felt a hot burn on the side of his face making him jump. Carrie smiled, nodding at him with a mischievous gleam in her eyes

"We'll take two slices of chocolate pie and two cups of tea please." He hated the idea of having tea but figured ordering tea was safer than dealing with the wrath of Carrie. The waitress snatched the menus back up and walked away. "You do like chocolate don't you?" Carl asked Carrie.

"What girl doesn't?" she said, a slight blush on her face, thinking she'd said it too enthusiastically.

The waitress brought over their order and set it on the table for them to dig into. Carl enjoyed watching how enthusiastically Carrie ate her pie. He was sure she could make better, but the pie was surprisingly very good, so they both ordered seconds. There's something about riding a motorcycle that gives you an appetite he thought

"So where are we heading to?" he asked as Carrie finished the last bite of her second piece.

"We're going to a magical village." She took a napkin and wiped the corners of her mouth. "That way when we use magic it won't be too suspicious."

"Is that how you think they found us, you using magic?" he asked, wondering how they found him to begin with.

"It's how I found you." She could see he wasn't buying it. "But, no I don't think it's how they found us. I think they followed me to you."

"So where is this village at?" he said not wanting to know more of how she had found him.

"It's still a ways away." She looked up as the waitress came over.

She sat the bill on the table and began to turn away but stopped suddenly, turning to Carl. "You know you look very familiar."

Carl had an uncomfortable feeling balloon up inside him. "I hear that often. I travel a lot on business and well…"

"Where are you from?" she asked, ignoring his last statement.

"Chicago," He lied without hesitation.

The waitress shook her head trying to figure out where she had seen him before. "I've never been to Chicago."

"Well, I work on a television talk show that's filmed there and I'm on camera a lot, maybe that's it," he said naturally as if it were true and not a lie.

Suddenly, she looked as if a light had been turned on. Her eyes grew wide as she started to rush away. Carrie flicked her wrist and Carl saw her casting a spell with her wand. The waitress immediately walked back to their table and sat down next to Carrie as if they were old friends. "How do you know him?" Carrie asked careful not to use his name.

The girl looked scared as she looked over at Carl. "It was on television I saw him. He's wanted for murder. He killed a man in a bar in Michigan. It's all over the television."

Carrie looked at Carl and saw the panic spread over his face. She was not familiar with local law enforcement and had hoped they hadn't responded too quickly. But, they had already posted his picture on their television and this annoying woman recognized him.

"They said he had fled from a bar in Michigan and they suspect he's armed and dangerous." Carrie looked over at Carl noticing the waitress' fear. "They had no clue where he was heading but they're asking for any information about his whereabouts."

Carrie pointed her wand again at the waitress. *"Seliminate!"* she ordered sharply. The waitress' eyes slid out of focus washing over glassy. Her brow collapsed as if about to fall asleep and a dreamy unconcerned look fell over her face. "You have not seen anything strange tonight," Carrie stated.

Carl looked at Carrie amazed. It looked like Carrie had hypnotized the waitress and was planting a memory. She began rambling about them heading to Chicago in dark car. She couldn't tell what kind it was. Carl put his jacket back on and tossed a twenty on the table. Two nights in a row he'd overpaid the bill he thought hurrying to catch up with Carrie.

"Hope they say how good of a tipper I am on the next update. What did you do to her?" Carl questioned outside.

"I just modified her memory." Carrie walked quickly to the motorcycle. "I never thought the authorities would be this quick to act."

"It sure ain't like the police I know. Surprising a television station would broadcast this far so quickly."

"What do you mean?" Carrie had a look in her eye telling him something was not right.

"Well, Michigan has three of the highest murder rate cities in the United States. It's peculiar we made the news." He hoped this helped her understand.

"They've had some help," Carrie finally said out loud but not to him.

"Come again?"

"I'll bet the police have been influenced by the Goblins." He looked as lost as he felt. "The Goblins have probably helped the police speed up their search."

"And extended it," he added.

"We need to hurry and make some modifications."

"What kind of modifications?" Carl asked, rising on eyebrow.

"Well first, we need to change your appearance." He thought they had already changed their appearance. "That's not the appearance I was talking about. She looked around to make sure no one was looking. *"Anoldbud!"* she exclaimed, pointing her wand at him.

He felt like he had been struck by lightning. He started to stumble and had to reach out to Carrie to regain his balance. He looked at his hands and watched as they became leather like. They been soft just moments ago and now felt rough and aged. He felt at his face a long dangly beard and mustache now cover his once clean shaven face. He staggered, trying not to fall because all of a sudden it felt like someone had jumped on him. He knew he had just gained 20 to 25 pounds instantly.

"What the blazes?" he exclaimed, eyes bulging.

"Sorry, but I'm sure no one will recognize you now." She stifled a small giggle with her hand. "I've just aged you twenty five years."

"What about you?" he asked in a much deeper voice than he recognized.

"No one is looking for me." She laughed putting the helmet back on.

Carl shook his head putting his own helmet on. Another change occurred as was attempting to pull down the face guard. It was gone. It had been replaced with goggles to protect his eyes from unidentified flying objects. He warned himself to remember to keep his mouth closed as he rode now with no protection there from the bugs that filled the night air.

He just kept heading east feeling his new beard dance in the breeze unsure where they were going but trusting the feeling he was going the right way. At the first highway heading north and south he instinctively turned south surprised they were heading away from Pennsylvania. He guessed they would be going to Massachusetts. It seemed Salem, Massachusetts would be the most obvious place for a magical community.

A voice inside his head answered, *precisely*. He smiled knowing Carrie was listening to his thoughts. He concentrated on hearing her as they rolled into the night. Carl could feel coldness of excitement. *Yeah, we're heading to West Virginia.* He felt Carrie thinking to him. She squeezed him tight. He was confused. Was she squeezing him because she was cold too or was she squeezing him because...

Don't worry about it. He heard her voice. She wanted him to feel her words but unsure of him sensing her feelings too. His head began to race as the bike roared down the highway.

Six in the morning they broke the West Virginia state line. The mountain air had been chilly in the night. Carl drove as if he knew where he was going but he was positive he'd never been in the state before. They rode for another half an hour before turning off the highway onto an old road that ran through some small villages.

Carl slowed the bike as they eased up a steep hill to one of those small villages. A warm feeling spilled over him as he looked over the little village. It felt like returning home after a long holiday. He felt a sense of security engulf them. He knew they had arrived. He tried to take everything in but the village still slept it was so early in the morning. He turned up an old beaten trail that led to a severely beaten up cabin. After parking the bike in front of the cabin, he started to tug off his goggles. They made a suction sound as he pulled them away from his skin. He felt Carrie release him and jump off the bike.

His legs buckled as he stumbled off the bike. He tugged off the leather helmet and felt his back scream in protest. He shook his head at the weather beaten cabin having the suspicion that they would not get much comfort in there. It looked like something out of a horror movie rather than a secluded magical hideaway. At first he thought it was an old outhouse.

Carrie looked very tired. She had taken off her helmet and gloves while strolling up to the cabin. Again her hair appeared perfect as if she had just finished styling it rather than having had it tucked into a helmet all night long.

"My hair is enchanted. It makes it easier to get ready in the morning," she told him, entering their safe haven.

Carl was amazed at the inside. The place was immaculate. There was no other word for it. From the outside it appeared a rickety cabin, inside it was a palace. There were three bedrooms, a huge walk down living room with a fine white fluffy carpet. Carrie set her satchel on a table. Carl followed her lead and set his next to it.

"Well, I'm off to sleep," she informed with a yawn. "I suspect we'll sleep the day away. Perhaps the village will be alive at night."

She closed the door to one of the rooms leaving Carl alone in the living room. Strangely he didn't feel the slightest bit tired. He sat down on the couch to soothe his aching back and closed his eyes. While thinking about the past two days, he slipped off to sleep.

CHAPTER 10

Carl awoke two hours later rubbing his stiff neck and regretting he had not selected one of the beds. He lay there a moment realizing this was the second night in a row he'd slept on a couch. He struggled to make sense of what had happened the previous night. He had so many questions about his past. Carrie was determined that he learn the rest himself now. After his last episode in the Chronicler, she wouldn't take him back in. There was no reason to even ask her to. He felt that they just may have over done it by venturing in three times in rapid succession. It was no wonder he had a reaction. He stood up and checked Carrie's bedroom making sure she was still sleeping. He snuck back to the living room and took the Chronicler from her satchel. He went out the glass sliding door searching for a safe place to attempt his experiment. He spotted a utility shed deciding it was the best place.

He stepped inside. It looked like no one had been in there for years all worn down and filled with cobwebs. That was the way he had expected the cabin to look. There was a stool in the corner covered with old newspapers. Carl tossed the papers on the floor causing a cloud of dust to mushroom in the air. He shut his eyes waving his free hand in front of his face to clear away the pollution.

Carefully, he sat the Chronicler Recital on the stool. He pulled out the wand Reginald had given him the day before out of the back pocket of his blue jeans. He placed the tip to the spot between his eyes as he had seen the others do. He concentrated on the memory he wanted to revisit. He wondered if this would even work or not. He had watched Carrie, Reginald and Sheba do it but they were real sorceresses and sorcerer. He on the other hand was... what was he now? He had been a sorcerer three years ago but for the past three years he had simply been Carl.

He took a deep breath thinking of the memory he sought careful to push all others out. Once he believed he had given it sufficient time he opened his eyes and plucked out a strand of his own hair. He took a deep breath looking down at the long hair which seemed transformed. He had expected to see a brown to black hair but this was brown and silver. He glanced at it hoping it would work and dropped it into the Chronicler. He began stirring the memory.

Silently, he chanted his intent while stirring, feeling a bit foolish. "It is my intent to visit the Embassy of Magic on the day I was attacked," he said once out loud and repeated it again while continuing to stir. He glared down into the Chronicler not satisfied with the results. He clinched his eyes shut repeating his intent and stirring.

He began doubting his success not knowing how long he had been stirring. The cloudy hurricane thing would not materialize for him like the others. Carl thought it looked more like milk than a cloudy substance. Resigned to give up because his hand was beginning to cramp up, he started to pull out his wand. At the same time, the milky substance transformed to a fluffy cloud and the cramp vanished. Excitement spilled over him as he began stirring vigorously. He marveled, surprised and proud at the success of his first try. A broad grin stole over his face as the fluffiness became the cloudy hurricane he desired.

It had taken a little more time than the others but still he was proud of his success. He had been a practicing magician again for only 24 hours. What could he expect? The next test would be to see how well it had worked.

He pulled his wand out of the Chronicler seeing silvery faces materialize beneath the clouds. It was the moment of truth. He was about to enter the Recital alone. He could feel his heart pounding in his ears like a drum. He took a couple of deep breathes trying to relax before taking the plunge.

On one last deep breath Carl leaned forward and was pulled magically into the memory. He was doing it on his own. He could not believe it. He was actually being sucked into a memory of his own. He wanted to scream, like you do when you're going down the first hill of the highest roller coaster, as success swelled inside him making him even warmer. He did a somersault going into the cloud.

He landed in a hallway of a strange building. Letting the air out of his lungs, he expected to smell the sea air but was surprised when he didn't. Strange, he realized there was no smell at all this time. Well, not exactly true. There was a kind of hospital type scent that hung just barely in the air as if all the air had been purified. He had hoped that by visiting this memory he might start recalling other pieces of his forgotten past.

The hallway ran about thirty feet long and was around four feet wide with two doors on one side of the hallway and three on the other. Two other doors stood at each end of the hall. The walls were a drab white with no paintings or any other decoration which normally covers bare walls. It made the place appear more like an asylum.

Carl stood fixed to the spot he landed on waiting for something, anything to happen wondering where he should go. In the other visits he had not been alone having guides to lead his way. There were also people in those memories helping him follow the memory. Right now though, Carl was all alone. There was no one in the hallway and no voices coming from any of the rooms to lead the way.

This was supposed to be a memory of his forgotten past. Maybe it had not worked the way it was supposed to. Where was he? Would he be able to get back? Would he have to wait here for Carrie to find him and get him out? He hadn't thought of how he was going to get out when he'd entered. He had always been with someone and they began the process of returning. Would he be able to do it? Where were the people in the memory? Fear began to rise up inside him as he looked around quickly for any sign of which way to go. How could he be here when his other self was not? *His other self*, he thought. This was so strange if he didn't know any better he'd think he was going mad. He began to wonder if this was how people with split personalities thought, calling the other personality its other self. People and friends talking to them about something they had no clue about whatsoever; maybe that was what was happening to him.

It was all too frightening. He stood alone in a hallway. He was beginning to feel like a seven year old lost in a foreign place hoping a grown up would find him. How would he be able to find a grown up? If he opened one of the doors would there be something on the other side? Or would there be darkness because he had no idea what belonged on the other side since he didn't remember this memory? He kept on doubting himself deciding that maybe he was just nuts. One moment he was sure what he was doing and what was going on, the next like now he was lost wanting to crawl back into bed.

Carl broke from his circle of thinking when Garrett came out from the first door on his left. Carl rushed over so he could walk inside the room if need be. He was afraid of being left alone again. This place did not feel right. Memory or not, he did not want to be alone. He felt better now that his other self was there.

"Mister Montgomery," a harsh woman's voice called from the other side of the door. She sounded like she was angry with him for something. "You will remember that I am the head of this department. Not you or your famous heritage."

"I understand and I'm sorry for the misunderstanding, Madame," Garrett apologized, trying to slip quickly away. She, however, would have none of it.

"I'm not through," she ordered as if her voice were a magic charm calling him back. "I want to be sure you understand that I am to be informed first of all and any discovery. I do not care who your father was. Your family is of no concern to me."

Garrett looked at her like an artist trying to capture every detail of her face. Carl knew he was attempting to read her mind the same way Carrie had read his mind over the past couple of days. Garrett did not appear to be as good at it as Carrie though.

"And don't try using *leer poma* on me. I am well practiced at *Brauchen* it is easy to keep your feeble attempts at bay. You need to concentrate your powers on your task and not on mind games. Save it for your party tricks."

Carl could see disappointment flood Garrett's eyes. "You may have charmed my husband while you were a student of his in your Orohunter training; but you have not charmed me. I am not a fan of the alchemists he teaches."

Carl wanted to get a look at the woman but was too afraid to try to slip by Garrett. He would have to brush against Garrett and he had no idea what would happen in a memory if he touched himself. Carl looked at Garrett trying to will him into opening the door a touch wider. He clinched his eyes shut thinking hard for to Garrett move. Opening his eyes again, Carl saw that Garrett still stood in the same spot.

"Yes Llewellyn, I'll be sure to deliver all my findings to you before telling anyone else." Garrett looked at her searching for acknowledgement of his promise. "I understand that it would be, and was, embarrassing not knowing what..." Carl could tell that Garrett had not used the best choice of words.

"You are darn right!" she exploded into a temper, sounding as if she had pushed her seat back. "How do you think I felt when the Chancellor of The United Magical World Federation congratulated our department on your findings?"

"I suspect that it was a very sticky situation." Garrett's voice sounded more like a little boy being scolded by his mother for taking a cookie without permission than a grown man standing up for himself.

"Indeed it was." Carl could not be sure but suspected Llewellyn was now pacing back and forth like a drill sergeant by the sounds of her footsteps.

"It shall not happen again. As a matter of fact I am on the verge of a break through," Garrett offered. "I just need an hour or two to sort out the details."

"What is it?" Her voice perked up with excitement.

"I promise, you will be the first to know, but I have to make sure it works properly." He cleared his throat. "It would be more uncomfortable if we go around bragging about an experiment that did not work."

"I think I preferred Orohunters better when they were out in the field rather than in offices developing new magic." The excitement left her voice. She sounded as if she had sat back down.

"I agree." Garrett pushed the door open a little more just enough for Carl to peek into the room. The office was rather small, about six feet by four. In the corner across from the door was a desk where Garrett's boss sat. She appeared to be extremely thin with long blonde hair which fell over her white lab coat. Her face was dominated by a nose that was too large for her face. It reminded Carl of a bird's beak.

"Well then you are dismissed," she said, sounding like a teacher. Garrett nodded and left so quickly that Carl had to jump back to avoid the door closing on his head. Garrett walked down the hall to another door on the same side of the hall. Carl hurried along and slid inside before the door closed.

This room was much larger than the other. It had a desk opposite the door and there was an old portly man with long grey hair working on something at one of the benches that ran against the long wall. His head turned a little as Garrett entered.

"Llewellyn sure is upset with you," the man teased, turning back to his work. "I could hear her in here and I'm nearly deaf."

Garrett nodded, putting a finger to his mouth to silence him then realized the man had turned away already. Garrett walked over to him with Carl following. Garrett leaned forward whispering into the old wizard's ear. "We need to watch our tongues around Llewellyn." It was not much of a whisper Carl thought. The old wizard must be closer to deafness than he thought.

"You're the boss," he said in his version of a whisper which was just slightly quieter than normal speech.

"This is an important stage of our work," Garrett whispered back. The old man sat back resting his back against the cushion of the chair. "When we finish this we'll not just prevent the *Mordirian* curse. We will have a defense against all curses thwarting the Goblins' activities."

"Aye, that would make the Goblins powerless," the old man said as if in a dream.

"That's the idea," Garrett said, putting on some gloves. "When we make them powerless, they will no longer put fear into society. They will no longer be able to harm people."

"They can still wreck havoc on the general public though," the old man contradicted.

"Well then, we shall develop a way of protecting them too," Garrett answered determined to defeat them. He had a certain gleam in his eyes that said he meant business and nothing was going to stop him.

"That will be some great magic." The old wizard shook his head.

"When we succeed, we will reestablish a new standard for all magical and non-magical people." Garrett's voice was strong filled with confidence and purpose. "I told Llewellyn we need a couple of hours. I think it should be completed in about twenty minutes."

"Aye, but shouldn't we wait for your lady friend before going any further." He looked at Garrett searching for the answer in his face. Carl looked too. There was something new in Garrett's eyes. Carl wasn't sure what it was but there was something wrong.

"We proceed as planned. Carrie Ann has her own priorities. We have ours." Carl continued to study Garrett trying to find out what was amiss. His voice had changed, the confidence had been replaced with something different, but he could not tell with what.

"Whatever you say boss," the man said.

"Stop calling me that. We are equals Rodney." Garrett shut his eyes taking a deep breath.

"No we ain't. I'm just an old alchemist." He turned around getting out of his seat. He limped over to Garrett peering down into the boy's eyes and putting a hand on his shoulder, another on his forearm. "Garrett you are the brightest and most talented sorcerer I have had the honor to work with. You are the greatest alchemist. You put your father to shame."

"Don't ever say that." There appeared to be tears brewing in Garrett's eyes. "My father was not an alchemist. He found fame when I had developed the metal not him. He couldn't combine peanut butter and jelly on a simple sandwich. If he had been in England he would have been exposed for the fraud he was."

"You have a heart of gold and are the only person I know who loves everyone unconditionally," Rodney continued not hearing or not paying attention to what Garrett had said. "You have purity about you allowing you to create such gifts. It is your love for your friends and people you don't even know that makes you so special."

Rodney sounded like a father saying goodbye. Well maybe grandfather was a better description possibly even great-great grandfather. He looked old enough to be. All the same, Carl was still touched by his words and there were silent tears slipping from Garrett's cheek. He was breathing deeply trying to hold them back but a few had escaped.

"All you have to do is trust your instincts and your feelings and everything will be just fine." Rodney patted his arm lightly.

"Thank you Rodney but my feelings are all mixed up right now. I would like to just disappear for a while." Garrett sniffled back his tears and blinked his eyes.

"There is no one that deserves a holiday more than you," Rodney offered, turning back to his work.

"Well the sooner we get this done, the sooner I get a chance at that holiday and to fix things with Carrie Ann. Perhaps you will get a well deserved holiday too." Garrett began to fumble with his gloves.

"My next holiday will be when I'm dead."

Garrett turned and walked to the other table. "Don't even joke about that. You'll probably out live me." Garrett stared into the old man's face. It was obvious that the words were coming straight from his heart. "You've got a safe job. Up until now I've been out in the field and once this is done I'll be there again. No more research for me. I'll be a hunted man. You'll probably out live most of us in the field."

"With all of your inventions, there is no way anyone can harm you. You have nothing to worry about."

"Let's hope so, for all our sakes." Garrett clapped the old man on the back returning to his work bench.

Carl watched as Garrett began working with a large golden nugget, a large diamond and an emerald. He waved his wand and tiny fragments of the emerald slipped away from the larger piece. He placed these fragments into a rectangle shaped container made out of pure silver that was sitting in front of him.

Garrett waved his wand to summon a brick of chocolate to the table. Then he began filleting the chocolate with a small silver dagger he pulled from the waistband of his white lab coat. Carl watched curiously as four slivers of chocolate were added to the silver container. By moving closer to the bench, Carl was able to get a better look at what was going on. He saw the chocolate liquefy once it hit the bottom of the container forming a little river surrounded by emerald fragments.

Carl peered into the container as Garrett added snow white hairs into the mixture. The hairs melded into the river of chocolate yet somehow remained snowy white. He marveled, watching the hairs jump in and out of the river like trout. It was an amazing sight.

"How many of those unicorn hairs are you going to use?" Rodney asked from his work table.

"None of your business, you know it's safer for you to not know," Garrett said, looking back at the old man and making sure he was not studying what he was doing.

Garrett took a silver flask and poured some of its contents, a clear liquid, into the container. A strange sound was coming from the liquid as it joined the chocolate and hairs. A profound sadness then filled the room as the liquid melded with the other ingredients.

"Be careful with those dolphin tears," Rodney squealed from the other table. "I'm not spying. I was the one that had to fetch them for you, remember. Besides, they have a way of making everyone feel sad. Anyone walking in here would know that dolphin tears were being used."

Carl glanced down into the silver container and watched as the dolphin tears blended with the chocolate and the unicorn hairs. Once the ingredients were fully mixed, the room did not feel as dreary. Carl wondered how it was that the chocolate had not lost any of its color. It was still dark brown but was now much thicker while the hairs were still leaping in and out of the chocolate river.

"*Poctome gold!*" Garrett ordered with a flick of his wand. The gold nugget immediately jumped into the air. Garrett pointed his wand at it and said another spell. A golf ball sized piece came off and landed in his hand. The large nugget then returned to the table. He placed the small piece of gold into the container and watched it liquefy just as the chocolate had done before blending with the chocolate, unicorn hairs and dolphin tears. The hairs stopped jumping as they were engulfed in the gold and the chocolate vanished. It was as if the gold was superior to the other ingredients and had ordered them to succumb to its greatness. Garrett had a pleased grin on his face as he surveyed the mixture.

Carl thought Garrett looked like he had when he sang, but a little sadder somehow. Garrett was extremely satisfied. "*Poctome lemon drops,*" Garrett said with another wave of his wand. There was a rattling from the desk as a package of lemon drops floated out and over to him.

"You and those non-magical candies," Rodney laughed, shaking his head as Garrett took off his gloves and tossed them on the counter. After opening the box, Garrett popped a couple of the lemon drops into his mouth.

"They're excellent. My uncle turned me on to them." Garrett put the box down beside the silver container.

"Well, he was a nutter too." Rodney continued shaking his head all the while aging coal into a diamond.

"That's what some people say. I wonder what they'll say about me when I'm gone." Garrett was excited about the progress he was making so he did a little jig as if there were music playing.

"Will you stop that?" Rodney ordered. "You kids, I just don't understand what you're thinking. So what if your girl's acting funny. It's not the end of the world."

"I'm fine." Carl actually thought Garrett was alright, except some of his word choices did seem gloomy.

"No you ain't. You're acting like a spoiled child. If you would be yourself, she wouldn't be so distant."

"What are you talking about Rodney?"

"Jeeze boy," Rodney slammed his hand on the table. "When did you become so dense? You used to be in here playing about and singing loud stuff you called music."

"You never liked my music?" Garrett sounded like this was news to him.

"No, I didn't and don't but I did like the way it made you feel; you and Carrie playing around being happy. Your uncle would have wanted you to have fun, he did."

"I thought we were happy, but now she's keeping something from me." Garrett's playful face disappeared and was replaced with a sad one.

"That's just how women are. Give her time. She'll tell you what's on her mind eventually."

"I don't know about that. She's keeping me shut out. I can't trust her if she's deceiving me." He took a deep breath as if relieved he was finally saying what he had been thinking. "We used to be here and we'd let each other know what we were feeling. At first we had fun with *leer poma* and *Brauchen,* but as our relationship grew we opened up to each other. But the last two weeks… she's been blocking me and she's been distant. I know she's hiding something."

"It's your imagination. She loves you. You two have just been cooped up in this awful place working too hard, too long. You've forgotten to have fun. Stop being such a baby."

"It's hard having fun when you feel alone."

"Perhaps she feels that way too." Carl thought he was watching a tennis match. They bantered back and forth so fast he could not keep pace.

"She say anything to you?" Garrett slowed down studying Rodney for a moment.

"Nope." Carl knew Garrett was using *leer poma* on Rodney. "I've just been around so long I can read people.

"I gotta get back to this before the gold hardens and we have to start all over again." Garrett returned to his table.

"Exactly what I mean, all work," Rodney shot.

"Once I'm done with this I will take some time off, I promise." This seemed to satisfy the old wizard as he returned to work.

Garrett glanced over his shoulder making sure Rodney wasn't still watching him. Carl walked back over to see what he was going to do. Garrett turned back to the silver container satisfied Rodney had returned to his work. He took out the silver dagger again whispering as he slid the blade over his thumb. *"The blood of unconditional love, given as a token of servitude to my fellow sorcerers and sorceresses."* Garrett squeezed drops of his blood into the container.

Carl cringed, watching Garrett cut into his flesh and squeeze out drops of blood. Carl glanced at his own right hand noticing a faint scar running on the inside of his hand from the knuckle to the meaty flesh of his thumb exactly where Garrett had just cut himself. That's where he got this scar.

"May my sacrifice be of benefit to all, BARCO!" The word barco was so loud that Rodney turned around in shock.

"What?" Rodney asked in alarm.

"Oh, I just cut myself." Garrett stated, showing him his injured hand.

"Again?" Rodney asked, coming over to examine it. "I'll get something to clean it up with before healing it."

Once Rodney turned away Garrett put his dagger back in its hiding spot. He smiled picking up a dowel that lay on the table. It had something at the end which looked like a large tooth. He began stirring the gold with the tip of the tooth while chanting the word barco over and over. Garrett stirred it counter clockwise three times, stopped for five seconds, stirred clockwise once, and then counter clockwise again three times again. He repeated this ritual three times.

Rodney stood at the desk shuffling through the drawers. "Where are the first aid supplies?"

"Must have run out the last time I cut myself," Garrett called out with a sneaky smile. "I have them over here," he whispered satisfied with himself. "I think there is another one in the office across the hall."

"Figures." Rodney limped slowly out of the room.

Once Rodney left, Garrett took out a gold chain from inside his coat. It was small and thin. Carl recognized it as a type used to make necklaces.

Garrett sat the chain down next to the container while picking up the diamond and shaking it over the container. To Carl it looked like little flecks of diamond dust were falling into the mixture.

"*Hardunous,*" Garrett ordered, waving his wand over the container. He quickly tipped the container over and six gold charms fell out. Garrett seized them then used the chain to make necklaces for each charm. He cocked his head toward the door listening for Rodney to return.

Garrett then picked up the necklace attached to the charm in the shape of the letter "C" and placed it in his hand. He then closed his eyes waving his wand over the charm. Setting his wand on the table, he began to chant. "*Aloh- ve- he adoni- eh- ha- atela,*" he chanted, clasping his hands around the charm as if he were strangling the life out of it.

Garrett performed the same ritual with the other five charms. Once finished, he picked one of them back up and put it in his hand. He clinched his eyes shut and a single tear rolled down his cheek. "For Carrie," he whispered, using the charm to wipe away the tear. The gold "C" charm was dazzling with little emeralds and flecks of diamond in it. It sat in his hand looking like it just came from a jeweler. With a flick of his wrist a small box appeared. Garrett slipped the necklace into the box and waved his wand again. The package wrapped itself and a card appeared saying to Carrie from Garrett.

The next necklace was a gold cross with an emerald in the middle with flecks of diamonds like mirrors on the top half. Carl's eyes bugged out as he looked at it. He had seen it before. It was sitting at home in his bedroom. He could not remember how he had gotten it, but he had had with him in the hospital after the accident. He thought it had been a gift but unlike the ring he could not remember from whom.

"*Mordirian!*" The curse came from the hallway followed by a thump. Garrett slipped the cross into his pocket and ran to see who had used the curse and who had been cursed.

His wand drawn, he slowly peered out into the hallway. There on the ground lay Rodney with bandages rolling out of his hand. Garrett peered down the hallway. A black hooded figure with a mask of bones concealing his face crouched near Rodney. Carl recognized the disguised assailant; it was the same person who had killed Danny at the bar.

Garrett cast a spell at the Goblin that stood over Rodney. The masked figure collapsed with a grunt. Trembling, Garrett went to unmask Rodney's killer.

Carl tried to warn him but it was a memory and Garrett couldn't hear Carl's cry. Another Goblin was standing further down the other end of the hall. Garrett had neglected to secure the scene his worry for Rodney overtook him.

Garrett's wand flew from his hand. Carl watched as another spell blasted Garrett in the face making him fall backwards over Rodney's dead body. Garrett's hand danced on the floor searching for his wand.

"He is wearing the ring," the masked figure Garrett had cursed warned unable to move. "That spell will not work on him."

"I know something better," the other figure said, pointing his wand at Garrett.

Carl listened closely but the masked Goblin did not say anything. Suddenly a jet of black light erupted from the tip of his wand sending the entire room into darkness as a gray funnel, like a tornado, appeared. Carl closed his eyes blocking out the stinging sensation the darkness inflicted. He heard a whooshing sound and felt a pull both as if he was being sucked inside a vacuum cleaner. He wanted to scream.

Everything fell silent. He opened his eyes finding that he stood alone in the shed. He returned from the Chronicler. Shaking, he fell to the dusty floor. Carl curled up into a ball squeezing his eyes shut once more attempting to prevent convulsions and the urge to be sick.

CHAPTER 11

Carl was not sure how long he sat curled up there on the floor. It seemed like hours but may have only been twenty minutes. Judging by the sunlight spilling through the grime covered window it was not yet noon. The pain searing through him seemed to make time slow down but his head was clear enough to realize he had not been out long. He forced himself to get up but not wanting to. Willing himself to, he picked up the Chronicler and with small movements opened the shed door.

Carl held the Chronicler in front of his face shielding his eyes from the bright sunlight that assaulted him. How long had he been in the Chronicler? How much time had slipped by while he lay unconscious? Panic seared his insides, wondering if Carrie still slept. He prayed she required a full eight hours of sleep dreading the thought of explaining his whereabouts. Her fury would reign down hard upon him if she found out that he had left the cabin. And if she found out what he had done... would all the stories he had heard about angry red heads come true? He could not help but smile at the prospect.

Each step he took seemed to be a monstrous task. His legs burned as if he were trudging through waist deep snow while wearing lead boots. He staggered the twenty feet to the cabin, pausing to take a deep breath when he reached the patio door. The door seemed to scream as he slid it open with a screech. "Still be asleep, still be a sleep," he chanted, sneaking into the cabin. He sighed, relieved to find the living room still empty. This is a good sign he told himself. Carrie must still be sleeping.

He tiptoed into the living room returning the Chronicler just as he found it in the satchel. So far so good, he thought taking a deep breath for the first time since entering the cabin. Luckily Carrie was still a sleep and the feeling in his legs began to return to normal, but his thighs had that tingling electrical echo sensation. The feeling you get when your arm or leg has fallen asleep and then the blood starts returning to it; that feeling.

He could not recall a time when his legs had ever fallen asleep before. Sure there were times when his lower leg or his foot had fallen asleep but never his thighs. When his legs fell asleep it usually happened when he was sitting cross legged for a long time. He wondered if the feeling could have been caused by that last spell he witnessed in the Chronicler. The one used to attack him. Could he bring back effects of events along with the memories themselves? What had the spell been? He could not remember the Goblin saying anything. He realized that some spells might be able to be sent telepathically.

He gingerly waddled into one of the bedrooms feeling as if it had been weeks since he had slept in a bed. He collapsed on the king size bed working his boots off with his heels and toes, too exhausted to change his clothes. He just unsnapped the clasp of his jeans making himself more comfortable and fell asleep.

In the other bedroom Carrie jumped awake as one of Carl's boots hit the floor. The strange noise startled her. She drew her wand ready for something to move. She cautiously slid out of bed pointing her wand at the door. She kept darting it from side to side while edging toward the door anticipating something or someone to leap out at her.

She went room by room checking for any sign of entry. She knew she had heard something. Before she'd gone to bed she had placed charms on the house so an alarm would go off if anyone besides Garrett or herself came within twenty-five feet of the cabin. Still, something or someone had made the noise which woke her.

Carrie stood with her head resting against her arm which was braced against the door of the room Garrett slept in. The poor guy had been so exhausted he was sleeping on the comforter, still wearing his clothes with one boot on the floor and the other cast to the end of the bed. She pointed her wand and transformed him back to the young man he was and exchanged his clothes with a pair of red and white pajamas.

She smiled pointing her wand at him once more as the comforter wiggled free from underneath him and gently covered his sleeping body. He shifted his head and mumbled something while he slept, "Doh't kidl ahe rodsee." He then rolled over with a loud snore.

Carrie jumped, not sure she had heard right. In the past she had spent many sleepless nights deciphering Garrett's sleep talk. She had concluded that "Rodsee," spoken while he was asleep, meant Rodney. After three years, could she still have the knack for interpreting his mumbles? There was no way Carl could know anything about Rodney. She wondered if she was just hearing what she wanted to hear. It could easily be a trick of her mind from the excitement of finding him combined with the adrenaline from being on the run and her lack of sleep.

She concentrated using *leer poma*, hoping to pull something out of his dream so she could be certain. She wished she had thought of this the night before. While he was asleep Garrett's mind would be resting and his subconscious would be exposed. It was an ideal time to see if subconsciously he was recalling his memories. Perhaps she had found a way around his amnesia and could get him to reveal more of himself to himself and her.

In her mind's eye she saw him dreaming of Rodney's funeral. The funeral that had taken place three years before and Garrett had not attended. Rodney had been killed when the Goblins had ambushed Garrett. The United Magical World Federation had concluded that Rodney had played the spy and had let the Goblins into the embassy. They had witnesses who testified that Rodney had been jealous of all the praise Garrett received and thus had turned traitor. No matter how much she argued, they would not change their position. She knew there was no way Rodney would have let the Goblins onto Garrett's ward. She knew the man would never turn on her or Garrett.

Besides, he had been under tight security while he was working with Garrett. Carrie would not accept it. She, Rodney and Garrett had worked closely together for over a year. There was no way Rodney would have been jealous of Garrett or plot to get rid of him. However, she had not been with them that fateful day and the only evidence she had was her memories of the times they spent together and how they thought of Rodney as the grandfather Garrett had never known.

She concentrated harder pulling up images of Garrett in the embassy. He was making... something. She could not see what it was at first but a tear spilled down her cheek; Rodney was still alive in this vision. He was glancing back at Garrett, concern showing in his eyes. Carrie wondered if this might be the day that Garrett had disappeared and Rodney was killed.

Excitement overtook her sorrow, he was remembering. These dreams were proof that he was subconsciously aware of who he was. She would not know if he would remember his dreams until he woke but she realized he may have been having them all along. Maybe, the dreams could be another avenue they could use to restore his memories. She would discuss this possibility with him when he awoke. Right now, he needed to sleep and dream; she hoped, remembering a life not so long ago.

In the corner of the bedroom sat an antique chair. It looked like it belonged in a castle or a museum. Carrie went over, sat in it and watched as Carl slept.

Carl slept for five more hours. Carrie never sensed another dream or memory that would have been Garrett's and not Carl's. It was possible that he had and she wasn't aware of it. He was getting stronger at blocking his feelings and she wasn't entirely positive she hadn't slipped back to sleep herself.

"How are you feeling?" she asked, seeing he was awake.

He just looked blankly at her as if he didn't recognize her. She tried to glimpse into his thoughts but couldn't, instead she felt a wall surrounding them. She wondered if he was trying to hide something from her. She opened her mouth to ask but stopped, thinking better of it. She smiled instead hoping for some sign that he recognized her.

Carl awoke with his eyes focusing on Carrie. He wondered why she was sitting in a chair watching him while he slept. Then he struggled to figure out where he was. It was not his bed. Then the memories of the past two days quickly came back to him and his mouth went dry.

Carrie said something he could not make out through his drowsy haze. He concentrated on building a castle around his thoughts and feelings. He could tell by her face it was working. He added a moat around the castle as an added layer of security to keep her away from his mind and his heart

"Hi," he finally mumbled without lifting his head off the pillow. "I feel like I ran from Michigan to West Virginia carrying you on my back." He pushed himself to sit up. He was not exaggerating about the way he felt. The motorcycle ride had taken its toll on his body and he suspected his Chronicler experience hadn't helped.

"Perhaps this will make you feel better." She pulled out her wand pointing it at him. He cringed away thinking she was about to curse him. She had found out about his excursion and now he would pay. *"Anotuha!"* she demanded.

Carl jumped, pulling the covers up to his chin. He realized the long hair and beard that had made him look old were gone because his hands hit his chin causing him to bite the tip of his tongue. He remembered that Garrett had not trusted her in his final days. Carl felt comfortable with her even though she was not being totally honest with him either. She was definitely holding something back.

The spell Carrie had used was a marvelous sensation. It felt as if hundreds of little hands were all over his body massaging his aching muscles. In his mind's eye he saw them as tiny stars each the size of a quarter. They were all over his body relaxing the tense muscles. It felt like each point of each star was a tentacle of an octopus seeking to comfort him.

"How's that?" Carrie asked, giving him a coy smile knowing exactly how it felt just by looking at the expression on his face.

There was something about her smile that grabbed at his stomach. He was confused wondering if his gut was correct. His head warned him not to allow himself to get too close. He had felt something sinister brewing when they were having dinner last night. No one had ever attacked him before. Could she have been involved in the attacks? No way, his mind protested. She had spent the past three years searching for him. Why would she spend all that time looking for him and why leave the bar last night? It did not make sense. None of it made sense. His head began to ache.

Still, he could not help but believe in her on some elemental level. Her presence was soothing and not just because of the massage spell she had just applied. "That is awe..awe... awesome," he stuttered, shaking off his thoughts.

"I thought you could use that." She smiled again with something sparkling in her eyes. She bit and sucked in her lower lip sending his stomach dancing again. Was she trying to hypnotize him? Maybe, she was most definitely trying some kind of magic on him and if he kept gazing into those eyes of her's, he would be succumbing to her every wish.

"I think I prefer the personal approach better," he said, breaking his eyes free from hers.

She felt the slap of his comment and her smile vanished. "Well, are you hungry?" she asked, needing to change the subject before she lost her composure completely.

"Starved." His stomach now voiced its desire for food and displeasure at being neglected for so long.

"Well, what are you in the mood for breakfast or lunch?"

"Actually, I'm in the mood for an old American classic. How does a bacon cheeseburger and fries grab you?" Carl began to feel better. The massage was soothing but the mere mention of food had gotten his motor running.

"With mushrooms?" she asked. The coy smile returned followed by a ginger bite of her lower lip. "Whatever you'd like, but I'll pass on the cheese. Cheese has not agreed with me ever since... well... yeah." He followed her to the kitchen.

Carl was surprised by the size and style of the kitchen. The room was huge. No way, a room this large could fit in this small cabin. It alone was larger than the entire outside of the building. Add on the three bedrooms, the bathrooms and all the other rooms he had not even discovered yet, you have a mansion.

The appliances in the kitchen were nostalgic with the exception of the refrigerator. A black cast iron stove with burners ignited by a fire that burned below stood against the far wall. Carl had seen one at Greenfield village back in Michigan but had never seen one that actually worked. Brass pans were floating near the ceiling.

"I was going to offer to help, but I have no clue how to get the frying pan down or how to use this stove." He shook his head feeling overwhelmed by all the new things he had to get used to.

"*Poctome frying pans!*" Carrie said with a swish and a flick of her wand. Two of the pans that were hovering near the ceiling began to float down to her. She then pointed her wand at the ancient stove and said, "*Pommes!* It's a spell that produces fire or light depending on your intent." The bottom of the stove erupted with flames as the steel door closed by itself.

She walked over to the stove putting the frying pan on top of the stove and patting Carl's jaw shut as he gaped in awe. "I think you'll find the hamburger meat, bacon and cheese in the 'fridge."

Carl shook his head walking over to the refrigerator. They hadn't had time to stop to pick up supplies and he was certain that any food already there would be way past spoiled. The modern looking refrigerator appeared out of place in the old fashion cooking room. There were two doors; a thin one on the left that Carl suspected was the freezer and a larger one on the right which had to be the 'fridge side. He opened the door on the right expecting to find a normal refrigerator.

Quickly, he slammed the door shut looking around the room to make sure his eyes still worked properly. Carrie stood by the sink monitoring some potatoes that were peeling and dicing themselves. She glanced over smiling her coy smile at him once more. He smiled back at her determined to fulfill his task with the refrigerator.

This time he slowly pried open the door with his fingers and glanced inside hiding all but the top of his head behind the door. To his dismay, Carl saw the same thing he had seen the first time he opened the door. Standing inside the refrigerator was a creature about two feet tall covered in white and black fur. It had pointy ears which stood up reminding Carl of the clipped ears of a Doberman pincher. The creature was gazing at him with large, black, shark like eyes that gleamed at Carl as if he were dinner.

"Awe sir would you like something from storage?" the creature asked as Carl eased around the door and gaped at the creature. He looked passed the creature and saw that the refrigerator seemed to go on forever. It was more like an aisle in a grocery store than a refrigerator. There were four metal shelves that ran down each side. It was the largest walk in refrigerator he had ever seen. He couldn't even see where it ended. He glanced down the outside side of it. It appeared to be a normal refrigerator, looking back inside, with a supermarket size aisle inside.

"Er... Er- um... hamburger?" he stuttered. Carl's watched as two wings sprouted out of the creature's back. It flew up to the fourth shelf, becoming a blur in the distance. It returned to the front of the center shelf with a container in its hairy little hands which he handed to Carl. "Er... thanks. I'll also need cheese and bacon." He cautiously took the container worried the creature might bite off one of his fingers.

The creature scooted off fetching the other items. The cheese was on the bottom shelf but the bacon was on the top shelf as the hamburger had been. The wings shot out of its back again as it flew up to retrieve the items. "Here you is sir," the creature said, handing Carl the items.

"Thanks again," Carl said with a half smile. The creature smiled back pleased to assist. Carl noticed that all of its teeth were razor sharp complimenting the shark eyes. Carl shut the door and stared at his reflection in the chrome.

"What was that?" he asked, turning back to Carrie. He rested his back against the door then jumped forward remembering what was inside.

Carrie clutched her side laughing at Carl's expression. "That was a furgoyle," she stammered through a fit of laughs.

Carl muttered the name turning back to the refrigerator. He examined it for a moment and then opened the freezer door to check inside. Sure enough there was another furgoyle waiting inside. This furgoyle wore ice skates and its fur was dark brown with khaki spots. It skated up to the door, stopped, spraying shaved ice out the door and onto Carl's bare feet. A minute must have passed as the two stared at each other waiting for the other to speak. Finally the furgoyle broke the silence with a scratchy voice that reminded Carl of what his voice sounded like when he had a sore throat. "What does master wish?"

"I'm sorry," Carl stammered. The voice had broken his trance. "I was just wondering if we had any raspberry ice cream."

"Why of course you have sir. Shall I fetch a tub for you?" The furgoyle skated around in a circle excited for the opportunity to serve.

"No, not yet," Carl smiled at the creature. It smiled back exposing teeth like those of a shark except one he noticed was chipped leaving a noticeable gap. "I just wanted to be sure. Perhaps after lunch we'll want some."

"Ookeey Dookeey," it cheerfully said and began weaving on the ice. Carl watched the creature. He took note that the freezer was like the refrigerator except for the ice floor. He imagined he could even skate in there even if there wasn't enough room to do the fancy turns the furgoyle was now accomplishing.

"Are you going to play with the furgoyle all day or can we eat?" Carrie asked still giggling.

Carl shut the freezer and turned his attention to Carrie. "How does this place and the…" He motioned with his thumb over his shoulder as if he were hitchhiking at the refrigerator. "How do they become so big?"

"Everything is enchanted," she said. She kept forgetting how all new this was to him. "On the outside this place appears to be an old deserted shack. Sometimes we make places so that Rubes can't see them at all. Other times we make them look so undesirable no one would want to visit them, like this place. Most of West Virginia is like that." She took the hamburger, bacon and cheese from him.

"I guess I could understand that but wouldn't some Rubes risk visiting the place?"

"Maybe, but there are other enchantments on the individual buildings to detour any non-magical person from attempting entry and even if they did look inside they'd only see what they expected to find." She waved her wand making the hamburger form itself into patties and flop into the frying pan. The bacon separated itself and floated into the other pan as she pointed her wand guiding it.

"It just seems weird that the house can be so large on the inside when it's so tiny on the outside. It's hard to comprehend." He sat at the table watching as Carrie cooked. He had planned on helping but she was using her wand and he would only be in the way.

Once Carrie finished cooking the food, they escaped outside to enjoy eating the meal outdoors. They sat at the patio table that overlooked a river that ran behind the house. Carl thought it hadn't been there when he went to the shed. "I'm sorry if I startled you when you woke up," Carrie apologized as Carl took a bite out of his burger. "It's just that I sensed your dream and it worried me. It was of a memory you couldn't have."

"What do you mean? What did I dream?" he questioned, setting the hamburger on his plate.

She swallowed the bite she had just taken. "Well you dreamed of things that happened after you disappeared. You weren't at Rodney's funeral." She studied his face looking for any sign that he recognized the name.

He looked at her realizing she had read his thoughts while he had been sleeping. He would have to be more careful. "It was a strange dream. I don't even remember the part you're talking about."

She looked at him wondering if he was being forthcoming or not. "Would you tell me what you do remember of it?"

He nodded. He wanted to tell her. It would be nice to get her perspective on it and perhaps shed some light on things. It might actually be advantageous for her to think it as a dream. He also knew that he would have to be careful not to tell her too much. He would also have to make sure it was choppy like dreams were. So, he told her the tale of his memory as if it had been a dream.

Telling her was even better than he thought. She shared with him the embassy's conclusion that Rodney had betrayed him. He agreed with her. That was rubbish. However, she did not tell him where she had been that day and he had a feeling that information was an important part of the puzzle. He wondered if she had been a suspect in the ambush. He thought of asking her but decided not to press the subject, revealing too much of his thoughts was a bad idea.

Later that evening, Carrie excused herself to take a long warm bath. Carl was thankful for the opportunity to sit alone on the couch and plan out his next course of action. He knew he had to go back to his house in Michigan but there was no way Carrie would allow that. He cupped the palm of his hands over his eyes, leaned forward placing his elbows on his knees and cried out.

"Please help me!"

He thought he heard someone clear their throat. His throat became tight thinking that Carrie was now standing before him. What could he say to her to explain his panic? Raising his head up, Carl peered through his fingers. Instead of Carrie standing over him, a black man sat cross legged hovering four feet off the ground. The man smiled at Carl.

A calm feeling raced over Carl. The logical part of his brain warned him he should be scared but there had been little logic in the past few days. The man radiated a feeling of peace. Carl could make out the scent of pine as if he were in the middle of a forest.

"There is no need to be alarmed," the man called out.

He was dressed all in black, shiny black shoes, black slacks and a black turtle neck sweater. Carl guessed he was in his mid- forties by the grey hairs that sprinkled the man's goatee.

"I'm not," Carl confirmed, sitting back and really looking at the man now. "I was just wondering where you came from and who you are? I suspect you're from the magical world."

"What gave me away?" He smiled motioning to the empty space below him.

Carl nodded.

The man smiled again folding his hands over his breast. "You can call me Larry."

"Weird, I was just thinking you reminded me of a famous actor named Laurence Fish..." The man cut Carl off before he could finish.

"No need to say his name, I'm not him but you can call me Larry as it pleases you."

"Why are you here Larry?" A chill stole over Carl as he worried about the answer.

"You called for help," Larry answered as if it were obvious.

The color washed away from Carl's face. "Did I, I didn't really think..."

"Would you rather I leave?"

"No!" Carl reached out toward him and quickly pulled his hand back afraid to touch him.

"Are you?" Carl raised an eyebrow wondering if he should explain further.

Larry roared with laughter rolling backwards. Carl expected him to fall to the ground as if he had been sitting on an invisible stool but Larry remained floating in the air clutching his gut, his legs still crossed.

Carl began to pout feeling stupid. "Why haven't you come before?" he demanded.

Larry sucked in a deep breath and returned to a sitting position. "Sorry about that. I forget how humans think when first meeting one of us."

"One of what?"

"It does not matter. What do you need help with?"

Carl looked at the bathroom door wondering how long Carrie would be taking a bath. Could this man take him back to Michigan and bring him back before Carrie finished. A mischievous smile stole over his face.

"I can only advise. I am not allowed to do or teach you anything." Larry's bottom lip stuck out further as if mimicking a pout.

"You mean this is like Aladdin and there are conditions to your help?" Carl asked, giving Larry a distrusting look.

"Garrett, everything has conditions. It is up to us to determine the limits of those conditions and manipulate them when we can."

"Please call me Carl," He said and really began to pout.

"I am here to help Garrett not Carl. You have been reacquainted with yourself. It is time that you embraced the real you."

"That sounds just too weird."

Larry laughed, "I guess it would. Now don't worry. Carrie will not come out until we are finished."

"That's convenient."

"Why don't you tell me what is bothering you?" Larry suggested.

"Well first of all I need to go back to my house in Michigan," he told Larry as if this was impossible.

"That's easy."

A flicker of hope bloomed in Carl as he expected Larry to take him there. However, the look on Larry's face told him differently. He had to hear it to believe it though. "You can't take me, can you?"

"No, but why don't you learn to do it for yourself?"

"How?"

Larry flicked his wrist and the satchel that held the Chronicler Recital drifted over to Carl. "Go back and relearn the fifth Pentacle of the Sun."

"How'd you do that?"

"As I said, I can advise not teach."

Carl examined Larry's hand noticing his right fingernail was colored with black polish. "Your fingernail is not natural it looks like…"

Carl's face brightened as Larry put his finger to his lips and shushed him, but Carl's eyes were still drawn to the nail. "I think that is enough for tonight."

"Why haven't you come before?"

"It has been awhile, but this is the first Sunday since you have found your true self and asked for help."

"You can only come on Sundays?"

He nodded with a smile. "I can only advise."

Carl got to his feet. "Yeah, you can't instruct." He looked back to Larry but he was already gone. For a second he wondered if he had imagined the man. Then he saw the satchel sitting beside him with the Chronicler inside it. "The fifth Pentacle of the Sun, huh?"

CHAPTER 12

Carl pretended to go to bed early that night. He wondered if he should ask Carrie about Larry, hesitant because he knew she would protest against his returning to Michigan. Besides, he was anxious to use the Chronicler Recital again, not daring to let Carrie know. She was too overprotective of him, not liking the effects of the last return trip she knew about. The fact was he did not look forward to the return trip either and the return trip she did not know about had been the worse so far. However, he believed that the knowledge he would gain far outweighed the ill effects he had to endure afterwards. Also, Larry had suggested it so it had to be safe.

Carrie on the other hand did not plan on going to bed early. She intended to stay awake and watch over Carl as he slept. After this morning she wanted to monitor his dreams again, hoping for any sign that he might be recalling a hint of his previous life. She sat on a chair outside his bedroom just out of sight, like a security guard sitting outside a room to protect a key witness.

Carl quickly became irritated at the surveillance feeling more like a child. He could feel Carrie's intention to use *leer poma* on him once he fell asleep. Agitation began to build inside him. He had no intention of falling asleep. He did need Carrie to go to sleep or at least forgo her attempt at monitoring his dreams. An idea to turn her plan against her brought a smile to his face. Carl knew it was difficult to use *brauchen* while exploiting *leer poma* but he needed to gain his privacy. It was reaching midnight and Carrie still remained stationed outside his room intent on exploring his dreams. He grew more annoyed with her constant vigilance and cursed the wasted time spent waiting for her to give up. It was time to exploit her meddling.

Through his practice with yoga meditation, Carl had become very good at shifting his brain into a relaxed sleeping state while actually staying awake. During meditation, he was able to clear his mind and not think about anything. Once he got to this sleep like state and he felt that Carrie was convinced he was asleep, he began projecting desire and passion. He thought of Carrie holding him the way she had on the motorcycle. Except this time they were facing each other, no helmets concealing their faces this time. He was holding her just as tightly. As they looked into each other's eyes, he could feel the thudding of her heart against his chest while she could feel his heart racing. He made them feel like they were falling in space almost as if they were going into the Chronicler Recital, suspended by their touch. His stomach fluttered with nervous waves as energy erupted from his solar plexus like a firework exploding in different directions. He felt her quiver in his arms surrendering to the same excitement and anticipation which was raging inside him.

He paused just before reaching her mouth. Her breath heavy now, he could feel her wanting exhale on his cheek. A slight groan of need escaped her throat. He could feel her moist wanting lips, a magnet trying to pull his lips toward hers. Her fingernails were digging into the back of his shoulders as she attempted to draw him those final longest millimeters to glory. He began to pull his head back, resisting as if realizing this was a bad idea. He felt her collapse with disappointment. His lips sprung forward as her mouth began to protest his pulling away, finding her lips with such force their teeth clicked on contact. Another hunger groaned from deep down inside her.

She squeezed him tight actually allowing him to sustain all her weight as she embraced him. Her arms clung around his neck which suspended her inches above the ground. There was another soft moan of passion echoing somewhere from within her or even him as their lips danced together. She needed this feeling, as if she had not eaten anything for a week. She ran her hand through his dark brown hair. Her feet still inches from the ground. An explosion of electricity erupted from her bosom sending tidal waves of current throughout her body. She felt as if her insides were a still pond and someone had tossed a boulder into the middle except the waves grew stronger instead of weaker as they moved outward. The trembles running through her veins carried each beat of her precious heart all the way to her curling toes. She never wanted to…

Outside the room Carrie's eyes shot open. She shook the image out of her head as the heat filled her. If she had looked into the bedroom, she would have seen him smiling looking at the open door. Garrett had returned. She could still feel the aftershock of the passion but it had been only a kiss. How had he dreamed what she was feeling? It was so not what she expected. The exploding feeling of anticipation washed over her again and again, growing stronger. It was like their first kiss, her first ever kiss. She wished he was still blocking his feelings. Was the subconscious mind this strong? She had to put distance between her and Garrett to weaken the power of the *leer poma*. She ran into the bathroom slamming the door shut behind her. She threw her back against it as if barricading the emotion out.

How did he do that she wondered again. She had underestimated how powerful of a sorcerer he had been. She retreated from the door taking a deep breath fighting to regain control of her emotions. She went to the sink, turned on the cold water and splashed some on her overheated face. She ran her watery fingers over her neck, stepping back to peer at her reflection in the mirror. "Get control of yourself, take a deep breath." She closed her eyes and followed her command. In her mind's eye between her eyebrows, she saw the numbers three, two, and one. She inhaled deeply picturing a large safe. She placed her feeling inside the safe locked the door, within it her feelings and memories were secure. She listened to the water running, taking more deep breaths thankful for the air that filled her lungs.

The electrical force which had raced wildly through her body vanished. She placed a furgoyle about three feet tall outside the safe. The furgoyle pointed a long boney finger at the tumbler of the safe, scrambling the combination. It had a clever face which looked like leather as if it had been in the desert for a long, long time. It bowed to the safe offering Carrie comfort. Calm spilled through her like a rainstorm cooling a hot summer's day.

From the bedroom Carl howled with laughter. Somehow, he had been able to magnify Carrie's feelings using her own abilities at *leer poma*. She had been so intent on reading his subconscious; she had ignored his conscious mind. He had surrounded his feelings with a moat and castle, protecting himself while her feelings were left unprotected. He felt like a triumphant king poised in his castle enjoying his victory.

He watched her protect her feelings with a safe and furgoyle. He felt confident that if attempted he would be able to easily dispatch the furgoyle and pick the lock on the safe. His confidence raged. But for now, there was no reason to attempt to break into her safe. It might be nice for future reference but for now he had more pressing matters to see to.

He climbed out of bed to fetch the satchels. He snatched the Chronicler Recital and quickly returned to his room. There would be no need for the shed this time. Carrie would not be near his room anytime soon. Just in case though, he arranged the covers to make it appear as if there were a huge lump under them. It should provide a good cover.

He put the Chronicler on a corner table out of sight of the doorway. He doubted she would even look towards the room but it was better to be safe and keep it hidden. He took his wand and pointed to the spot between his eyes, concentrating on the memory he wanted to retrieve. "I want to revisit the day I learned how to *reanesce* and *vanerialize*." He repeated this over and over. Once satisfied with his mantra he lowered his wand tucking it into the waistband of his jeans. He plucked a long brown hair with silver at the end of it from his head.

Carl studied it for a moment. It seemed different from the one he had used the last time. He finally realized that he had been transformed back to his normal self. He tried to remember when but it didn't matter. He pulled his wand out again wondering why he had tucked it away in the first place. He shook his head placing the hair in the Chronicler Recital. Stirring the contents of the Recital with his wand, he concentrated on *reanesce* and *vanerialize*.

Tonight, he was pleased to see the cloudy surface appear quickly. He smiled at his success feeling confident and powerful as he watched the hurricane like cloud appear. It had only taken four stirs to materialize. He smiled down spying trough the eye of the storm the old castle he had visited before.

He pulled the wand from the Chronicler returning it to the waistband of his jeans. He took a deep breath and held it as he closed his eyes. It was not the venture in he worried about but the return trip out which frightened him. He leaned forward feeling the familiar tug. He figured a fish which had just bitten into the bait would have that feeling. He experienced the same underwater somersault sensation until his feet found the firmness of solid ground.

Carl stood in a large beautiful oval room, filled with funny noises and smells. When he inhaled a feeling like he had just eaten pumpkin pie filled him. In front of Carl stood a large mahogany desk upon which sat a Chronicler Recital which looked similar to the one he had just entered. He wondered if it was the same one he had been using the past three days. It looked so much like a television screen that he first thought it was until he noticed that the screen was hollow. Surrounding the Chronicler was a half circle of large pillar candles. Carl was amazed. The candles were all different colors and heights but there was no melted wax. In front of them sat a silver dish Carl thought looked like the container Garrett had been using back at the embassy.

A door opened behind Carl causing him to jump. He turned to watch Garrett enter with a satchel that appeared to be the same one he had used to carry his pillows. Garrett tossed his on one of the old fashion chairs, as if coming home from school, and ran over to another chair by the window where a large cat or a small tiger, lay gazing outside.

"Hello, Titan," Garrett greeted the feline, scratching behind its ears.

"Oh, thank you Garrett," the cat purred, rolling its neck. "I sure love to have my ears massaged. My claws are so rough and clumsy."

Carl shook his head wondering if he had heard the cat speak. Was the cat a magical creature with the ability of speech or had Carl use his magical ability to understand the creature?"

Neither Garrett nor the cat spoke again. Carl took advantage of the silence to examine the rest of the room. There was something about being in a round room which made his stomach queasy as if being on a merry-go-round that suddenly stopped. Bookcases had been magically manipulated to nestle perfectly against walls of the round room. The only places not covered in shelves were the floor, ceiling, window and two doors. It looked like there was no way another book could be stored on any of the shelves. Carl felt like he was in a library.

"How are lessons?" the cat asked, standing up and stretching.

Garrett stopped petting Titan, looking as if he had just been caught doing something he shouldn't be doing. "They are going well."

"What's wrong then?"

"I've been offered a couple fellowships and I'm worried my uncle will want me to accept one of them?"

"What would be wrong with that?" the cat asked, jumping up on the lip of the chair balancing only as a cat can. It pranced back and forth displaying the grace of a trapeze artist.

"I finally feel like I belong somewhere." Garrett glanced out the window watching the waves of the sea roll in. "Uncle is the only family I have left and I've learned so much here. I finally have friends."

"Friends are important." The 'r' in the cat's words began rolling together as if it was purring the words. "However your education is just as important."

"I am learning here, in fact I have learned more here than anywhere."

"Perhaps." The cat pounced onto the window sill.

"This is the greatest learning institution in the world. How would I be better off at any other facility?"

"Exactly," Belarus, added walking in from another door.

"Good afternoon Dean Belarus," Garrett greeted, again looking like he had been caught doing something he was forbidden to do. "I was just explaining to Titan my desire to remain at Sitnalta."

"I understand." He walked over and took a seat behind the great desk. "With your talents, opportunities will arise which others only dream upon." Belarus pointed his wand at the window. Carl noticed that he did not speak as the window sprang open.

"Thanks," Titan smiled, showing his tiger fangs before jumping out of the fourth story window.

"You're most welcome," Belarus shouted out the window.

"Uh-sir," Garrett called, running to the window just in time to witness Titan gliding to the ground. He had all four of his paws stretched to the side enabling him to drift to the ground like a flying squirrel.

"No worries, Titan can take care of himself." Belarus opened the silver container sitting on the desk and offered a candy corn to Garrett.

"No, thank you," he said, shaking his head.

"Go ahead or perhaps you would care for a lemon drop. I hear they're excellent for the voice. Although, you sing so wonderful I doubt they would help you."

"Yes sir," Garrett answered, looking down at the floor of the office obliviously embarrassed by the compliment.

"That reminds me of two points I have before we begin tonight's lessons." Dean Belarus picked up a paper on his desk. Garrett took a seat in a chair facing the desk.

"With the blessing of your uncle I have procured two jobs for you this summer." Garrett's face slid into obvious disappointment. "Yes, I'm sure you were hoping to make your own plans, but don't be alarmed these are not as bad as you may believe."

Garrett nodded, trying to wash away the emotion from his face. "Yes sir, it's just I was hoping to spend some time in Canterbury over the holiday."

"I understand, young love is so demanding and the participants believe they'll parish if they are separated for even a minute." He nodded as a slight smile curled at the corner of his mouth. "That is why tonight's lessons are most important."

Carl watched Garrett pouting, "Yes sir."

"First let me explain the jobs which I am sure you will find rather enjoyable and meet your special talents. First, you will be helping some wizards in Africa that are on safari there. It seems they are having difficulties with some lions that just had some cubs. You shall act as a translator. Your uncle expects the knowledge you gain there this summer will be most helpful in your future."

"Sir, I don't wish to sound ungrateful or disrespect my uncle's wishes..." He swallowed hard trying to stand up for himself. "But Africa is awful far away."

"Yes, it is," Dean Belarus agreed.

"The second job will rely on your other very special gift." Now Belarus looked to the paper in his hand. "It seems the band Phoenix is looking for a replacement singer this summer. They had planned on taking July and August off but had originally agreed to perform at a festival in Canterbury." Dean Belarus handed the slip of paper. It was a flyer announcing the band Phoenix would be playing for an extended time at the Canterbury Festival.

"But how?" Garrett asked not believing his eyes or ears as he studied the parchment before him and listened to Dean Belarus.

"Your uncle was very impressed as well as very touched with the song you performed at the Winter Solstice Celebration as were the band members themselves. The lead singer will not be able to perform at the festival for the same months you are on holiday. However, the band is choosing not to back out of the engagement. Thus, they are requesting your services on a temporary basis."

Garrett stared at the flyer dumbfounded.

"Yes, yes, sorcerers don't understand the amazing strength of the magic in music even while it flames their emotions. The call of a dolphin is much like a song stirring love."

Garrett looked at Dean Belarus in disbelief. Carl thought Garrett was going to jump out of his skin with repressed excitement. "I...I...I can't wait to tell Carrie," he stuttered, regaining the ability to speak.

"With your uncle's consent I have already begun scheduling your rehearsals with the band. They will be in Kenosis at the end of the week rehearsing for their spring magical tour."

"Ahhh... Yes sir... I er... can't believe it."

"Yes, yes it shall be very exciting indeed. You are going to have a very busy holiday I believe. Thus, I have arranged, despite strong opposition, for you to be permitted to teleport between Africa and Canterbury regularly. The Embassy was not too pleased with granting this privilege. However, due to the nature of the two events involved they relented."

Garrett's eyes were on fire as he thought about being able to travel with such ease. Carl even smiled remembering the driver's license he had gotten at sixteen; but wait, that was not really him or was it? He still had the memory of feeling of that freedom that Garrett must be experiencing now and the memory still made him feel happy. I tear fell from Carl's eye as he struggled with his past. He felt like a father watching his son, not like he was watching himself.

"I also suspect that having such a power will be very useful to you in your other endeavors." This time Carl thought Belarus had spoken to him rather than to Garrett. He was looking directly at Carl with a twinkle of understanding in his brown eyes. Any time Carl had been in the Chronicler with Belarus it looked like the man could see him.

"So, let us begin." Dean Belarus turned to face Garrett now. Carl shook his head wondering again if Belarus actually knew he was there. Carrie and Sheba said it was not possible but this could not be just a coincidence.

"There will be an Embassy of Magic official here next week to test you." It looked as if Belarus was not too pleased with this. "I dare say I doubt I shall be able to arrange special circumstances like this in the future. I see a falling out of favor between the embassy and myself but that is not your concern."

"What do you mean sir?" Garrett asked, looking very concerned at this prospect.

"It is neither here nor there; we have before us another pressing task to set our worries upon. I believe that your attention will be better served if we focus them upon your studies rather than what might be."

Dean Belarus waved his wand and a large bamboo hoop appeared in front of the door. It reminded Carl of a hula-hoop that kids played with in his old world. "The embassy official will first expect you to know Eli's coming. Eli's coming is energy, location, and intent." Garrett crinkled his nose as Dean Belarus mentioned Eli's coming. "Ah yes, I do feel the same way, yet it is vital to know for your exam."

"Yes sir, Eli's coming is energy, location and intent." Carl repeated the Eli's coming mantra over and over in his head so that he would remember it. "Location is important because one should know where one is going. It's like a person should always have a goal in life, know what they are striving for. Otherwise you stumble, going forward in no particular direction." Garrett glanced up hopefully to see if Belarus was pleased with the definition.

"Most impressive," Belarus said, studying Garrett. "I see you have been doing some research on the subject. Were you already aware of what we were going to be studying? Is your *leer poma* that developed?"

"Oh, no sir." Garrett shuffled his feet nervously studying the floor. "I was talking with some sixth levels who have already begun their lessons and I got curious, so I took the opportunity to read about it in the library."

"Yes, I see that you would. That is most wise of you but a fifth level to study this alone is most disturbing, lucky for us you are no longer studying this on your own." Belarus looked impressed in the preparedness Garrett displayed. "Please proceed with the definitions and your understanding of Eli's coming. I am most interested to see what else you are aware of."

"Of course, sir," Garrett stood at attention as he had in the memory with Sage Skopector. "The energy of the Eli's coming mantra represents the complete control one must have of their energy while traveling to their location. Their energy cannot be focusing on anything else but their destination. It's being so focused on your goal that you don't wavier in the slightest or you'll miss your location." He paused to be sure he was on the correct path.

"Very true, I could not have explained it better myself." Belarus appeared very pleased with his pupil. "And the third?"

"The third is I for intent. One must have a firm intent with regards to their energy and location. It would be unwise for a magical person to falter in their intent. When a magical person does not have complete intent when *reanescing* or *vanerializing they* will in most cases find themselves "buchstabiened" in their travels. By the way buchstabien is the term used to describe the person being frozen at two different locations. It's said to be painful. However, I don't think it would be."

"Why do you believe it's not painful?" Dean Belarus looked to be even more impressed with this theory the three definitions given before.

"Well sir, I have no proof and am only working on theory." He looked directly into Dean Belarus' eyes for the first time. "It is my belief that the person is in shock and the person's brain transmits a phantom pain when it realizes that the body frozen. It is like when I get a small cut. It normally doesn't hurt until I'm aware the cut exists. Then it seems to be annoying and sometimes excruciating painful." Garrett held up his finger showing a cut along the side of his finger he probably received on a roll of parchment.

"It seems so logical that the body would actually feel more like it was asleep, as if one had been sitting for too long with their legs crossed." He stopped to take a breath.

"Very good Garrett and you came up with this theory on your own?" Belarus smiled as if he already knew the answer.

"Well, I guess Sage Harding helped me a little," he said shyly, turning his eyes back to the floor.

"Please do not turn away. I understand that your old school reprimanded you for direct eye contact with a Sage but we do not believe in that here at Sitnalta. It is a sign of respect when you look into our eyes when you speak to us." Belarus smiled waiting for Garrett to make eye contact with him. Garrett returned the smile when he saw the look of pride on Belarus' face.

"Now you have spoken of this subject with Sage Harding?" he asked, still smiling and holding Garrett's eyes in his gaze.

"Not actually, no." Garrett began to look away but Belarus shook his head.

"Garrett," Belarus said and Garrett's eyes returned to look into the peaceful brown eyes of his instructor.

"Sage Harding suggested that I attend a few of Sage Rasmovich's lectures to prepare myself for my standard magical practice classes she figured a few lectures would be wise to acquaint me with a history of magic from the perspective of European society rather than... umm American folklore."

Garrett cleared his throat at the end as if he may have been a little offended by the word choice.

"Well I had to endure two double sessions of pure lecture with Sage Rasmovich. The first was with my own class; the second was with the second levels. Well, in the middle of the second lecture my bottom fell asleep. I thought at the time that this was what it would be like to buchstabien. I had heard the word earlier in the day and it was still dancing in my thoughts."

"I see," said Belarus, brushing his stern face, "and you credit Sage Harding with helping you?"

Garrett nodded. "Yes sir or maybe Sage Rasmovich helped me."

Sage Belarus nodded and walked out from behind his desk to stand beside Garrett. "I want you to take my arm now," Belarus instructed, extending his arm as if he were going to help Garrett cross the street. "Hold on tightly." Garrett did as the dean instructed and with a sound of broken glass they disappeared and reappeared inside the hoop.

"It felt like I had fishing line stuck in my belly and it yanked me into the hoop. I also felt like I was being pried away from you." Garrett panted as he let go of Belarus' arm.

"Aye yes, it does take some getting used to. I believe it would be good for you to experience it without much preparation." Belarus smiled as if he were looking for a certain reaction.

"Well sir, I did feel like I was falling into a dream."

"Well, let us do it again but this time pay more attention to your feelings." They walked back to the desk and Garrett took hold of Dean Belarus' arm again. As the breaking glass sounded, Belarus was gone but Garrett remained. Well, at first Carl thought Garrett had remained then he saw that Garrett's body had gone with Belarus while his head was floating where they had been standing by the desk.

"I thought you should experience what it was like to buchstabien in case it should happen." He waved his wand, returning his student whole. Garrett shivered as if coming in from the cold. Belarus smiled as the terrified look vanished from Garrett's face. "I wonder if it was what you had imagined it would be like."

Garrett stumbled on wobbly legs. He let out a big breath turning back to the Sage. "Well sir, I guess it was and is. My legs still feel like they're asleep."

"You are most wise," Belarus said, waving his wand. Immediately Garrett stopped stumbling around and was walking naturally. "Most sorcerers would have given into their fear, succumbing to the pain that they claim transpires when they buchstabien themselves. You seemed to have embraced it, interesting most interesting"

"So that was buchstabien?" Garrett asked as he stopped testing his legs for balance.

"I thought that you should have the answer to your theory," the dean said with a smile. "What we did was called *reanesce*. It is very legal to do with those without a license once you have passed your own teleportation exam."

Garrett smiled as if he understood the meaning to way Dean Belarus had shown him *reanesce*. "Thank you, sir. I can see how that can be important over the holiday."

"I thought you might." Belarus walked back behind his desk and sat down. "You will also be examined upon your knowledge of the Pentacles of the Sun."

"Pentacles of the Sun?" Garrett asked looking confused.

"Specifically, the fifth Pentacle of the Sun." Belarus held a smile that said he was pleased Garrett didn't know what it was. "A teacher enjoys instructing and when a student as bright as you does not know something, we rejoice at the opportunity to further their brilliance."

"There are others smarter than I." Garrett stated modestly. An even larger smile bloomed on Belarus' face.

"That is what makes you so extraordinary. There are few that rival your brilliance and those that do make excuses for your achievements rather than accept them graciously."

"Like my father?" Garrett let slip out not realizing he had said it out loud.

"Ah-ha, my brother Ollie was a little dim. It still surprises me that he fooled so many people, taking credit for your accomplishments in alchemy."

"You knew!" Garrett stumbled back as if someone had shoved him.

"Easy son," Belarus warned, snatching hold of Garrett to steady him. Carl never saw Belarus get up, but he had appeared next to Garrett instantly. "I knew Ollie better than anyone else and there was no way he could have made a discovery as clever as that."

Garrett looked at Belarus trying to think of something to say. "Well, back to your studies."

"Yes, we were discussing the fifth Pentacle of the Sun." They were in silent agreement not to speak any further on family matters.

"The fifth Pentacle of the Sun serves to invoke spirits that who transport someone or something from one place to another over a long distance in a short time. You understand that the sun is the ultimate source of energy?"

"Yes," Garrett answered, feeling more comfortable.

"The Pentacles of the Sun that are keys to magic that only gifted few can grasp. The fifth Pentacle of the Sun allows for the manipulation of light which is how we teleport."

"Now, I would like you to try to *reanesce* alone," Dean Belarus said, folding his hands in front of him on the desk.

Carl and Belarus watched as Garrett struggled with *reanesce*. Try after try it seemed like nothing would happen. Then after nearly an hour, Garrett made the leap. At the sound of breaking glass, Dean Belarus gave a light clap.

"You will need to come back and practice every day for the rest of the week. Keep in mind; you are not permitted to practice inside the palace unless you are under the supervision of a sage. I am very pleased and surprised at your success. Most of the sixth levels are not able to *reanesce* until they have spent four weeks practicing and then a majority of those do not succeed inside the palace."

Garrett smiled at the compliment, bowing his head to hide his smile.

"Now, I want to teach you a charm I think will be most helpful in the future." Belarus put a hand on Garrett's shoulder. "It's a nice charm that will allow you to put your victim into a slumber."

"We've already learned that in rituals and ceremonies class," Garrett interrupted as he looked at the dean, puzzled that he did not already knowing that.

"Yes, I am aware of that. However, this is a different charm that acts more like a potion. The subject of your spell will feel like they have fallen asleep of their own accord and they will not awaken until you perform the counter curse or a full ten hours has passed."

Carl's eyes lit up at this. This sounded like a good spell for him to know. It would permit him ample opportunity to visit the Chronicler Recital anytime he wished. Smiling, he caught the twinkle in Belarus' eyes as if Belarus knew what a great gift he was bestowing upon him. Carl rubbed his hands together in anticipation of the knowledge.

"Yes sir, it sounds like that would be very advantageous," Garrett said with a twinkle in his eyes also.

"I must advise you; this is another powerful lesson and should not be abused." Belarus' face was stern as he studied Garrett to make sure that his meaning had sunk in.

"I shall not abuse the privilege of the spell sir," Garrett assured him as he pulled out his wand.

Dean Belarus must have been satisfied with this statement for he drew his wand out also. "The name of the spell is *Slumberopus* and the counter spell is *Reviverate*." Both Garrett and Carl repeated the words. "We shall practice them later in the week when I have arranged for a subject on which to use them." Belarus nodded to Garrett and walked back to the other side of the desk.

"Yes sir," Garrett said as he returned his wand to the inside of his toga bowing his head slightly.

"That will be all for tonight. I shall see you tomorrow here at the same time. Goodnight." Dean Belarus turned and strolled out of the office.

Carl smiled, time for home.

CHAPTER 13

The next morning Carl awoke feeling as if he had been in a fifteen-round prize fight. He did not want to get out of bed but forced himself to sit up anyway. The sun was already beating into his bedroom demanding he get on with the day. Carrie would be up already, wondering where he was. He looked at the Chronicler Recital in the corner and recalled last night's adventure and the tough return he had experienced again. This time he had not experienced the attack in his stomach region. It had been his arms. They had pulsed as if snakes were running through his veins instead of blood.

Gingerly he took off his pajama top tossing it over the Chronicler to conceal it from view. His arms felt heavy as he pulled on a black t-shirt. He rubbed his hand over his biceps surprised to feel they were hard as if he had done three hundred pushups in his sleep. He tried rubbing them to loosen them up but they remained firm. He worried they would cramp if he could not get them to relax.

He headed into the living room. His legs felt like he was running and he could feel the beating of his heart in his throat. He took a deep breath and closed his eyes trying to wish away the feeling and prepare himself for the confrontation with Carrie. He could hear her on the other side of the door.

He opened his eyes pushing the door open. Carrie stood at the counter putting the finishing touches on some banana nut waffles. Her hair was pulled back in a ponytail this morning. Carl noticed her face seemed puffy and pale as if she were sick. Her movements were clumsy as she set the waffles on the kitchen table. It appeared she struggled with each step, too. There was a thud as she dropped the plate on the table instead of setting it down gently. A hint of sympathy washed over him as he watched her move. Carrie had not realized he had entered the room.

"Is everything all right," he asked, alerting her to his presence. He walked over to the table, smiling at her.

"Oh, good morning," she said without a smile. There was something wrong. She was too mechanical. She moved slowly and cautiously as if afraid her actions would betray her. He lowered the drawbridge of his mind and projected his concern. She stopped pouring the fresh squeezed orange juice and turned to face him.

"I'm okay," she answered, trying to reassure him without looking into his eyes. "I just didn't sleep well last night."

"Oh," Carl said, wondering if she had tried to see into his mind, his dreams last night while he slept even after the false dream he had planted. "Usually when someone has something on their mind they're unable to sleep. I found talking about it sometimes helps."

She looked at him and for a moment he thought she might tell him what was bothering her. She opened her mouth and closed it again. It was like she wanted to tell him but could not find the words. He tried to use *leer poma* but she was guarding her thoughts very carefully. He wondered if he could step into her safe. Even though, he was concerned with the furgoyle guarding it he was still confident he could break into it.

"It's all right if you don't tell me. I don't want to pry, just figured it may help." Carl sat down starting to add bacon and sausage to his plate of waffles.

Carrie sat down next to him staring at him for a couple of seconds before she responded. "I really do want to tell you something. Actually, I have two important things to tell you. It's just that I made a vow not to until you've regained your memory or at least the part related to what I want to tell you about." She looked at him as if she was going to cry.

He studied her a moment. He believed she wanted to tell him. He could see the anguish in her face, the torment she was battling. She was a good person. He felt like such a fool to have thought otherwise. She was keeping things from him for his own protection he told himself. She had made a promise. There was no deceit in her, no malicious intentions. He should have trusted his first impression, she was... is a person he could and should trust.

"Well, I reckon that I'm beginning to recall some things." He saw excitement bloom in her eyes. She no longer looked pale and her eyes raced back and forth.

"What is it?" She grabbed both his hands in hers and pulled them to her. She just missed knocking over the pitcher of freshly made maple syrup.

"It's not that big of a deal. I just remembered my dream from last night."

She pulled her hands free from his, sitting back in her chair. She peered out the window above the sink. He thought that she was probably thinking about the dream he had pretended to have the night before. He regretted having done it; it seemed to have caused her pain

"It was the sage we saw dancing in your memory of the Winter Solstice Celebration." He looked at her happy to see the excitement return to her face realizing it wasn't the one she had saw.

"What was it about?" she asked, cautious not to get as excited as she had been before.

"Well, did I have lessons with him?"

"Yeah," she answered moving closer to him again.

"I was in his office and we discussed S.M.P.'s. What are they?" He needed to fill in some pieces of the puzzle. There had been some things in his memory he had not understood and he wanted a better understanding of it all before filling her in on any of it.

"They're the exams we took at the end of our fifth level. S stands for Standard, M for Magical and P is for Practice. There was an exam for each class we had taken."

"What classes are taught?"

"Well, there is crypto zoology, which we all ready discussed along with alchemy." She started counting them on her fingers to remember them all. "History, spells and charms, magical lost worlds, magic versus non magic, rituals and ceremonies, music, magical mixtures and elements, religions of the magical world, astrology and magical folklore, and magical plants and herbs."

"And Sage Rasmovich taught magical history?" Carl asked cautiously not knowing the best way to bring it up.

Carrie almost jumped out of her seat. "You remember Rasmovich?"

"Well, not exactly. I just told the dean that I had sat in one of his lectures."

"Actually, you sat in two of his lectures. He also taught magical folklore. Classes were very boring, hundred percent lecture and Sage Rasmovich has a monotone voice. The rest of us all struggled just to stay awake."

He nodded finally understanding why a double session would put his bottom to sleep. "And Sage Harding taught?"

"History of Goblin lore, we learned about Goblins and the charms used to combat them." She took her wand out and waved it at the cup which turned into a mouse that scurried off the table and ran to the darkness behind the refrigerator.

"So what does Dean Belarus teach?"

"He was the spells and charms sage before becoming the dean of the school." Carrie paused as a tear rolled down her cheek. She was remembering a sad memory. He did not need *leer poma* to figure that out. "He only took a couple of students for private lessons. They were very secretive and I only know of you and Sheba having taken them. You and Sheba seemed to take Belarus' death the hardest."

"He died?" he asked with a sudden slamming in his throat as if he had swallowed something a little too big.

"Yeah." Her eyes were close to tears again. "That was when you became obsessed with becoming an Orohunter and gave up singing."

"I see." He told her about being in the office with Dean Belarus and talking to Titian. She had never known that Belarus had a cat and looked strangely at him when he told her about it. He quickly changed the subject. He told her about the silver container that was on Belarus' desk that was filled with candied caramel corn.

"Thank you for sharing this with me." She smiled but still had a look of puzzlement on her face.

"Are you sure you're all right?" he asked, hoping she had not figured out that it had not been a dream.

"Yeah, I think you're on verge of a break through. I also think that I do need to talk to someone as you suggested. So, I'm going to see if I can have someone sit with you while I go do that."

"I don't need a babysitter." He was hoping for an opportunity to practice what he had learned in the Chronicler Recital

"I understand but I would feel better if an experienced sorcerer were here with you." He could see by the look in her eye that there was no reason to argue. He nodded, acknowledging her concern and agreeing to the supervision. "Good, I'm going to be back in just a moment while you finish your breakfast." The sound of breaking glass announcing she was gone. That sound was another thing he was not ever going to get used to.

He went to the refrigerator once she was gone and opened the door. He looked in and saw the furgoyle smiling at him happily waiting to fetch something for him. "What can I get for master?" it asked in its squeaky little voice.

"Yes, I need…" He took his wand out of his waistband and pointed it at the furgoyle. *"Slumberopus!"*

The Furgoyle yawned deeply. "I'm sorry sir but I need a little lie down before getting you anything." It then curled up into a ball, falling asleep. Carl smiled pleased that the spell had worked so well.

"Reviverate!" he said, pointing his wand at the sleeping creature. The furgoyle stirred as Carl tucked his wand away.

"Sorry master wanted?" the Furgoyle asked as it staggered back to its feet.

"Nothing thanks." Carl shut the door returning to the table of food. Well, that was easy he thought. He believed he was regaining Garrett's ability. It was like just hearing the spell gave him the power to perform it. He was not sure how but he thought it might be because he had possessed the ability before it just needed to be tapped into as Sheba had said. What was he saying? Once you learn how to ride a bike you never forgot how. He smiled waiting for Carrie to return.

Instead of Carrie returning, twenty minutes later Reginald showed up. Carl had just finished cleaning up the breakfast remains. "Oh, it's breakfast time here," Reginald said, walking into the kitchen. "I forget about how time is different from area to area. It's strange, don't you think? I don't know how your body is supposed to understand the difference. I am nearly ready for dinner."

"I guess it can be confusing."

Carl watched as Reginald examined the kitchen for any remains of food that may have been left behind. "I put the leftovers in the refrigerator if you're hungry."

Reginald smiled greedily going to the refrigerator and throwing open the door. The furgoyle was delighted to hand him a stack of waffles as well as bacon and sausage. Reginald took out his wand and waved it over the food. Carl guessed to warm it up. He doubted a sorcerer needed a microwave.

Once Reginald was finished eating they adjourned to the living room. "So what's the plan?" Carl asked as he took a seat on the couch. Reginald stood in the middle of the room and coughed into his hand.

"Well, I'm going to teach you some more spells." He took out his wand, gave it a wave and a book materialized. "This is *The Age Book of Elementary Magic* by Natalee Hawkshank. It's what we learned in one of our level one classes at Sitnalta."

Carl leaned forward. "Excellent." He was confident he would only need to know the proper pronunciation of a spell to perform it. Therefore, he carefully slid his wand out from its hiding place, pointed it at Reginald, and quietly said, *"Slumberopus!"*

"What did you say?" Reginald yawned, not noticing the wand in Carl's hand that was pointing right at him.

"I was saying you look very tired. Perhaps we should start the lesson after you take a nap."

Reginald stretched his arms out and yawned. "I think I could use a lie down." Reginald yawned again sitting down on the couch next to Carl. "I should be good as new in a moment."

Carl stood up as Reginald stretched out on the couch and fell asleep. Carl smiled looking down at Reginald. Pride welled up inside him. He was very pleased at the success of the enchantment. He was not sure how long he would have. Dean Belarus said it was supposed to last for ten hours but how long would Carrie be gone. Plus, he wanted to examine the book Reginald had brought with him but it would have to wait until he returned. He had more important matters to see to at the moment.

He concentrated hard squeezing his eyes shut. He went over Eli's coming in his head; energy, location, and intent dancing through his head as he thought about his house. There was a clanging in his ears and he felt like he was being pulled from the inside out. A burning sensation coming from his lungs, he felt like he was suffocating. His body begged him to take a breath which he couldn't. He fought to breathe but it was impossible. He thought he could see his skeleton as if all the flesh had been ripped off it. As quick as the pain began, it vanished. He was standing in his living room.

The house was in disarray. He imagined the police had given the place a thorough search. He did not think they would have left the area in such a mess though. He had no idea why they would have gone through the cushions of the couch scattering stuffing all over the floor. He shook his head picking up a piece of fabric that used to hold some of the stuffing.

He cautiously stepped over broken knickknacks that were scattered on the floor. He cringed at the crushing sound he made with each step he made on his way to the bedroom. The mattress and box spring had also been dissected; their insides tossed all about the room. It looked like he was going to have a right job of trying to find the item he wanted. He realized someone else must have been searching for something specific as well. The police surely would not have disassembled his furniture. He thought back to the two Goblins in masks of bone that had murdered Danny. It was possible they were the ones who had ransacked his home. He had no idea what they could have been looking for though. Could they have been searching for the same thing he had returned to get; or had they been searching for a clue to where he and Carrie had gone.

That seemed more likely. He picked up an overturned nightstand that had been next to the head of bed. The two drawers had been ripped from their home; the contents scattered around the room. He picked up one of the empty drawers and put it back in the nightstand as best he could. He studied the floor where it had rested. The item he was looking for was not there. He picked up the second drawer and put it back as best he could. He then sat down on the table scanning the floor for objects that had been on or in the nightstand.

He took a deep breath rubbing his face with his right hand. There was probably something in the book Reginald had brought that would help him find it. He shook his head wishing he had brought the book with him or at least taken a few minutes to go through it. He thought back to the lessons Reginald had given him just a few days earlier. He thought of the castle where he had studied magic by visiting a memory. None of the spells he had learned so far seemed appropriate to the situation. Why had Belarus not taught him a spell that would help him find lost objects or make items float in the air?

He stood; his eyes bugging out. "I got it," he shouted to himself. He took his wand out. *"Poctome golden crucifix!"* He looked around sure that whoever had searched his house had found the necklace. Then he saw to his amazement something struggling at the end of the bed. He shook his head and chuckled. A pair of boxers began floating toward him.

He roared with laughter as he watched Santa Claus' face on a pair of red boxer shorts drifting magically toward him. He wondered what had gone wrong with the spell he had attempted. The underwear landed in his held out hand, allowing him to feel something heavy entangled in the fabric. Fumbling with the boxers as it was wrapping paper on a Christmas present, he grew more and more confident he had what he wanted. He tossed the boxers on the floor freeing the necklace that was hiding within them.

Smiling, he looked down and studied the diamond and emerald golden cross charm hanging on the necklace. Inside of it, he knew there was unicorn hair, dolphin tears and chocolate. He wondered how it had gotten here with him. He had made it in Brussels. Somehow the necklace and the ring had come with him when he had his memory erased and Garrett had become Carl.

"Well, welcome home," a muffled voice greeted from the doorway.

Carl spun around looking in the direction of the voice expecting to see a police officer or one of the masked assailants. He saw neither. Instead standing in the doorway stood a scruffy looking man about twenty-four years old. He appeared and smelled as if he had not showered for weeks. In one hand was a sandwich, which explained the muffled voice, in the other hand Carl saw the metal gleam of a gun pointed at his chest.

"What are you doing in my house?" Carl demanded, trying to buy some time to figure out how to get out of this situation alive. He was afraid to try to teleport. What would happen if he buchstabiened himself while this guy was holding a gun on him? Would the guy shoot at whatever body part was frozen before him?

He was not going to find out. He would to stall for time. "What are you looking for?"

The guy finished his sandwich before answering the questions. "I've been waiting to kill you. You've a nice place here." Carl guessed the guy had dark hair but was not positive what with all the filth. He was about five foot eight, large taking up most of the doorway in which he stood.

"So, do I have you to thank for the new décor?" Carl slipped the necklace into his pocket, distracting the man by taking a couple cautious steps with his hands up to show that he was not armed.

"Keep it slow and easy," the man ordered, motioning with the gun to make sure Carl knew he had it.

"So what do you want?" Carl asked, coming to a stop.

"Haven't decided, I've been hoping to find something of worth but unless you're into reading there isn't much here." The man leaned against the inside of the doorway crossing his legs.

"Well, what is it you are hoping to find? I might be able to help you." Carl glanced around trying to figure out what he could do to get an advantage over the gunman. He could hear the echo of his heart pounding hard in his throat.

"Not sure actually," he said offhand. The guy's eyes seemed glassy as he stared at Carl. "I just thought this place looked like a good place to hang out for a while."

"I'm sure it is what with all the police around here," Carl said, hoping the police were outside watching the house for any signs of life. They would come in if they saw someone in a house that was supposed to be empty. How could he manage to get their attention though, without getting caught himself? There was no way anyone was going to see him in his room. He was going to have to get the man to go out into the living room or kitchen.

"I didn't expect that," the man said with a vacant expression on his face. He looked flushed, like he had a fever.

"Did they find the bag in the living room?" Carl asked as the man looked at him with a more alert face. This seemed to be music to the man's ears.

"What's in the bag?"

"It's my take from the robbery. You must've read about it or saw it on television." Carl figured this would be enough bait for the guy to take a look. If he was lucky the police might notice the movement and come in to investigate.

"Show me," these words were like music to Carl's ears.

He walked toward the door, the man backing away allowing Carl to pass by, but not close enough for him to make a move for the gun. Carl slowly walked into the other room hoping the guy would get really close to him or that he could somehow draw the attention of the police.

"It was right over there behind the cabinet against the wall." Carl was surprised the guy had not mentioned the wand in his hand. Sure, it would appear to be just a piece of polished wood, not much of a threat. However, it was strange.

Carl was pleased the guy did not seem to be too bright. The wand was not the only mistake he had made so far. He stopped looking at Carl and began feeling behind the cabinet for the phantom bag.

Carl pointed his wand at the cabinet, *"Poctome!"* The cabinet began to move toward Carl smacking the guy in the face. The gunmen stumbled falling to the floor. He reached up and cupped his hands, with the gun still in one, around his now bloody nose. Carl jumped away as the cabinet landed on the ground near his feet.

The guy cursed. He looked at Carl and the cabinet, shaking his head, trying to stop the blood that was streaming into his hand. "How did you do that?" the guy gurgled through the blood.

"Do what?" Carl nearly laughed as he pointed his wand at the lamp by the door. *"Poctome lamp!"* he whispered. The lamp lifted off the table and started floating in the air banging the guy in the head. The lamp kept beating at him trying to get through him to Carl. It was also struggling to free its cord from the wall. It took a moment or two, but it finally wiggled free.

The man stared at the lamp as it floated to Carl. Carl grabbed the lamp and tossed it against the wall loudly, hoping the noise would reach outside. There was a loud smash as it shattered against the wall. They guy just stood there not believing his eyes as more furniture began to float in the air.

"You didn't know this house is haunted?" Carl laughed as the guy turned white watching the items float to Carl. The television tried to obey Carl's magic but fell to the floor instead, the electrical and cable cords still securing it to the wall. The man looked at it in disbelief as it lay smashed on the floor.

"Stop it," he screamed as magazines started flying through the air. Carl eased back toward the bedroom. He enjoyed scaring the guy but he did not want to be in the room when the police came in. He slipped to the doorway just as the man began shooting at the floating objects. Carl smiled sure the police would hear the sound of the gun blasts. The man squeezed the trigger three more times. One bullet slammed into the television which had still been trying to wiggle its way free.

The second bullet tore into the cabinet that had given the gunman the bloody nose. There was a crack as the dark wood splintered and turned violently white where the bullet had entered and exited. A smash was heard as the china within the cabinet shatter. He would not be able to those for the next holiday season.

The third bullet tore through one of the magazines floating toward Carl. The ripping sound was followed by a stinging of Carl's left shoulder. The bullet burst into his arm sending angry pulses of burning pain through his body at the same time, he felt blood erupt from the wound. Squeezing his eyes shut against the pain, he stumbled against the door keeping himself from collapsing. Why hadn't he had the darn gun come to him instead of the bullets?

He managed to stumble through the doorway into the bedroom just as the front door burst open. "Stop right there!" one of the police officers ordered. Carl heard laughing just before the roar of gunfire raged through the room.

Carl rested against the wall opposite the gun battle, breathing hard trying to concentrate. He had not meant for the guy to be killed just caught, but he was sure the police had taken him out. Now, he just wanted to get away. His shoulder was roaring with pain. He breathing was very short and shallow. He was trying to calm his mind, to concentrate. He had to control his energy. He had to be intent on the location he wanted to go. He had to be sure of his intent. He had to focus, concentrate on the location. He had to think... He had to think... What was Eli coming for? He could not think past the spreading pain. His fingers were numb.

"Hey Charlie," a voice from the other room called. "Look at this. There's someone else here."

Carl realized that they must have noticed the splatter of blood against the wall. His blood had splattered when fell against the door, leaving an imprint of his existence. They would be there just outside the door any second now ready to come in. Revolvers would be ready to finish him off. He only had a few precious moments. How long would they wait before barging into the room?

Carl took a deep breath trying to fight through the pain. Energy, intent and location was it, but location was second and intent was third, right?

"Okay in there, come out!" a voice ordered.

There was a loud crack of breaking glass but from where did it come? Carl forgot about the pain in his shoulder. He felt he was being squeezed like an orange. The pain exploded in his shoulder, darkness fell.

CHAPTER 14

Perspiration drizzled into Carl's eyes as he held his hand against the hole in his shoulder. The blood had slowed but it was still trickling through his fingers, his mouth was very dry and he felt dizzy. He fought the urge to be sick.

His location was off a little. He had wanted to return just outside the back door. Under the circumstances he figured he was lucky to have returned at all. He was not sure if Carrie was back yet. Materializing right in front of her would have been a bit funny. He did not know what he would tell her but at least it would have been safer coming in from outside. It would have given him more options with his story. Instead he had materialized right in the middle of the living room. If Carrie was back, this is here she would most likely be. He darted his head around searching to see who was there with him, relieved to only find Reginald still sleeping. He let out a deep breath as Reginald snored from the couch.

Carl lowered his right hand to examine the hole in his shoulder. He struggled to pull off his t-shirt hoping to get a better look at the wound. Other than a twinge of pain, he managed to get his right arm free. The left was a different tune. He pulled the shirt up to the shoulder but the dried blood clung to the shirt and his skin like glue sealing the two together. His legs wobbled as he tried to force his arm free. He needed to sit down but was afraid of what would happen if he did.

He tugged his wand free as pain roared through his body. He pointed it at Reginald and stuttered, *"Reviverate!"* Tucking his wand away, he stumbled against the glass coffee table sure he was going to fall onto it and break it. He closed his eyes trying to fight back the light headedness. He waited for Reginald to wake up. Would it take longer because he was human? Maybe, the longer one slept the harder it was for them to wake up. He swallowed hard closing his eyes praying to God that Reginald would wake up soon. He tried to cough up some moisture, anything to relieve the aching dryness of his throat and mouth.

Reginald began stirring on the couch. Carl watched as Reginald's eyes blinked open but fell closed again. Then he took a deep breath, stretched his arms wide and arched his back like a cat. He opened his eyes and blinked again and this time they remained open focusing on Carl. There was blankness on his face as he tried to register who Carl was. It was like he did not even remember where he was. His eyes sprung open when he finally realized who he was looking at.

"Sorry." Reginald wiped his eyes with the back of his hands. "How long have I been sleeping?" He looked around the room to see if they were still alone.

"Don't know," Carl said as he staggered backwards. "Listen Reginald there's been some trouble and I need your help." His voice seemed too calm, not sounding like the panic in his head. He wanted to scream that he had been shot but the words would not come out. It was like it was someone else talking while his brain screamed, look at me you imbecile!

Reginald stood up still not registering the blood that covered Carl as he clutched his shoulder. Reginald drew his wand, looking around the room again for the source of the trouble. "What kind of trouble?" Reginald looked prepared for someone to jump out at him at any moment. He kept bouncing around.

Carl moved his hand from the hole it covered. Reginald kept glancing around the room expecting someone to attack. He failed to see that Carl had his shirt half way off and had blood all over it. Instead he kept looking from left to right, from the front door to the back door over and over. His eyes took a detour to the kitchen as he debated if she should go in there or not.

"This kind," Carl pointed at his wounded shoulder as his wobbly legs gave way and he stumbled to the floor. He balanced on one knee as Reginald gaped at the wound.

Reginald pointed his hand at Carl and gave it a flick *"Limpiaro!"* The blood that had covered Carl disappeared.

Carl struggled to free the shirt off the rest of the way. The agony on his face almost caused Reginald to scream. Carl sighed in relief as he pulled the shirt free of his injured arm.

"Can you do something to repair it before...?" Carl asked as his eyes rolled back into his head and he passed out.

Carl heard voices coming from what seemed like far away. He could not make out what they were saying but he could tell there were at least three other people there with him. His eyes wanted to open but he forced them to remain shut while he listened, trying to figure out where he was and who they were. He wanted them to think he was still a sleep until he could figure out something to tell them to explain his injury. It was sure to be the topic of discussion when he woke.

"As I already said, I don't know what happened." This had to be Reginald. "I was taking a nap and Garrett woke me up covered in blood. I nearly got sick myself."

"He did lose a lot of blood," a female voice said. Carl did not recognize the voice. It was neither Carrie's nor Sheba's. It was a new voice, someone he had not met before or didn't remember or maybe even Garrett did not know her. Whichever was the case, he did not know who it was.

"He looks awful pale." This was Carrie's concerned voice no doubt.

"That's because of all the blood he's lost. I used root of a willow tree to slow the burn from the bullet. Garrett would have liked that old Indian custom. Indians used to chew the root and put it on burns. It acted like a magnet pulling the poison, as they called it, away from the vital tissue," the new female voice explained. "I was able to heal the wound and repair the damaged tissue easy enough thanks to the root that's easily found here. However, reproducing the blood he lost is up to him alone. There's only so much magic can do."

"I thought...," Reginald began but stopped. One of the girls probably looked at him sharply or he decided that what he was going to say was unimportant.

"Orange juice and rest are the best remedies to replace blood. All the others are just old wives tales," the new person added. Carl was not sure but he thought he heard someone fall against the wall.

"This is entirely my fault, again!" Carrie stuttered through tears she could no longer fight back.

"No, it's my fault; I never should've taken that nap," Reginald said gloomily.

"You're right; it is your fault," Sheba's voice said as if she had turned away from the bed. That meant there were four people there,

Carl began to be overcome with guilt. Neither of them was at fault. It was his fault. He was responsible for the mess he had gotten himself into. It was his fault entirely. He had been playing around with the gunman. If he had not been having fun tormenting the guy with magic, he would never have been injured. He should have left the minute the man was distracted. He wanted to tell them that he was responsible for the entire mess not them. He struggled to speak but his mouth would not open. He needed to tell them that he was the one to blame. He tried to open his eyes but now they would not follow his command. He tried to move his right hand but nothing, his left hand, again nothing. He tried moving his arms, kicking his feet. There was no more pain. Why couldn't he move? Then it came crashing down on him, he was paralyzed. All he could do was listen to them as his gut wrenched with guilt.

"Don't be silly Reggie and don't be so hard on him Sheba." Carl could hear the liquid sadness as Carrie inhaled. In his mind's eye he could see her tears ruining her beautiful face. "I should never have left. He's my responsibility not yours. It's just... I wanted to tell him so bad. I..." His gut twisted wondering if it was Sheba, Reginald or the newcomer that was comforting her.

She could no longer hold back the flood of tears. Could she have been about to say what she promised someone she would not? He did not know. He wondered if there was a spell that would prevent her from telling her secret to anybody.

"Stop dwelling Carrie," the new bossy female voice said. "He'll wake soon and you'll see he will be alright."

It was like those words were the charm needed to break the curse that had him immobilized. He felt his arm twitch as his muscles came back into life. First there was a tingling in his fingers on his right hand as they slowly curled and released his fist as if he was squeezing an invisible sponge. He took a deep breath as the ghost of pain came haunting through his body. It began in his shoulder where he had been shot but washed down his body to his toes like a wave traveling to shore in the ocean. He slowly opened his eyes seeing the blurry outline of six people standing over him. He squinted trying to figure out who they were. The light was bright stinging his eyes as he fought to recognize their faces.

Two of the six people leaned closer to him. The bitterness of the light softened as the shadows of the two people fell over his face. He could smell the sweat of fear on them and felt nausea building in his throat. "He's opening his eyes." It was Carrie but something was weird, both of them were Carrie.

"There are two of you," he weakly whispered. Was that his voice he was hearing? It sounded so distant and like a mouse if it could actually talk.

"A little double vision is to be expected," the newcomer added matter-of-factly as she leaned down and shined a beam of light from her wand into his eyes. "It should pass shortly."

"Who are you?" Carl asked, trying to pull his head away from the heavyset person.

"This is a friend of ours," Carrie began to introduce the stranger to him. "Garrett I would like to introduce you again to Susan Medico."

Carrie had called him Garrett not Carl. He wondered if that was because of the new person's benefit or had something changed?

"Susan is a doctor at Saint Luke's Magical Medicines. It's a hospital for magical folks in Kenosis. She came here as a favor to me." The second part was stressed pretty hard as if implying he should watch his manners.

"How are you feeling, Garrett?" the two Susan's asked as they smiled at him.

"Thirsty," he mumbled to all of them. He closed his eyes and slowly shook his head trying to clear his vision. The double vision added to the queasiness in his stomach but shaking his head hurt his teeth. It was strange. He felt as if he had lost a tooth or something. He blinked his eyes and tried not to think.

"Here's some orange juice," Susan said as the two Susan's moved two glasses towards him. It was not the injury or the weird vision but he was sure the glasses were steaming. "It's a sleeping draft with an accelerator potion added to it. We should be able to rebuild those red and white blood cells with a good night's rest."

"Wait a moment," Carrie interrupted. "We need to know what happened."

"I'll tell you everything but I have to do something first." He swallowed hard expecting her to argue. "Don't worry we're safe."

Susan put the glass in Garrett's hand as he was having trouble finding it. "I think some more rest would be best."

Carrie was looking, wanting to know now what had happened but she relented. She could see that he was in no state to recall what had happened to him.

Carl took a sip of the orange juice tasting cinnamon with a hint of ginger in it. There was a warm feeling as the potion went down his throat. He looked up at Carrie, smiling as his vision blurred. There was three of her now. That was nice. He bet she was worried about him but it looked like all three of them were smiling at him anyway. He felt like he was floating. He wanted to shut his eyes but fought to keep them open. She looked so pretty. He tried to talk but nothing came out. Susan took the glass out of Garrett's hand and put it up to his mouth, tipping the remainder into his mouth.

"That's it. You can go to sleep now and when you wake up you should be ready to talk."

He closed his eyes, smiled, and pulled the covers up to his chin. He took a deep breath and gave in to the overwhelming urge to sleep.

Carrie sat alone watching Garrett as he slept. Susan had told her he would probably sleep for at least eight hours if not longer. Carrie was determined not to let him out of her sight. Every time she did something happened to him. No matter what everyone else said she could not help but feel responsible for what had happened. She had left him out of her sight and something bad had happened *again*. He had nearly died this time. Next time he was attacked, she was going to be with him. Anyone who attacked him would have to go through her first.

She thought about using *leer poma* on his dreams but remembered the last time. She had allowed her feelings to get involved that time. It had been three years since they had been together. It was natural for some of those old feelings to resurface. No matter what she felt now, she had to control her feelings and her responses to those feelings. She wished there was a spell that could suppress those feelings. She bet Garrett could come up with a spell like that; even this form of Garrett seemed to possess unique magical powers.

Garrett lay dreaming. Well, he thought he was dreaming. It was difficult to determine the difference between dreaming and being in the Chronicler Recital. He had a strong desire to go back into the Chronicler again. He did not want to sleep anymore, feeling like he had already spent three years sleeping and now he longed to be awake. Yes, he was sleeping he decided. This had to be a dream; he was dreaming that he was dreaming. Only in the dream he was in control of what he could do, could actually make his dream go where he wanted it to go. Lucid dreams they were called.

He was standing on the edge of a cliff. He was not sure but he thought it was the white cliffs of Dover in England but Carl had never been there. This was a memory of Garrett's. He was looking out at the sea. Closing his eyes, he heard the call of the seagulls as they searched for food on the seashore. He opened his eyes as a white dove chirped in a pear tree at his side.

He walked over to the tree and took a pear from it. After taking out his wand, he silently waved it over the pear which then divided into eight parts. The pieces floated in the air just above his head like stars in cartoon do when someone is struck in the head. The dove floated to one of the pieces and began to peck at it in the air.

"There you are mister dove. Enjoy your breakfast." Garrett smiled as the dove chirped back. There was a loud crack of thunder far off over the sea drawing Garrett's attention from the dove.

"You are most generous," the dove said, but it was no longer a dove. It had transformed into Dean Belarus.

"Hello sir," Garrett said as if Belarus' transformation was a natural thing.

"You had a pretty close call there." It was like Belarus was talking about what had happened to Carl back in the house in Michigan. Well, it was a dream so anything was possible he told himself.

"Yes sir," Garrett said, looking out at over the sea admiring the distant thunderstorm that was sending lightning to the water. "I was careless and abused the power I have. My fun nearly cost me my life."

"Yes, it was a rather painful lesson to learn if I do say so myself." He took one of the pieces of pear and nibbled at it. "The non-magical community is most dangerous especially if you underestimate them as you did. I hope you will be more prepared for further confrontations."

"There are going to be more confrontations, sir?" Garrett looked down the cliff at the surf pounding violently against the shore.

"I'm afraid so." Belarus plucked another piece of pear out of the air but did not eat it straight away. "You have only begun to experience the vengeance of a very evil warlock or in this case warlocks that are using the Hyvindeis curse."

"What is the Hyvindeis Curse, sir?" Garrett asked, realizing there was still so much he had to relearn.

"It's a spell the Goblins use to control non-magical people." He continued nibbling on the pear as if he had never eaten one before.

"Is that what happened today, sir?"

"Yes, the gunman waiting for you was under the Hyvindeis curse, a curse that can make even some of the strongest minded individuals surrender themselves to the bidding of the Goblin casting the curse."

"So, the gunman was being controlled by the Goblins that want me dead. They were unable to kill me with dark magic so they're now using other means."

"I believe so." Dean Belarus began to eat another piece of the pear as Garrett continued studying the waves.

"So along with the two Goblins that at are after me I have to be on guard for everybody else I come in contact with."

"I'm afraid so." He turned, looking out at the sea now like Garrett. "You see when there are real terrible Goblins in the world; there is an evil non-magical person as well that is doing harm. We are in a connected circle with non-magical society. In fact it usually through a Goblin's actions that brings the other to power. For example, in 1942 there was a very evil Goblin that I will not name."

He paused and looked at Garrett to make sure he was listening. "And the rest of the world was living in fear of Adolph Hitler," Garrett said, his face growing hard.

"Precisely and in the early 21st century the magical community was in fear of another goblin as the Americans were fighting the tyranny of Al-Qaida." Belarus nodded his head as he saw the recognition erupt on Garrett's face.

"So the non-magical community is going to have a new tyrant that has to be taken care of while I and others in the magical community have to deal with the two Goblins that are after me?"

"Not precisely, it is my opinion that the two Goblins you are aware of are actually acting on the orders of another while Al-Qaida is still the cause of much pain in the world."

"So there are three?" Garrett shook his head.

"Or more, but I think there is one Goblin that is more important than the others. They are merely taking orders from the one. I'm afraid that when you return to Belgium you will find that the Embassy of Magic will not share your understanding of the situation," Dean Belarus informed him.

"What should I do then?" Garrett asked, looking like a young child asking for help from a parent.

"We need to be quick. First, you must learn a new spell and I think it is important that you hide a piece of wood in the cushions of the couch." Belarus smiled with a nod.

"Why's that?" Garrett asked, looking puzzled.

"It feels important that when you are being captured you get to the couch and have there a stick resembling your wand."

"Anything you say sir." Garrett took out his wand. He started to wonder if he was really in the Chronicler again after all. This was not just a dream. It really felt like being in the Chronicler except this time it was him now and not a memory. He was aged to his current age. The only difference was that he looked more fit than he remembered. He had the look of a professional athlete, his muscles tight and ready for a fight.

Dean Belarus nodded with a smile. "Well, then let us begin. This spell is a freezing charm."

Garrett turned squaring his body to Sage Belarus. He bowed like karate student honoring his sensei. He thought he noticed a tear in the corner of one of Belarus' brown eyes as he looked into them. Garrett tried to smile at the sentiment but the rest of Belarus' expression discouraged it.

"The charm is *schrankes!*" Dean Belarus waved his finger pointing it at one of the remaining pear pieces still floating in the air. He then plucked it out of the air and handed it to Garrett.

Garrett was surprised that it felt like his hand was experiencing the burning, freezing feeling cold things gave off. He juggled the fruit from hand to hand for a couple of moments as if it was an ice cube. Finally, he let it rest again in his hand amazed that it felt ice cold. Belarus nodded and Garrett pressed his other hand against the pear and it shattered into little pieces. The pear had been frozen solid and even the small pieces were not warming.

"Now, I hope you can see the importance of this charm. I also want to impress upon you that this spell can be cast with different degrees of strength as with all magic. It is all based on your intent."

Garrett looked at him as if he did not understand. Belarus said the charm again, *"Schrankes."* Another piece of pear froze. Belarus nodded to Garrett directing him to investigate the frozen piece.

Garrett took the fruit. It did not feel as cold as the first piece. He tried to break it like he had the other. It remained solid. He juggled it between his hands as he started to feel the same burning sensation from earlier. He smiled and nodded as Belarus transformed the pear piece into a seagull which then promptly flew away.

"I understand, sir," Garrett said, waving his wand at the remaining piece which suddenly covered with frost. He then took it and broke it in half before taking one half and shaving off slivers and eating them like frozen treats.

Belarus laughed as Garrett handed him the other half of the frozen pear. "I had forgotten how wonderful your mind works." He began nibbling on the frozen treat and smiling. "Aye, magic that touches the tummy is most yummy."

They both laughed enjoying their treat as they watched the storm raging over the sea. They watched as lightning shot the water and loud cracks of thunder fought to be heard over the pounding surf at the bottom of the cliff. There was something beautiful about a storm far off in the distance. The dark black, purple and grey clouds contrasting with the light blue skies just overhead gave a tingle down the spine. It warned something fierce was on its way and you should be prepared.

"Sir, I was wondering, where is your wand?"

"That is something else I was hoping you would discover." He held up his hand showing Garrett his painted nails.

"Larry had painted…" Belarus smiled tucking his hands into his pockets.

"I believe it is time for us to return."

"I'd rather stay here with you," Garrett said surprising himself when he heard the words.

"Yes, it is nice to remain in the slumber and comfort of a nice dream, but it is only a dream." He put his hand on Garrett's shoulder like a father rather than an instructor. Again Garrett felt the tingle of excitement race down his spine. "We need to battle on and try to make our days as good as our dreams. It is only in reality we can truly find our happiness for in a dream it is only a fantasy and fantasies are only useful in fairy tales."

Garrett crinkled his nose as he listened. It seemed more of a riddle than advice. He smiled anyway figuring in time he would understand. For now, he would just try to remember it and recall it when it is was important to do so.

"I wish you could come with me."

"I would like that too. However, I have my own way to go."

"Before you go I have a question, sir."

"Shoot," Belarus smiled. Realizing his pun, his mouth formed an "O". "I guess a poor word choice under the circumstances. Anyway, no more than three questions."

Why was that, he wondered but he did not that to be one of his questions. "Yes, sir. How is it that I'm able to perform these spells so easily?"

"I am not positive." He smiled as if he did know. "Your situation is unique. No one has had happen to them what you have. Thus, we can only vocalize our ideas."

"You mean guess?"

"Yes," again the man smiled. "I think it is because you already knew the spells and magic has always been inside you. You only have to be reacquainted with the magic and yourself."

"It makes sense in a bizarre sort of way."

"Yes it does but I suspect you have more inquires."

He nodded at the older man. "When I visit memories in the Chronicler, why do I get so sick when I return?"

"Again, I am working on theory and not fact." The confidence on his face shined bright. "However, I believe it has to do with Garrett's consciousness being lost for three years. While it was, for lack of a better word, gone, it had to keep itself occupied. In this case, I would guess that it performed mental aerobics. Now as the two consciousnesses begin to meld it seems natural the physical will also meld."

Garrett looked confused. "My last question is, when I'm in the Chronicler, you see me there. Don't you?"

"Yes."

"How?"

"That would be four," he answered, vanishing as thunder rolled over the sea.

CHAPTER 15

He took a deep breath and opened his eyes. The first thing he saw was the dark sky through the window. It was night and he felt alone in the room. Becoming more aware of his surroundings, he realized Carrie was asleep in a chair by the door. Gingerly he pushed off the covers and slipped out of bed. His legs were weak but they sustained his weight. Still he did not trust them to hold him up for long and he was not sure he would be able to walk. He tried to take a couple of careful steps towards the door. There had to be a better way he thought as his legs shook in protest of the movement.

"*Poctome parchment!*" He waved his wand clutching the side of the bed for support. A dozen or more papers began floating in the air towards him. He shook his head as he saw the dilemma of all the paper in the house flying to him. "My intent needs to be more focused," he whispered to himself. He concentrated harder, all but one of piece of paper returned to their original place.

"*Poctome pen!*" he waved his wand again, this time focusing more intensely. Only a single pen floated to him. He snatched the paper out of the air as it reached him followed by the pen which arrived seconds behind.

My Dearest Carrie,
I do not want to alarm you more than you already are, but you need your sleep. I know that you did not sleep enough last night. So, I did not wake you up. Please, don't be mad.

Once you wake up you can find me in the Chronicler. Yes, the Chronicler Recital. Another thing I'm sure you won't be thrilled about. The truth is, I have been going in the Chronicler at night. That's how I've regained more powers so quickly. I'll explain once you join me. I'm sure you will enjoy the memories I've chosen.
Carl

He was not looking forward to seeing her once she learned that he had not only been going into the Chronicler but that he had been going in alone. He looked back at the little table on which the Chronicler Recital was sitting. He wondered if he had enough energy to withstand the trip into the Chronicler and more importantly the trip out. He would have to risk it.

He put his wand between his eyes thinking about the memories he wanted to visit. He took a little longer this time than he had before because this time there was more he wanted to remember. Once he was sure he had given it enough time to materialize, he lowered his wand and pulled out the long silver, thread like hair that was glowing like a butane flame. He placed it in the Chronicler Recital stirring it in with the tip of his wand. Carl wondered if he would be able to stir memories with his finger once he accomplished his goal.

The mixture was ready but he had another task to complete before venturing into the world of memories. He was pleased to find that his legs were more supportive as he exited the room and headed for the plate glass door. Would Carrie have added extra protection? Would a magical alarm go off when he opened the door?

There were no alarms on the door as it slide open but something warned him not to go outside. He decided to use his wand instead to summon the stick like the pen and paper. After he tucked it away as he had been instructed, he returned to his room.

He glanced back at Carrie thankful to find that she was still sleeping. He did not know exactly how she would react if she saw him preparing to go into the Chronicler, but she would probably try to stop him. He could not allow himself to marvel at her as she slept. He knew she would be angry when she found out he had gone. He took a deep breath sighing heavily. He hoped he was doing the right thing, a twinge of doubt still plagued him. He hoped she would forgive him and rush to follow.

He turned back to the Chronicler. The whirlpool he had stirred into existence greeted him. The silvery clouds of a hurricane smiled back at him with its one eye like an old friend. He leaned forward feeling the pull of the Chronicler clutching his wand for what he expected would be the last time. He had to go fast. There could be no indecision. He did not dare give himself time to retreat. He felt the familiar tug from his belly as if doing a summersault and squeezed his eyes shut. His body was still weak and the ghost echo of pain twisted in his recently healed shoulder.

Carrie jerked her head just as he disappeared. The paper he had left on her lap slipped to the floor as she jumped up cursing herself for falling asleep. She blinked hard trying to send the heaviness of sleep away but it lingered waiting for another opportunity to posses her. She focused her eyes on the empty bed as fear shot through her erasing all traces of exhaustion. Like a mother frantically searching for a lost child, Carrie raced through the empty house calling for Garrett. Overcome with fear and anger at herself for falling asleep, she returned to the bedroom when she could not find him elsewhere in the house. The charm she placed on herself to warn her when he left had worked.

She stood beside the empty bed looking at the chair in which she had slept. She should never have sat down. If she had remained standing, she would never have fallen asleep. She had allowed herself to get too comfortable, too relaxed. She could not afford to relax. Every time she did something bad happened. She sniffed back tears that began to well up inside her. This was not a time to cry. She had lost him again. Panic began to swell as she scanned the room for any clue as to what had happened to him.

She noticed a piece of paper with her name on it lying on the floor at the base of the chair. It could have fallen to the ground when she shot out of the chair she thought, picking up the note. Relief began to spill over her realizing Garrett had not been abducted. She scanned the note quickly shaking her head in disbelief. She looked over at the corner table where the Chronicler laid waiting for her. How had she never noticed it before? Some Orohunter she was turning out to be not to have noticed such an obvious clue. She cursed herself.

She ran over to it and looked in. What memory had he gone to visit? What was he playing at that he could not have waited for her? Well, his luck was running out; just wait until she found him. He had some answering to do. He had no right to be making these kinds of decisions. She did not know what to do with him but knew whatever she chose he would not like it.

She leaned forward and was pulled into the Chronicler. Her eyes narrowed with anger. The Chronicler had been in his room this whole time. He had used it without telling her, more than once! What was he playing at? "AH, men!" They were supposed to be a team. Her temper was as red as her hair as she landed on solid ground.

"What are we doing here? Why are you in this bloody thing?" she demanded, seeing Garrett smiling at her.

His smile slipped a little as he motioned for her to take a look at the memory. She glared at him but then reluctantly turned to witness the scene. "You just wait 'til I get you home," she threatened before noticing what he had been smiling at.

Instantly her eyes began to tear up. They were visiting the summer holiday after they had first met. It had been the greatest summer of her life. There she was with Garrett sitting in a field in Africa holding a couple of lion cubs. She was actually feeding the cubs with a milk bottle as if it were her baby. The mother lion prowled up to her making her nervous. She remembered how scared she had been but Garrett had assured her everything would be alright as long as she remained calm. The mother brushed its head against her leg as if scratching her ear.

The father sat watching a few feet away. He growled a couple times scaring her but Garrett had told her, he just liked reminding them of his presence. The large lion showed his large teeth almost as if he was smiling. She was scared and excited. The cubs were so playful while they ate that she had to take care not to get scratched with their large claws when they swatted at her.

The older Garrett turned back to her offering his hand. Carrie took it surrendering her fury not noticing that the fingernail on his index finger was now a dark, dark brown. She could no longer be mad at him. He had chosen a wonderful memory. She wondered if it was hers or his. Had he used *brauchen* while she slept and taken the memory? Or had he retrieved this memory from himself? Was he himself this quickly regaining powers that none she known possessed?

The older Garrett waved his hand, a fog rolled in. "I never knew you could do magic inside the Chronicler," he told her.

"I can't." she said, trying to perform a simple spell. He was getting stronger.

The warm African air hung still for a moment. Then suddenly, they were standing on a cobblestone road she knew well, having grown up here just outside the village. They were in Canterbury, England, her home town.

She looked down the cobbled street, her eyes drawn to the familiar Canterbury Cathedral. She remembered the tragic story of Thomas Becket. On December 29 in the year 1170, four knights rode horses into Canterbury. Richard Brito, Hugh de Moreville, Reginald FitzUrse and William de Tracy had come to confront Archbishop Becket and former Chancellor of England. He once had been a friend of King Henry II. However, now they were the bitterest of foes. A long standing quarrel between the King and the Archbishop resulted in Becket's six year exile. He had only just returned. Fresh evidence of Becket's intransigence reached King Henry in Normandy, France. King Henry had burst out in rage, 'Who will rid me of this low-born priest?' The knights, eager to please their King, set sail for Kent, determined to deal once and for all with the Archbishop's stubborn opposition to royal interference with church affairs.

The older Carrie and Garrett followed their younger selves up to the cathedral. The young Carrie looked down at the ground wondering if this was the spot. This could be the exact spot where the four knights had heatedly debated Archbishop Thomas Becket. The older Carrie closed her eyes watching in her mind what the young Carrie was telling her Garrett, the tale of the four knights rallying an angry mob of supporters outside the sanctuary of the cathedral. Some of the monks had persuaded the archbishop to retreat into the safety of the cathedral.

It was late in the afternoon; the service of the vespers was being sung. The older Carrie strained her ears thinking she might just hear the music fill the air. After a tense siege, the knights burst into the church calling for Becket through the darkness. He in turn cursed their names for barging into the house of the Lord. They attempted to seize hold of him. Beckett threw one of the knights to the ground with a clash of chainmail.

Young Garrett and Carrie entered Trinity Chapel where from 1220 to 1538 it was home to Becket's shrine. The older Carrie watched as her younger self continued whispering the story to her Garrett. He was holding her hand just as she now held the older Garrett's hand. She did not need to hear her young self tell the final passage of the confrontation. Instead, she squeezed her Garrett's hand continuing to watch it in her mind's eye. Knight William de Tracy cried out, 'strike, strike!' Thomas Becket prayed for the last time to an earlier Canterbury martyr, Saint Alphege. 'For the name of Jesus and the defense of the church, I am willing to die.' Richard Brito gave the death blow as the sword pierced deeply into Beckett's head.

The older Carrie shuddered at the force of Brito's strike which took off the crown of Becket's head and shattering the tip of his blade on the stone floor. Garrett squeezed the older Carrie's hand giving a slight bow of respect. Carrie offered a brief smile of gratitude watching as he waved his hand again. Instantly, they were outside the cathedral. She wondered how he was doing that without a wand. They had not gone far when she finally noticed the dark, dark brown look of one of his index fingers. Now, she knew why.

This was memory was a moment she had been reliving in her head for the past three years fueling her heart with hope as she had searched for him. It was a beautiful memory. They were in a field for the summer festival. The twilight sky line was dominated by the Bell Harry tower of the Canterbury Cathedral. Garrett was singing with the Phoenixes.

He looked so silly and yet so sexy all dressed up in leather. It really did not suit him but her stomach still quivered seeing his naked chest behind the leather vest he wore. The black makeup around his eyes reminded her of a raccoon. She should have applied it for him; men were so clueless. As far as she knew, it was the first time the Phoenixes had ever played for both magical and non-magical people. Many of the magical community were enjoying themselves disguised as non-magical people in order to take part in the festivities. Her own father was standing with her younger self frowning about to meet the boy about whom she had talked so much.

"Good evening Canterbury," the younger Garrett greeted the cheering crowd. "We are Phoenix and we are going to slow it down now with a song I wrote for a very special lady."

He sat and began playing the piano. The beginning was a blend of piano and bells, a salute to the cathedral she had cherished so much back then. Carl smiled at himself mesmerized as the drums and the guitar joined the song. It was the end of his hold on Carl. He completely accepted Garrett now.

> "I love the shine in your eyes; I can't believe the way I am feeling. Please don't speak it's taken me all this time to find the strength to say. That I never knew friendship 'til I met you, never thought I could act the fool, but I am still afraid to show how much I need you, tell me what makes a magic man feel this way."

The older Carrie could feel her younger self melt while her father turned to stone knowing that Garrett was singing to his little girl.

> "Carrie, don't ask me why, baby I work so hard just to hide my emotion. Carrie, words can't explain the way I feel in my heart. Girl I can make you smile."

The drums and the guitar stopped leaving Garrett to his keyboard solo.

> "Our hearts, never quite beat in time. Oh no I am going crazy with love. Search to find a perfect rhythm. You show me the rhyme. You know I, have many issues. This I promise to you. I'll never lead you through doors of deception or bind you with chains of lies. You know my dream for you will only be perfection. What I give to you will last 'til the end of time."

The band joined in with the chorus again. The older Garrett looked into his Carrie's eyes, this time she saw the tears in his eyes. She could not hold her tears back now. "Damn romantic fool." She could feel herself falling for him all over again.

> "Take a little time, to realize, I love you faithfully. Just take a little time and you'll see, baby it's me."

She wanted to embrace him but fought the urge. She shook her head trying to shake away her desire and tears. He took her hand bringing it up to his lips kissing her fingers. Her heart quivered.

The music carried another verse as Garrett pulled her into a slow dance. She trembled at his touch. He was not playing fair. She laid her head on his chest inhaling his warmth and listening to his racing heart.

> "Carrie don't ask me why, baby I work so hard to hide my emotions. Carrie my words can't explain the way I feel in my heart. Ohhh, ohhh, ohhh, Carrie. I love the shine in your eyes. Girl I can make you smile!"

The crowd went nuts as the music ended. Carrie trembled wanting to kiss him just like in his dream. She could not let go. Neither could she look at her younger self standing, crying, gazing up at her Garrett on the stage with her father looming close by. Her father did not approve of Garrett and she could not look at him without losing your heart. She could feel him gazing down at her but she would be lost if she lifted her eyes to meet his. She just swayed to the memory of the music squeezing her eyes shut for protection.

She felt his arm move and the air changed. She smelled the cool scent of a misty morning fog. He, thankfully, had taken them to another memory. Which one would it be this time? She pushed away, eyes still closed. She peeked through her lashes and tears trying to see where they were now. They were standing in front of a castle surrounded by water. Not a moat, but a lake. They were at Leeds Castle, the one that movies so often misrepresent as a castle with a moat. Garrett had taken her there during her sixth level, his seventh, just before his graduation.

They were supposed to be in Kenosis on their last trip there for the year. However, the weather was frightfully miserable in Kenosis at that time so Garrett had surprised her with a romantic getaway. They had stopped at pub and picked up a picnic lunch with a nice bottle of ginger wine. The younger Garrett had teleported them to the castle instead of the dreary village they had visited so often. It was such a foolish thing to do with all the problems in the area. Yet, they had been young and in love. They had believed that their love made them invincible.

So, they had taken flight with their romantic picnic to the most beautiful place in all of Britain. It was peaceful, seeming to shield them from the horror that was surrounding them. They were sitting comfortably on a blanket by the shore watching black swans swim feet away from them hoping for scraps from their sandwiches. The younger Carrie was resting her head in younger Garrett's lap as he feed her grapes. It was like something out of an old movie.

The older Carrie raised her hand to her mouth in shock realizing what was coming next. She quickly grabbed hold of her Garrett's hands and led him to the water. "Just take a look at that black swan!" she yelled so loud that he had to put a finger to his ear to be sure it was still there.

He smiled at her enthusiasm over the sight of such an amazing animal. She was right though. It was a beautiful sight. He wondered if he would see his younger self have a conversation with the animal. He watched the swan, marveling at the orange beak feeling the anxiety that filled Carrie. Just down from the two swans were a couple of strange looking ducks swimming in search of treats but cautious of the bigger fowl.

"Those are called Shelducks," Carrie informed him, noticing the Shelducks had caught his eye. They had a magnificent orange bill, black head and neck with a mostly white body. There were brown and black markings along the white area of their bodies. They were, in one word, beautiful. He thought of how peaceful they appeared gliding upon the water but knew that just under the waterline they were paddling their legs like crazy.

There was something very special about being here. Garrett enjoyed a feeling of fulfillment about the being here, about being with Carrie. He took a deep breath sensing the misery just miles away. It felt like something tainted the air but the castle grounds repelled the outside world.

Garrett looked back at young Garrett and Carrie. They were lying on a blanket locked in a passionate kiss. It would be so nice to go back to a time when all they worried about was where they could go to escape. Carrie looked back, blushing as if apologizing for her younger self's lack of self control. He believed it was just teenagers doing what teenagers did best.

He gave his hand another wave. The mist came, washing the scene away to reveal five people sitting around a dining room table. Three of them he knew Belarus, young Garrett, and young Carrie. The other two he could only guess at who they were. He assumed the man with sandy blond hair that he had also seen at the concert was probably her father. The other was a woman with fiery red hair. He concluded that she was Carrie's mother.

"That's my dad and mom," Carrie confirmed. The older Carrie resembled her mother so much. She was quite a combination, very beautiful like her mother and defiantly stern like her father.

"Now that we are all here," Belarus began. "These are troubling times and I assure you that I usually do not take such a personal interest in my students."

Carrie's father grunted as if upset already with Belarus' meddling. Carrie's mother shot an agitated gaze at her spouse.

"I am here on behalf of Garrett's uncle, his only living family member," Dean Belarus began explaining, taking no offense in Carrie's father's behavior. "It seems that Miss Stephens and Mister Montgomery have been in a relationship for over two years which you..." Belarus looked pointedly at Carrie's father.

"No, I do not approve of it," he said, folding his arms across his chest glaring at Garrett. "I do not want my daughter to associate with the likes of him."

"The like of what?" Carrie's temper flared. She shot out of her chair, standing nose to nose with her father. Garrett and her mother jumped back in their chairs while Belarus smiled, watching and enjoying the boldness of the young woman. "What is it that bothers you so much about him?" Carrie demanded.

"He's different from what we are," her father said, moving his head away from her so they would not collide. "I do not want my daughter tramping around with a musician."

"Sir," Garrett said, standing up. "I have not played in a band for over a year and do not foresee myself ever doing so again. I enjoyed last year's experience but I feel that my gifts of magic can better serve in other areas. Music is nothing more than a hobby now."

Carrie's dad just shook his head not believing him.

"Ah music," Belarus said. "It is a magic beyond even all that I know. However, I suspect that there is something deeper which is troubling you that still needs to be addressed. What is really bothering you Marcus?"

Carrie's father shifted in his chair not making eye contact with anyone, not even his wife. "Well, dad is there some other reason you don't want Garrett and me to be together!" Her fierce determination to get to the bottom of this was reflected in her voice.

"Come on now Marcus." Belarus smiled at Garrett as if to assure him that everything would be okay. "You have doubts about the boy besides his music."

"Yes, I do." It seemed Carrie's dad had been pushed to his limits. "He's not from here. He doesn't know what it is to be…"

"Dad, this is the same battle the magical community has always been fighting." Carrie took control while Belarus willingly surrendered it to her. "It is deep sided jealousy. He is different. So what? I don't have blond hair does that mean I'm not worthy of being your daughter?"

The glare he gave her told her that it was not the same.

"Exactly, and just because Garrett was not born here does not make him any less British. In fact, he may be more so because he appreciates what it means so much more. Where do we draw the line?"

"Sir, it is true I was born in the United States and I am thankful for the time I lived there with my family. My father was an ambassador for the English Embassy of Magic. My mother was a Native American. I have endured not fitting in here or there. I think the problem is that no one is good enough for Carrie and I agree."

Mr. Stephens looked at Garrett as if trying to determine if he was lying or not.

"Carrie is the most precious being I have ever had the pleasure of meeting and no matter what I say nothing will persuade you that I am good enough for her. I just ask that you judge my actions not where I've lived. Allow me the opportunity to prove my worth to you."

Carrie returned to her seat. Garrett's voice was soothing, easing her anger with her father. Her father looked like he was losing some of his momentum also. "All I can tell you is that there is no one else in the world who can or will respect, love or take care of Carrie more than me."

Dean Belarus stood up, putting his hand on Garrett's shoulder. He smiled at Carrie. "I have seen these two together and have witnessed many marvelous deeds. I suggest that you take the time to get to know Garrett. I apologize that the school term is about to begin, not giving you enough time to truly get to know him that much more deeply. To facilitate this endeavor, I have arranged for Garrett to stay in a flat here in town."

"There will be no need for that," Carrie's mom said, standing up and taking charge. "He will stay with us so we can get to know him even better." Marcus raised his eyebrows but did not dare protest. "In different bedrooms," she added.

"Again, I regret that it will only be for three days," Belarus apologized. "Thank you Cassidy for your hospitality."

"We also regret that it will only be for three days." Cassidy remarked as Marcus stared down at the floor perhaps ashamed of the way he had been behaving.

Garrett walked over to Dean Belarus. "I was expecting to go back with you to Belgium."

"I know you would like to help but that is not for you. You must remain here and get to know Carrie's family better. You, beyond all others, know the importance of family. Carrie is prepared to go anywhere with you, but there will be a time that she will be thankful she still has her family. One day you will understand."

"There are many things I will understand one day." Garrett glanced down at the floor disappointed not to be returning with Belarus. Carrie walked over to him, taking his hand. It gave him comfort.

"Now, if Carrie will walk me to the door, I will take my leave." They were all surprised he requested Carrie to walk him to the door. She obliged, leaving the other three staring at them. As they walked away, Belarus whispered something to Carrie who smiled in response.

The older Garrett swallowed hard before raising his hand and returning them back to West Virginia.

CHAPTER 16

His reaction to their return this time was mild compared to the past ones. A pulsing of pain burned in his legs like he had just run two miles while a suffocating tightness in his gut stung as if he had just completed two-hundred sit ups. Another burning pain in his arms and chest made him feel as if he had just completed two-hundred pushups. Finally, there was stiffness in his neck echoing the feeling of working out on a weight machine used to strengthen neck muscles. He normally would have been bothered by this kind of reaction but after Belarus' explanation, he welcomed it with open arms. However, he was worried about Carrie's reaction to his condition.

The haunting feeling of the bullet had disappeared. His mind still registered the weakness of the tissue but the pain he had felt was but a mere memory. He tried walking but his legs wouldn't work right, sending him stumbling into the table, knocking the Chronicler to the floor. It clanged violently, screaming out echoes that could be heard throughout the house as if in pain. He looked to Carrie with an apologetic smile trying to imply that she need not worry. He regained his balance and smiled at her again trying to appeal to her forgiving nature.

"Well- well- well- look who has returned," a strange voice sarcastically greeted from the doorway. She didn't think to check the Chronicler Recital."

Garrett and Carrie cringed in utter shock, surprised by the voice. Standing in front of them, blocking the doorway was a black-hooded figure wearing a grotesque mask made of bones. Garrett had seen this same man twice now, once with Carrie back at the bar and then in the Chronicler when Rodney was killed. Where was the other? Each time there had been two of them. He quickly deduced that the other must be searching somewhere outside for them as he or she had not also come to the room after the commotion they had made resounded through the house.

Garrett's stomach lurched; the outfit the man wore reminded Garrett of the robes the Ku Klux Klan wear to spread terror in the United States. The mask itself reminded him of the china masks worn in plays like *Phantom of the Opera*. This one, however, was not made out of china or porcelain but of what looked like rib bones.

The masked figure forcefully pointed his wand at them not having to tell them to remain still. They were, for the moment, at the man's mercy. Garrett opened his mind to Carrie. He was afraid to look her way, giving away his intentions to the villain standing in front of them. But, they had to do something before the other Goblin showed up and evened the odds.

"Keep your hands where I can see them if you please." The man tipped his wand menacingly at Carrie. She had tried to reach for her wand. Reluctantly, Carrie and Garrett raised their arms as if the man were holding a gun on them.

How could I have let this happen? Garrett heard Carrie say to herself as he felt her guilt. She was blaming herself for their capture.

It's not your fault. He tried to reassure her. *I was the one to go into the Chronicler and asked you to follow me.*

It is my fault. I should have made sure we had sentries. Her thoughts commanded, her voice warning him not to argue about this. *I should have found us a new place to stay once you were injured.*

If I had not gone back to the house, they would never have found us.

What? They? She glanced around, realizing that he meant there was another thug somewhere near.

There have been two of them in each of the attacks. I bet the other one is in another room or more likely outside looking for us.

You went back to the house! You stupid idiot, why did you go back there? It's not safe,

You're telling me; I was the one that got shot.

He rolled his eyes thinking about why he had gone back to the house and shaking his head when he realized the necklace he had retrieved was still tucked in the pocket of the jeans. How would he be able to activate it with this guy threatening them? His mind raced to the memory of the chant he would have to use the cross. Would he be able to teleport without being cursed? It was risky. Would they both be able to teleport? He figured the odds were good that at least one of them might be able to get away. However, Carrie would probably not take the risk.

Don't even think of trying it. I don't know how you learned to teleport by yourself but it is not safe. She glowered at him making sure he understood. *We don't know who these people are nor do we have a safe place to teleport to.*

Garrett stumbled to the floor. Carrie took a step to assist him but the masked Goblin threatened to use his wand. She backed off. Garrett clutched his knee to his mid-section as if he was cramping up again.

"What's the matter with him?" the man asked, brandishing his wand between his two captives but focusing more on Carrie, thinking that Garrett was not much of a threat. This could be the advantage that Garrett needed. That is if the other Goblin did not appear to even the odds.

"He has attacks each time we return," she claimed, tears swelling up in her eyes.

I'm alright, just need a distraction; trying to make him think that I'm weaker than I really am. He projected to her, hoping to ease her fears. *I know he was there when my memory was erased and I bet he doesn't consider me a threat. He believes they erased my abilities forever and therefore I am no threat.*

You're not a sorcerer. You only learned a few simple spells over the last of couple days! She screamed at him through her mind. He cringed back as if struck.

I am equipped enough to take care of this guy. He looked at his painted index fingernail. *I can actually do magic while in the Chronicler. Remember?*

Don't do anything stupid, again!

You know me.

That's what I'm afraid of.

Your faith in me is touching. He thought sarcastically even though he was smiling.

"He needs to lie down," Carrie said, motioning to the bed, hoping Garrett would reconsider his stupid plan.

"No," the masked man barked. "Bring him out to the couch. That way I can see him more clearly and keep a closer eye on you. You just could not leave things well enough alone." He motioned them out of the bedroom and into the living room.

Garrett nodded, his eyes locked on Carrie. This was better than he could have had hoped for. With any luck he could manage the rest. Once they got to the couch he would be able to lie on his side. How had Belarus known? He should be able to...

Belarus? To what? Carrie thought. *Don't do anything yet. Let's try to find out who he is and why he's after you. And, what do you mean you're going to use your finger? I don't understand.*

Garrett rolled his eyes. He had his own agenda but he worried that Carrie would stop him if she knew. He cautiously slid the necklace out of his pocket. He clutched it in his hand watching the masked man attentively. "Chippewa, Foxes, Huron's, Kickapoo...," Garrett began mumbling. The Goblin glared at him suspiciously. Garrett faked another cramp. His body began to support the action as a sudden real urge to be sick grasped hold. It was like his body understood the importance of what he was doing and thought an authentic retching would help.

"What is he doing?"

"They're names of Indian tribes that once lived in Michigan. Menominee, Miami, Neutrals, Noquet, Ottawa, Potawatomi, Sauk and Wyandot." Garrett continued with the ruse.

"Make him stop!"

"I can't when he's in this state. He's like a child." She glared at him in protest.

"Why did you return to the house?" the Goblin demanded venomously, staring at Garrett as if he were not human.

"Did you know Noquet means bear foot not bare foot," Garrett giggled, trying to support the idea that he was not a threat.

"*Jolar!*" the Goblin cursed. A wave of pain shot through Garrett forcing him to curl into a ball. Carrie nearly fell to the floor as he jerked in pain. The Goblin lifted his wand breaking the curse. "Like that smart guy, do you want to experience it again?"

"No," Garrett panted, straightening out.

"What's that?" the Goblin asked, spotting what appeared to be Garrett's wand. Carrie tried to snatch it but the Goblin summoned it to himself with a flick of his wand. "Well, well you were clever leading me to believe it was my idea to bring you out here." He snapped the wand in half, tossing the remains behind him as he pulled Carrie from the sofa.

"Easy," she protested as the Goblin quickly searched the cushions for other weapons.

The Goblin pushed Garrett to the floor. Rolling, Garrett quickly slipped the necklace around his neck, tucking the charm under shirt. Carrie watched, amazed at the speed and grace of the maneuver. Garrett panted the entire time as if out of breath.

"Now where was I?" The Goblin paced in front of them confident now that the couch held no more surprises. "Oh yes, you were just about to explain why you had returned to your home last night."

"I felt it would be important to return." Garrett said, feeling it was safe to return to the couch. He wanted to know why the Goblins were after him. This had to end here and now, he decided. "I'd been trying to persuade Carrie to go to the police. She wouldn't agree. So, when she left me with one of her friends, I conned him into taking me back."

Carrie studied him with a crinkled up nose, knowing he was a lying. However, she pretended he wasn't in order to buy them time. Besides, she wanted to know why he had returned to the house and how he had learned to teleport. Reginald had sworn to her that he had not taught him and she knew Sheba would never have taught him. The book of spells Reginald had brought with him only carried easy, level one spells. Teleporting involved manipulating the fifth Pentacle of the Sun. And, how had he been injured and by whom? She felt the heat of anger swelling inside her as she pondered all of this.

"As I said, I tricked someone into teleporting me back to the house. I told him I needed to get a magical item," Garrett said louder confused with Carrie's concerns rolling through his mind. He kept his eyes on the Goblin not allowing himself to be distracted from his plan. "That's when we ran into your man at the house. He was a non-magical, like me."

The Goblin smiled, stopping in front of him. He stuck the rough point of his wand to Garrett's throat. "To bad he did not kill you."

"What was he doing in my house anyways?"

"That was in case you returned, like you so predictably and stupidly did. Not as bright as you once were are you?" The Goblin was very pleased with himself now. "We figured you would feel safer at your own place."

"You're right there." He wanted to keep the Goblin talking; hoping the delight he was taking with his success would cause him to not watch him and Carrie so closely.

"Yes, you are not as dangerous as before. The others are fools to worry about you." The Goblin beamed, taking up his pacing again. Garrett smiled, realizing it was a habit he could use against him. "I have used a curse on a number of non-magicals to kill other non-magicals and you if you should arrive at their location." He laughed spying the shock on their faces.

"So, the guy that shot me…," Garrett began.

"Shot you?" Carrie asked.

"Yes, this non-magical person was in the house when we got there. He was going to kill us but all of a sudden items began floating in the air. Your friend was brilliant." Carrie nodded, understanding.

"He shot me while he was shooting at the stuff that was floating at him. The police burst in and killed him," Garrett retold the event, feeling the guilt of the man's death erupt in his heart.

"So, with your man wanting to kill me and then actually being shot, I was unable to locate the item. It didn't seem wise to talk to the police at the time."

The intruder had his wand pointed at Carrie, directly at the center of her chest.

"Who are you taking orders from?" Garrett asked, knowing that if the man answered at all it would be a lie. He was hoping he could use *leer poma* on the guy as the truth surfaced in his mind in response to the question.

"That is none of your concern." The man turned the wand back on Garrett. In his mind, Garrett saw a figure in a bright orange robe, no mask concealing the villain. However, the face was in the shadows still hiding the identity of its owner. He or she was standing on a platform while the two Goblins were kneeling before it.

"Who are you working with? There were two of you at the restaurant the other night," Carrie asked.

"*Jolar!*" the Goblin cursed, sending Garrett back into a ball of pain.

"Stop it!" she pleaded as Garrett tossed in pain.

"I am the one that is asking questions. You need to mind your tongue." The Goblin lifted the curse.

Carrie slid back, preparing to attack him, ready to rip into him with her bare hands. Garrett began mumbling, clutching at the pendent under his shirt.

"What's he doing? It sounds like a chant." The Goblin looked concerned.

"He's just mumbling, incoherent from your torture," Carrie reassured the Goblin through her tears. "Besides, you busted his wand."

"I don't like it," he said, looking perplexed.

"I guess you shouldn't have cursed him and erased his ability. I'd love to have watched him kick your ass when he had powers."

The Goblin pointed his wand at her. "Silly girl, I was that one that removed his powers in the first place. What makes you think he could kick my ass?"

"So you killed Rodney?" she asked, hoping Garrett was finished with his chant.

"Old fool was in the way. No witnesses you understand."

"If you weren't so gutless and fought fair, that old fool would have kicked your ass."

"Enough," the Goblin cursed Carrie making her freeze like a statue.

"What'd you do to her?" Garrett shot up, touching Carrie. She felt like a statue.

"Not to worry." He began pacing again. This time it was Garrett's turn to be annoyed. "You tell me what I want to know and do as I say and maybe she will live."

Garrett slipped back down on the couch pretending to be too tired to complain.

"Now I will only have to keep my eye on one person." The man gloated with a little laugh. "Where were we?"

"You were about to tell me about the female you're working with." Garrett knew this would enrage the man again but he wanted to pull the woman to the front of the man's mind.

"I was not!" the man boomed, pacing fiercely back and forth.

The man's temper would have to be dealt with but Garrett's goal had been attained. He had seen the lady's face in his mind, no mask. He knew her name, it was…

"What are you looking at?" The man looked scared, realizing he had somehow just given away some secret.

"I was just wondering how to revive Carrie," Garrett remarked, hoping the knowledge would surface in the man's mind.

"Why would I tell you that?" the man asked before resuming his pacing.

"So she could get her wish and watch me kick your ass." The Goblin looked frightened for a moment as Garrett attempted to push himself up on his elbow then relieved as he collapsed back against the back of the couch.

"Well allow me." Carrie's head jerked to see what she had missed. "Welcome back. Your man wanted to rouse you to witness his kicking my ass." The Goblin laughed at Carrie's surprised look. Without looking at Garrett he cursed him, watching Carrie's expression.

"Potawatomi means bear foot, huh," the man gloated.

"*Todaviz.*" Garrett barked.

The Goblin's arms snapped to his sides, his eyes turned glassy, and his legs sprang together and froze just as Carrie's had. Garrett snatched the wand out of his hand and handed it to Carrie. Carrie took it, rushing to stand next to Garrett. Garrett snapped his fingers and the Goblin's head was freed while the rest of his body remained frozen.

"Potawatomi were the people of the place of the fire. Noquet were bear foot."

"Let me loose," the Goblin howled.

"Hmm, no; I don't think so."

"How did you…"

Garrett took the necklace from its hiding spot, squeezing his hand shut around it and closing his eyes. "*Aloh- ve- he adoni- eh- ha- atela,*" he chanted. The cross started to glow.

The Goblin and Carrie looked confused.

"I'm not as weak as I let on. I should kill you now for Rodney."

"We were ordered to do it," he pleaded now.

"By whom?" Carrie asked.

"I won't tell you." Carrie pushed him. He swayed back and forth before falling face forward. Garrett cringed, hearing the crunch of his nose breaking underneath the mask. He turned the Goblin over with a kick of his foot so they could see his face. Carrie broke his wand in half as he had done to Garrett's clone.

"Your wand?" she asked Garrett.

Garrett held up his hand, showing her his finger. "As I said, you can do magic inside the Chronicler."

"But how?"

"Belarus," was all he had to say and she nodded in understanding.

"You used *todaviz*?" Carrie asked, watching him hide one half of the wand in a vase and the other in a magazine. "Don't worry. It's ruined. It'll be no good to him or anybody else." She retrieved her wand, producing a green ropelike vine and binding the Goblin's legs and arms with it.

"We need to hurry up. His wife is outside somewhere looking for us," Garrett urged. Carrie was scribbling a note on a piece of paper. She paused her writing when she heard this.

"You know his wife?" Carrie turned, looking suspiciously at him.

He nodded. "Llewellyn is in the backyard searching around the shed."

"How do you know that?"

"While you were out," he said playfully, as if she had just been taking a siesta, by choice. "I used *leer poma* on Sage Skopector. He's the one that wasn't too bright. All I had to do was ask him the questions and the answers came to his head as if he were saying them out loud."

Carrie looked at the man on the floor. His face now covered in blood. She walked over to him, pointing her wand down at his blood stained face. "*Limpiaro*," she said. The dried blood disappeared from his face exposing his mangled nose. She put a hand on Garrett's chest. "It's not too bright to underestimate you," she said in apology.

"I wish I could've really kicked his ass for you." She smiled in response.

"This is not good," she said, falling back onto the couch. She sat there shaking her head not knowing what to do.

"What's the matter?" Garrett asked, coming over and sitting next to her. He put a comforting arm around her shoulders.

"There is no way anyone is going to believe that Llewellyn and Nathaniel Skopector are the ones that attacked you and killed Rodney."

"Why not?"

"Well for starters, Llewellyn is the head of the Oro Department and Nathaniel teaches at the Palace of Sitnalta." She closed her eyes, taking a deep breath. "There is no way anyone at the embassy is going to believe us."

"No worries." Carl smiled, looking up at her. "We've got the Recital."

She jumped up with him following his idea. She threw her arms around him, giving him a quick kiss. "You are brilliant," she said, running back to the table. She picked up the note she had written and scribbled out a new message with more enthusiasm than she had the first time.

Garrett watched as she ran to the bedroom and returned with the Chronicler in her hands. She set it down next to their prisoner. Looking around the room, she went over to a cupboard, taking out two crystal bottles with cork tops. Handing one of the bottles to Garrett, she took her wand and put it between her eyes. She closed her eyes and concentrated for a moment, focusing on the memory of what had just taken place. She pulled out a hair and placed it in the bottle, sealing it tightly with the cork.

Garrett nodded, understanding what he was to do. He thought of the attack back at the embassy when he had first lost his memory. He added the attack from the restaurant, the attacks of today, and Skopector's admission of being his attacker. He pulled out the hair containing his memory and sealed it into the other bottle.

Carrie took both bottles and wrapped them with the note she had scribbled just moments earlier. Waving her wand, the package disappeared. Next, she turned her wand to the Chronicler sending it to follow. Last to go was their prisoner. This teleportation took more time but he finally did disappear.

Looking around, she looked for anything she could use as evidence. Carrie took a deep breath, feeling safe for the moment. "How long have you been going into the Chronicler?" She turned on him.

He whistled out a breath. "I wondered when we'd get to that. I really don't think this is the time to discuss it, what with that hag out there."

"Don't give me that rubbish," she warned not to be distracted.

"Okay." He walked over to her looking deep into her eyes. "I've been going into it ever since we got here." He motioned with his hand around the house.

"It's not safe for you to go in it"

"Yes, it is. My reactions, my fits are just the result of my learning and becoming Garrett. Belarus told me so."

"You can't talk to Belarus in there." She looked at him, questioning what he was saying.

"I didn't. I talked with Belarus in a dream after I was shot."

"And another thing, who taught you to teleport?" she ranted.

"Belarus taught me in the Chronicler," he said, throwing his arms in surrender. "But you're wrong. He can talk to me in the Chronicler. He told me in the dream that it's because we're related. That's the reason he can see me visiting."

"That's impossible."

"Belarus also told me that while I'm becoming Garrett he can communicate with me temporarily."

"What do you mean, becoming Garrett?"

"Belarus' theory and I agree with it, is that for the past three years, Garrett's consciousness and body have been trapped in my body. He hasn't been able to do anything. So, he's been running, doing sit ups pushups anything to keep himself physically and mentally fit."

"I don't understand," she said confused.

"Neither do I. To simplify the theory let's just say that Garrett's mind and body are merging with my mind and body, one effects the other." He looked at her. His hope that she believed him reflected in his eyes.

"I don't know." She shook her head, starting to walk away but he grabbed her, making her face him.

"Just look at this." He took off his shirt. "Take a look at my stomach and my arms." He flexed his arms. They were very tone as if he had been working out for years and his abs looked like the type most men dreamed about.

"This is not possible," she said, rubbing her hand over his stomach.

He pulled away from her touch. The caress was sending tickles of pleasure to his stomach. "Now you sound like I did just a few days ago," he said with a little laugh.

Shaking her head, she turned away.

"We are married, aren't we?" he blurted out, sending her mind whirling.

She stopped and looked up at the ceiling, biting her bottom lip. She was thinking about the best way to answer. Finally, she turned to him again, tears fighting to escape her eyes. She nodded. He walked over to her, taking her hand, forcing her to look at him.

"I didn't see our wedding in the Chronicler," he stated slowly with a slight question in his voice as he looked deep into her eyes. "I proposed to you that day at Leeds Castle; didn't I?"

She nodded, "The magical community doesn't call it being married. We call it being sealed to each other."

He took both her hands, bringing them to his lips. Her eyes followed her hands. "I want you to know, for the past three years I have not been with anyone."

She laughed, finally smiling back at him. She freed a hand, caressing his cheek. "You silly man, being sealed is taking a vow. That vow, that seal cannot be broken. You could not be with anyone else without dying. It's how I knew you were still out there somehow, lost."

He looked at her very confused. "What do you mean?"

"In the magical world when you are sealed together you can't break that seal that binds you, that promise. That is why my dad was so against it. If the vows are made in seal fashion neither person can break the vow without dying." She took his hand, giving the tips of his fingers a gentle kiss.

"So you never…"

"I never," she said.

"I was never even interested in anyone either." She perked up at this unexpected news. "It was like I waited for someone special and I was. I was waiting for you."

She threw her arms around him, squeezing him tightly. She held him tight and wept into his neck. "We eloped right after Belarus' funeral. We were determined to become Orohunters." He covered her mouth with his, framing her face in his hands.

"*Jolar!*" a voice suddenly screamed from the back door.

CHAPTER 17

Two earth shattering screams echoed in Garrett's ears. One came from Carrie surprised by the attack. The second came the open glass patio door. On the ground, cringing in pain was the Goblin that attempted to attack them while their backs were turned. She wiggled on the ground, in the pain from her own spell. Her mask had slid partially off her face exposing the beak like nose of Llewellyn.

"I don't believe it," Carrie said as she began to take a step towards the Goblin. "How did that happen?"

Garrett smiled at her, pulling the necklace out from under his shirt. "I think it goes well with the ring. Don't you?" He smiled as he and Carrie started walking over to their former boss.

A loud slam sounded from the front door, someone was trying to force it open. Carrie grabbed Garrett's hand, bounded over Llewellyn, kicking her wand out of her hand in the process, and turned around to watch a large man burst through what remained of their front door.

They were out the back down door as a storm of bullets started to fly over their heads. "Where's my wand?" they heard Llewellyn scream as they fled past the shed, fleeing into the woods behind it.

They ran, stumbling down the steep hilly woods, stopping behind a large oak tree to catch their breath. "What're we going to do now?" Carrie panted, clutching at her side.

"You've been a practicing Orohunter longer than I have." He glanced back around the tree to see if they were being followed. They heard someone curse as he or she fell down as they entered the woods. "The one thing I do know is we had better get going."

"Yeah, but where?"

"Anywhere, as long it's not here," he answered, sending them off again, skidding down the hill, bouncing against and round trees like the silver ball in a pinball machine.

The slashing sound of a bullet ricocheting through the pine trees behind them rent the air. "What was that?" Carrie screamed.

He looked at her a moment before realizing that she was not familiar with non-magical weapons. "It was the sound of bullets being fired from the guy's gun."

"Is that what went through your shoulder?"

He nodded, glancing around trying to see which way they ought to go next. Sweat beaded down his face stinging his eyes. He worried that the shadows that concealed them now would quickly dissipate when the sun rose higher in the sky.

"Could we teleport?" he suggested, looking down at Carrie.

"We could but where would we go?" Her eyes darted around as the sound of leaves crinkling from their pursuers grew louder behind them. "It wouldn't be safe to just show up anywhere. Remember, non-magical people are looking for you, too."

"It's not safe *here* right now if you haven't noticed," he argued. She nodded in agreement as he took her hand, proceeding further down the hill.

"Where are we going?" she asked moments later as they seemed to be going in a specific direction even as they ran between trees trying to put distance between them and their pursuers.

"Do you hear that?" he asked. She stopped to listen.

She heard something that sounded like a heavy wind blowing through the trees. "What is it?" she said, following him over a mound of large rocks.

"I think it's a river. If I'm right, we can follow it into town." He helped her around a rather tricky patch of earth. "I still think we should teleport," he urged.

"It would be too dangerous." Letting go of Garrett's hand in disgust, she slid a little bit down the hill, skinning her knee. "They were able to track you the last time you teleported. I don't know how but they did. Maybe, they somehow put a tracking spell or something on you."

"Sorry about that. I went back for the necklace I made for myself the day I was attacked. I'd made five of them actually." He was taken aback by her reaction to this information. She looked at it as if she did not know what the big deal was about the necklace.

"What is it?" She wrinkled her nose as if he could not be serious about how important the necklace was. "Other than a crucifix?"

"I charmed it to repel all magic." He looked at her, confused by her reaction. "Didn't you get the one I made for you or did the Goblins get the other four?"

"Yeah, I got it but I never knew what it was." She got back to her feet, heading for the river.

She kept glancing over her shoulder at him but said nothing. Suddenly, Garrett grabbed Carrie's shoulder, stopping her. He put a finger to his mouth, instructing her to remain silent. He had noticed that he no longer heard any more sounds of breaking branches, crackling leaves, or any other sounds one would naturally hear in a forest other than the ones they made themselves. The eerie silence bothered Garrett.

He looked around suspiciously; the feeling that something was very wrong growing inside him. What exactly it was, he could not tell. There was no sign or sound of Llewellyn or the gunman. However, he could sense them somewhere out there lurking, waiting for them.

"Get down," he whispered, pulling her down to sit on her haunches just like him.

"What's wrong?" Carrie whispered the question, putting her hand on the ground to keep from tipping over.

"It's too quiet," he whispered back.

Carrie looked around not seeing anyone. "So," she said, starting to get up but he tugged her forcibly back to the ground.

"Just stay put!" he warned quietly. "I can feel them. They're still too close."

Carrie looked at him wondering how he knew that but decided to do as she was told. She could hear the beating of her own heart, pounding fiercely in her chest. It was so loud she worried that it might betray them to Llewellyn. "I don't know about this."

Again Garrett put his finger to his mouth silencing her. "What happened to the sound of the river?"

"I don't..." The realization spilled over her; she could no longer hear the river. He tossed a rock toward where he thought the water might be.

There was no responding sound of the rock hitting the water or hitting the ground. "She must have put a muffling spell on the area," Carrie guessed, seeing Garrett's confused face.

"Yeah, and we almost walked straight into a trap." He looked around nervously.

"What are we going to do now?"

She looked to him for the answer. She was out of ideas. This had been his place three years ago, coming up with the ideas. "Do you know a spell that will increase our sense of smell?"

She looked at him puzzled by the request. "Do you want to enlarge our noses?"

"No," he answered, shaking his head. "I was just thinking that if we can't hear them…well, maybe we could smell them instead like an animal would." He hoped she knew of a charm.

"Well, there is one spell that we can use." She took out her wand, pointing it at him. *"Sinoate tensious,"* she cast the charm at him, hoping his plan worked.

Garrett's head bounced back as the spell hit him. His eyes began to water as he felt his nasal cavity expand. The inside of his nose felt like a gust of warm air rushed into it. He let out a deep breath trying to mellow the uncomfortable feeling, fumbling to the ground when he lost his balance. Trying to rid himself of the burning sensation, he shook his head violently. As quickly as the sensation began it vanished. He took a deep breath through his mouth afraid that it might return.

"I think only one of us needs the spell," he said, blinking water from his eyes.

"Are you all right?" she giggled.

He nodded, allowing her to help him to his knees. "I can smell the river; it's about twenty paces that way. By the way your scent is succulent." He pointed in the direction they were already heading. He closed his eyes, taking a deep breath followed by four short sniffs like a dog searching for a certain scent.

"Well, what's next?" she said anxiously.

"I think we should go that way." He pointed south. "The guy is a little to the north, Llewellyn is waiting by the river, and to the south, someone is cooking breakfast."

It was good enough for her. She nodded, following him back the way they came. They were just about to a clearing when Garrett stopped quickly. He sniffed around. "Come on." He tugged her arm, leading her forward at a quicker pace.

In the large clearing was a campground with a cabin larger than the size of a house nestled in a stand of large pines. In front of it at the water's edge was a short dock with about half a dozen rubber rafts. Garrett led Carrie up the flagstone walkway and through the front door of the cabin.

The room they entered was the reception area for the campground. The large room was filled with souvenirs, most of them boasting about having survived the rapids. There were some others advertising the great adventure of West Virginia and a few advertised the campsite itself, Little Big River Bend. They browsed around trying to pass as guests as others began filing into the cabin in search of breakfast.

They followed a few of them into a hallway leading to the restaurant. They descended two steps, stopping by the host. A man looking like he was ready to go on a fishing trip escorted them to a table near a picture window looking over the river. Carrie sat facing the doors, watching anyone that entered. Garrett figured that as of right now, she was more accomplished at magic than he was so he did not object.

He had trouble concentrating on breakfast; the abundance of scents floating in the air was overwhelming. On the plus side, he was pleased that his hearing expanded along with his sense of smell. Unfortunately it was so acute that people talking three tables away sounded as if they were yelling. He struggled to subdue the intensity of the two senses. They were very useful but right now they were giving him a headache and making him feel nauseous.

"Are you all right?"

"Yeah," he whispered, nodding. "I'm just trying to get used to all the smells and sounds. My hearing improved also when you enhanced my sense of smell. It sounds like you're yelling at me."

"Sorry," she whispered. "Why don't you think of your hearing like a radio?"

"What do you mean?"

"Well, if you had a volume control in your head you would be able to turn the sound up or down as you need."

He sat back closing his eyes, trying to do as she suggested. She watched concerned as he took a deep breath holding it as he focused his attention only to the couple that had walked into the other room. It was working. He smiled no longer overwhelmed by all the voices or smells in the room able to focus on the couple. A low static informed him they were there.

"Thanks," he said, pleased to find his voice was not ringing in his ears. "You know you're pretty smart."

She laughed, returning her focus on observing their surroundings. Garrett followed her gaze. His eyes roamed the room as well, stopping on a police officer who had just entered the dining room. He paused by the host's station as if waiting to be seated while his eyes moved from table to table, slowly scanning the room. Garrett concluded that he was searching for someone specific.

Garrett studied the officer closely. He looked familiar, but he couldn't place him. He had dark hair and deeply tanned skin. An uneasy feeling squeezed Garrett's gut as realized that the officer was looking for them.

"We need to get out of here," Garrett warned Carrie, nodding his head toward the law official.

It was like Garrett's voice was a beacon because immediately after the words left Garrett's mouth, the officer spotted Garrett. Garrett felt a sudden chill shoot down his spine. The officer had recognized Garrett. He started toward them, his right hand casually lying on top of his revolver. He walked deliberately, closing the distance quickly. Garrett panicked. His intuition told him what was coming, but he couldn't move. All he could do was watch. He wanted to scream, to tell Carrie to run, but he felt paralyzed. Out of the corner of his eye, he saw the officer walk around a nearby table.

"Garrett?" Carrie questioned, tilting her head to one side.

Her voice broke his trance, throwing him into action. The officer was now only steps away. Garrett saw the man's hand remove the strap securing his gun. In a sudden explosion of activity, Garrett snatched the tablecloth from the table, sending the plates, glasses, and silverware tumbling to the floor as Carrie leapt to her feet with a shriek. People turned to see the cause of the commotion.

Garrett rushed the policeman, flinging the tablecloth over his head, pushing him backward into a neighboring table, knocking it over and sending more plates and glasses to the floor. He had attacked a police officer. The people at the table screamed in outrage, stumbling as they tried to get away from the fallen police officer. However, several were caught in the tangle of overturned chairs and tumbled to the floor themselves, adding to the chaos.

In the commotion, Garrett grabbed Carrie's hand, yanking her out of the room. They rushed out of the cabin. "He was under a spell. I saw his eyes; they were glazed over."

Behind them, Garrett could hear the door of the cabin crash open. They were being pursued yet again. This time there was no way they were going to make it to the woods and the road was too open. Instead, he pulled Carrie toward the water. Racing for the dock, Garrett dared a glance back at the cabin. He could see a figure run to the porch railing, shouting and turning for the stairs. He must have headed for the parking lot first Garrett guessed before coming their way.

Carrie tried to jerk her hand free, but Garrett tightened his clasp, yanking her forward. "I don't know how to swim!" she shouted.

"It doesn't matter. He wants to kill us. That's what counts." He motioned behind him at the officer sprinting toward them, his gun reflecting the bright sunlight.

Stumbling on, they sprinted to the end of the dock. Garrett shouted for Carrie to help him untie all the rubber rafts and send them off down the river. When coming upon the last raft, Garrett helped Carrie climb into it. Scrambling in after her, he pushed them away from the dock with his foot. One of his shoes slipped from his foot, splashing into the water. They began drifting downstream, following the other rafts. Garrett could hear a man standing on the dock unintentionally stall the officer by complaining about his stolen rafts.

"Get down," Garrett ordered. There was a violent sounding pop immediately followed by a dull thud somewhere in the boat. Garrett forced Carrie to lie down, covering her body with his own. Almost simultaneously, they heard the sound of air escaping the raft. Garrett groaned. Another pop was followed by the sound of a bullet going through one of the paddles. The third pop was followed by a slapping sound in the water.

Garrett was relieved; realizing that although a bullet had deflated one section of the rubber boat, it was not sinking. It was somehow sustaining them. A few more shots drove innocently into the water just short of the raft. They were safely out of range. He sat up, glaring at the police officer.

The officer turned, running back up to the cabin, realizing that the bullets would not reach them. He didn't get that far. Garrett watched as Llewellyn and another man intercepted the officer. They grabbed a canoe from a nearby rack and carried it over to the water, climbing in after placing it in the water. They began paddling furiously, attempting to catch up to Garrett and Carrie. Soon they would be in range of the officer's weapon or worse Llewellyn's wand.

Anxiously, Garrett grabbed one of the paddles and began paddling. Carrie went for the other paddle. "Stay down! You don't know how to swim." She slipped back to the bottom of the rubber raft.

The officer stood up, pointing his gun at them, cocking his head while squinting down the sight and taking aim. He had a clear shot, in range to bury a bullet into Garrett's chest. He was just about to squeeze the trigger when the other man in the boat put his paddle in the water.

The resulting events occurred better than if Garrett had shot a spell at them. The canoe quickly capsized, spilling all three pursuers into the water. Garrett let out a shout of triumph, pounding his fist in the air and almost sending himself overboard. He staggered back, regaining his balance. He pointed at the two men and one woman sputtering in the water. "*Schrankes!*" he shouted, casting a spell that caused the river to freeze all around them.

"How do you like me now?" he taunted. He knew it would not hold them long but should provide them with enough time to get away.

He inspected the extent of the damage done to the boat as Carrie remained curled up in a ball on the floor of the raft. A section of the right side, the bow, was soft as was a portion of one of the seats. Otherwise the vessel was intact.

"Okay," he called to Carrie, beginning to paddle. "It's safe to sit up.

Carrie rose gingerly from the bottom of the raft, running her fingers through her well kept hair. Her face was puffy, perspiring from their strenuous activities. It was the first time he could remember her not looking like she had just left a beauty salon.

"We'll head down river until we find another campground or village or something. There's got to be plenty of places along the way," he said, looking hopefully at the shore.

Carrie sat still, breathing sharply. He thought about talking but did not know what to say. She was out of sorts and he had no clue how to comfort her. He was worried enough already for the both of them.

They had been floating on the river for over an hour with no sign of life. Garrett gauged their speed by observing the shadows of the trees lining the river. He calculated that their speed was about that of a fast walk. He began wondering if it would be safe now to stop at another campsite. After all, their pursuers should have thawed by now and could be anywhere in the woods.

After another half hour, there was still no sign of life. There was just the menacing forest taunting them as they floated down river anxious about what may happen once they left the relative safety of the boat. "It'll be okay," he said.

"I know," she whispered. He took a deep breath, thinking he tasted salt. No, it wasn't salt. It was blood. Had he bitten his lip sometime during all the commotion?

He noticed the bordering trees closing in rather suddenly and they were now moving a lot faster. Listening more intently, he heard an ominous sound. It was a deep growling roar like a train. They had reached a stretch of white water rapids.

"Oh God," Garrett mumbled, remembering the souvenirs they had seen earlier in the gift shop. Frantically, he tried to angle the boat toward shore. It was too late; they were trapped in the strong current. They came around a bend in the river and all hell broke loose. Garrett and Carrie were sucked into the unforgiving clutches of the river as it narrowed to a rocky gorge

Around the top edge of the rubber boat was a rope secured at intervals by eyelets. Garrett, realizing that neither one of them was skilled enough to navigate the rapids, grabbed hold of the rope on each side, spanning the craft with his outstretched arms. He yelled for Carrie to do the same. She could not hear him over the roaring water. However, she was watching him attentively and understood that she was to do the same. Unfortunately, her arm span was not as long as his. Therefore, she clasped both hands to one side instead and shoved her feet against the bottom of the opposite seat that Garrett was straddling.

At the exact moment, they hit the first serious turbulence. The boat twirled around like a bottle being spun by some invisible hand. Water rushed into the raft in blinding, drenching sheets. Garrett sputtered, trying to keep an eye on Carrie. The water was pelting his face making it nearly impossible to see her. Suddenly, he felt Carrie's body hit up against his. Desperate, he anchored her with his legs as best he could, still clinging tightly to the rope in his hands. The raft slammed into a rock, throwing the boat into a counter-clockwise spin.

Garrett strengthened the grip of his left hand then forced his right arm between the rope and the raft all the way up to his elbow. He bent that arm back around the rope, feeling the rope tear at the inside of his elbow as he tucked his fist under his chin anchoring himself to the boat that way. He then let go of the rope with his left hand and blindly searched for a way secure Carrie. He pulled her up to his chest, clutching her firmly around her waist with his legs.

They hit another grouping of rocks. She clung tightly to his neck as he clung tightly to the ropes once again with both hands, but still with his right arm bent under the rope. Water filled the cockpit as the raft pounded into a third set of rapids.

After what seemed like an eternity of hell, the water finally smoothed out. They were still spinning, churning downriver but without any sudden violent upheavals. Garrett cautiously opened his eyes, glancing out. It was not over. He continued to clutch the ropes, tightening his hold on Carrie.

With a tremendous upward surge the violent beating resumed. Garrett could feel his elbow start to burn in pain in response to the combination of pounding against the boat and rubbing against the ropes. He doubled the strength of his grip on the ropes and tightened his hold on Carrie even more as she bounced around as if she was unconscious. A new fear, one he had never felt before seized hold of him.

He was losing her. She was sliding down his body. He tried shifting to secure her more effectively with his legs more but during his attempt, she slipped free. Thankfully, as suddenly as the nightmare began, it was over. Carrie was still safely in the raft even though she had fallen once more to the floor.

Slowly still spinning, the raft all but stopped moving forward in relatively placid water. As the thundering noise of the rapids faded, the sides of the river fell away. Inside the raft, only ankle deep water remained as a souvenir of the nightmare. Garrett glanced around, spotting one of the oars floating in the water next to the raft. Luckily, it had been tied to the raft. He fished it out and used it to stop the raft from spinning.

"Well that was exciting," he said, smiling back at Carrie who remained sitting on the bottom of the boat in the water. The rush of adrenaline running through his system disappeared as he came to the realization that Carrie was still not moving. "Are you alright?"

Carrie took a deep breath, jiggling her head slightly. She tried to tell him yes but her appearance betrayed her. Garrett noticed for the first time that she was covered in blood. He fell on his knees next to her, spotting a bullet wound. She looked up at him lovingly, giving him a weak smile, saying not to worry. Yet, worry was what he did.

CHAPTER 18

Llewellyn led her two slaves through the woods. Her quest to capture and hurt Garrett burning through her veins as she battled through the wilderness with the two fools. She did not care what happened to her as long as Garrett died at the end of her wand. She was so angry; she nearly killed the men instead of just torturing the one that had stood up, causing the boat to capsize.

She glanced down at the little crystal ball she carried. It was hovering just above her hand. Inside of it, a foggy picture of Garrett and Carrie shone brightly. It was leading her toward her most hated foe. A smile crept across her face, spotting the blood on Carrie's body. One of the fools had actually injured her. The Rube had been useful after all.

"Well, it looks like you fools managed to hurt one of them but we need to get the other one. He is the key." She pushed a branch of a pine tree out of her way. Hearing the sound of the rapids just ahead, a sinister smile grew on her face. "They are just beyond those rapids!"

Using one of the paddles, Garrett guided the raft to shore. Jumping out and wading in the water, he pulled the boat the last four steps to solid ground. With the front safely on shore he went to the back of the raft that was still floating in water where Carrie was laying. She caressed his face with her right hand, squinting in pain. He worried she was slipping away, hearing her labored, shallow breath. A creaking sound escaped from her throat as she tried to speak. He turned the volume control up inside his head. The spell she had used on him earlier was still functioning.

"There is something I need to tell you, my love." She opened her eyes wide as if trying to memorize every atom of his features. "You are a father."

He was not expecting that. His legs buckled in shock and he stumbled on the slimy rocks which rested on the floor of the river. She smiled lightly at his surprised expression. "I found out the day you disappeared. That was the appointment I had."

Garrett took her hand. He could not believe what she told him. He felt anger raging inside him. He should have been with her instead of at the embassy. She touched his cheek, sensing his emotion.

"I am so sorry," he said, embracing her caress.

"I love you," her voice croaked weakly. "You must take care of our daughter now." She sucked in a shallow breath as a wave of pain prevented her from saying anything more.

He took her hand, feeling the wrath of pain that was searing through her veins. A crackling of leaves from the tree line startled him. Garrett looked up, expecting to see Llewellyn. Instead, standing at the tree line was a female white-tail deer, looking puzzled at seeing Garrett and Carrie there.

"Don't be afraid," Garrett said.

"Were you speaking to me?" Garrett focused on the deer. He could not believe the deer was speaking to him and he had heard it, her.

"No, but you can hear me?" Garrett asked, clutching Carrie.

"You can hear me?" The deer retuned, cautiously walking up to the waterline. She looked at Garrett, then back to the woods, ready to dart away at the first sign of danger. "I don't believe this. You can understand me," the small doe said in a quiet voice.

"You're telling me," Garrett said, battling tears that were struggling to break free. "Could you excuse me for a moment?" Garrett turned back to Carrie who was tugging on his shirt.

"They can help you," Carrie whispered, struggling to keep her eyes open. "You'll find our daughter at my parents. Tell her, tell her…" She blinked tears. Some were already dribbling down her cheek. She clutched his sleeve as another wave of pain pulled her into darkness.

"Noooooooo!!!!!" he screamed, looking up to the sky praying to God asking Him to intervene. The deer scrambled back to the safety of the tree line. Garrett did the only thing he could think of. He pointed his finger at Carrie. "*Schrankes!*" he cried. Tears exploding down his face like a waterfall. He swiveled his head looking for the deer.

He spotted her just at the tree line but it was no longer alone. Other animals had come to witness what had caused such an agonized cry. There were a couple of squirrels, a rabbit, a pair of chipmunks and a bear had just burst through the trees. They looked sorrowfully at him as they huddled about. The bear ventured the closest, coming near the raft and studying Garrett and Carrie. He could smell the scent of death hovering near. Looking back to the other animals, he shook his head sadly. He peered down at the ground, ready to go back into the forest.

"Wait," Garrett yelled, still clutching Carrie's frozen body. "I need your help." Garrett blinked his eyes as the bear stopped walking and looked over his shoulder at him. The animals treated the bear as if he were their leader.

"What," the bear grumbled. It was a deep, burly male voice that demanded respect.

"Your kind protected my ancestors just as my ancestors protected your ancestors." He gazed back at the unconscious Carrie, knowing he did not have much time. He hoped his plan would work. It had to work.

"Are you trying to tell me that you are a descendent of the boy who lived with bears?" the bear asked, confused; if bears could actually be confused.

"Have you had many conversations with humans?" Garrett asked with a forced smile, fighting the grief that was strangling his heart and throat. It felt like his throat had shrunk three sizes and was now too small to swallow properly.

The bear turned, studying Garrett. After a few moments, the bear laughed. "What do you want us to do?" Garrett walked up to the animals before beginning to whisper his instructions. He could smell the three villains closing in. Llewellyn was tracking him somehow. He could hear her telling the two rubes, "He's this way." Time was running out. The bear nodded in agreement before turning and rambling off into the woods followed by the others.

Garrett went back to Carrie. He grunted, lifting her out of the raft. She did not look heavy but still he struggled to carry her to shore. His arms were cold from carrying her. He wondered if the freezing charm had made her heavier. More determined than he had ever been in his life, he focused on energy and location. He was already as intent as any husband could be while his wife's life was hanging in the balance. He would not allow himself to be distracted even though he was aware of all that would be asked of him when returned.

The loud breaking glass echoed through the woods. Llewellyn gazed into the crystal ball and watched as Garrett teleported with Carrie in his arms. She cursed the officer in front of her. He fell to the ground, shaking in pain. There was no sign of Garrett in the glass orb. She clung to it, shaking it violently as if that would make him materialize. There was no way the charm she had put on him at the house could have worn off this fast. She knew that it should have allowed her to track him for at least a week.

Her fury rose. How could Garrett have relearned enough magic to thwart her so quickly? Yet, he had somehow perfected a charm to repel her greatest assets. Her bones still tingled with the ghost of pain caused by the curse she tried to perform on him.

Enchanting the non-magicals had been helpful. Garrett's troublesome wife would be out of the picture due to their efforts soon enough. Perhaps using these miserable creatures for other attacks would produce similar results. Right now, however, she needed to find Garrett and there was no way these fools could help her with that.

"Reveal your secrets?" she demanded of the crystal ball as she pointed her wand at it. In response to her command, the fog turned into a red haze. She turned it over in her hand, preparing to hurl it at the nearest tree. She screamed, making a throwing action with her arm but held onto the crystal knowing it was too vital to part with.

"Be quiet you two," Llewellyn ordered, silencing her slaves. The spell was removed from the cop. He staggered to his feet to continue searching for Garrett and Carrie unaware that they had vanished.

Llewellyn stared into the crystal. The red fog had returned to white. She glared at it, expecting to see where Garrett had gone. She turned away from the crystal with a scowl to silence her two companions again. A low growl began to grow louder. "I thought I told you to…" Her eyes caught the yellow glow of a grey wolf's eyes as it stalked out from under the cover of the bushes surrounding them.

She pulled out her wand, pointing it at the beast. "*Mor...,*" she began as a hawk soared down from the sky, snatching her wand before she could finish the murdering spell. "*Mordiiee... noooo...,*" she squealed, realizing her wand was gone.

Her two minions turned their weapons on the hawk. Before they could get a single shot off, two more hawks swooped down, snatching the weapons and dropping them deeper into the woods. They stared at the birds not believing what had just happened. They had been disarmed by birds of prey. Llewellyn turned to her two goons and saw that they were now empty handed and completely useless. She flung the crystal at the slowly approaching wolf.

The wolf caught the globe like a dog would catch a ball thrown by its master.

Behind the wolf stood the bear Garrett had talked to earlier by the water. He let out a heart stopping growl, slashing its claws in the air. The men's eyes bulged as they stumbled away from the beast, turning, ready to run. However, two of the wolf's pack were blocking their escape, silently snarling their teeth at them. The animals circled their captives as the hawks swirled overhead. More animals joined the group, securing the prisoners taking away any means of escape.

"Do Something!" Llewellyn ordered but the two men only watched as the animals kept circling, snarling anytime someone made even a slight move.

* * *

"Oye," a round sorceress yelped as Garrett and Carrie appeared. "Don't you know, you can't teleport in the middle of a health center? You need to enter through the door like normal civilized human beings. What would happen if everyone just showed up, bursting into your home without the chance to be invited in?" she ranted. Her blonde hair looked like a Dolly Parton wig. She wore dark red lipstick and a pink uniform. The uniform looked more like a business suit than the scrubs Garrett associated with the medical community. There was only one word for the uniform, ugly.

"I'm sorry," Garrett muttered breathless. He tried to say more, but he couldn't yet catch his breath. Therefore, he tried to lift Carrie higher in order to show the woman that he was carrying a person in dire need of medical attention.

"Well of course you're sorry," she continued lecturing, still not noticing Carrie or Garrett's struggle to remain standing as he continued to support Carrie's dead weight. "Young man, this is a place of healing not a place where you can just barge in like a barn party."

"I understand but I have an injured person here." The woman finally looked at Carrie.

"What would it be like if everyone that was injured just teleported here?" she started back up with a hint of disgust. She touched Carrie's bare arm, jumping back, surprised Garrett could hold on to something so cold. "She is terribly cold."

"I put a freezing charm on her to prevent her from passing on," he explained, saying the last words no louder than a whisper.

Just then Susan Medico came around the corner. Looking up from her chart, she spotted Garrett. "Garrett, you're not supposed to be here." she whispered harshly.

"Susan, thank God. Quick, Carrie's been shot." He lifted Carrie higher, hoping to get their full attention and focus on the fact that she desperately needed their help.

"Did you say that she had been shot with a non-magical weapon?" Susan asked, taking a curious look at Carrie.

"Yes," he said, exasperated with their lack of action. "I put a freezing charm on her, hoping to prevent her from..." He could not say the words again. He was too afraid.

"What made you think to do that?" she asked, beginning to run her wand over Carrie as if it were a rolling pin, just inches from actually touching her.

"It was the only thing I could think of. I recalled people surviving from falling through thin ice; the cold, the ice actually helping to keep them alive." He thought of having gone into the Chronicler Recital and Dean Belarus teaching him the charm. It did not seem like a wise idea to tell her.

"I just hoped it would be a good idea."

Susan waved her wand, summoning an examining table. "Please, set her down," she advised, crinkled her nose.

"This is not a drowning accident, Mister... umm?" The rude nurse added now looking at Carrie.

"Montgomery," he answered, beginning to worry that he might have actually harmed her more.

"Well Mr. Montgomery, I will advise you to not practice healing in the future. You are not a trained healer." She began to slowly move her empty hand over the wound.

"This girl is barely alive and is in need of immediate attention," Susan said to the round healer who was still standing there gawking at Carrie.

Garrett felt like curling into a ball as he looked at Carrie's pale white face. Closing his eyes, he felt his throat tighten.

"You're lucky Mr. Montgomery." Relief erupted inside of him from those few simple words of encouragement. "If you had been just a minute longer I doubt I could have saved her." She flipped her palm over, showing the single bullet which only moments ago had been buried inside of Carrie.

Garrett jumped as a cacophony of cracks announced the appearance of sorcerers and sorceresses teleported around him. The healer who had chastised him shook her head, mouth gaping open, indecisive on who she should yell at first. She kept looking at the ten armed Orohunters who had just broken one of her precious rules.

"Garrett Montgomery?" a sorcerer wearing an emerald green uniform asked, pointing his wand at the center of Garrett's chest.

"Who's asking?" Garrett did not know what to do. He was surrounded and very much overmatched. He did not know enough magic yet to get out of this. He could try to teleport but he suspected that the Orohunters had cast a spell over the healing center preventing his escape. That would explain why it had taken them so long to appear.

"My name is Thaddeus Louganis." He wore a brown fedora hat with a white silk sash around it, taking it off as he introduced himself, revealing his semi bald head. Garrett eyed him suspiciously. Thaddeus had lowered his wand but the other Orohunters kept their wands aimed directly at him. "I am the Commander of the United Magical World Federation."

"Am I supposed to be impressed?" Garrett couldn't help being cheeky, nervous at being outnumbered. "Couldn't come up with a shorter title?"

"I guess that would not impress you in your current state." He moved his hand in the air palm downward signaling for the other Orohunters, wearing purple uniforms and green berets, to lower their wands. Garrett noticed that they still held their scowls. "We heard you had lost your memory. That's a terrible fate for a sorcerer, to have spent three years without magic."

Garrett nodded; watching as a third healer came over and motioned for the other two to move Carrie from the area. Susan glanced back over her shoulder at him with a wink, a nod, and a smile as they wheeled Carrie away on the gurney. Satisfied Carrie was in safe hands with her childhood friend, he was ready for whatever the commander had in mind.

"Don't worry. She's in good hands here," the commander said.

Garrett turned his attention back to Thaddeus but his heart remained with Carrie. "What do you want with me?" Garrett asked.

"We have Nathaniel Skopector in custody. I understand his wife is also involved in the attacks against you."

"Yeah and I bet she's wishing she were with Nate right now," Garrett said, concluding that the commander was not a threat.

"What makes you say that?" Thaddeus asked, playing with his hat.

"She is being held captive back in the United States by some friends of mine."

Now it was Thaddeus turn to look puzzled. "I don't understand. Friends of yours have captured Llewellyn, the head of the Department of Orohunters?"

"Well, not actually people." A huge smile rose on Garrett's face imagining Llewellyn being chased through the woods by the animals.

"Where is she?" Thaddeus demanded, losing his patience; his tone growing sterner.

"She's in West Virginia." A blank look replaced the puzzled one on the commander's face. "You know, West Virginia a state in the United States." He told them how Llewellyn had used spells to get two people to hunt down him and Carrie and Carrie being shot. He went on to tell them of his gift, being able to communicate with animals, and how the animals had agreed to detain the three villains until the authorities arrived. He gave them directions to the woods but they all agreed that it would be wiser for Garrett to accompany them.

"Let me get this straight." The commander was shaking his head. "There is a forest full of animals that have captured the head of the Belgium Orohunters and two armed men?"

"I don't think the men will be armed anymore." Garrett smiled at the thought. He wanted to stay with Carrie but Thaddeus had convinced him that the healers would not let him anywhere near her. "Let's make this quick then" he dictated.

"Lead the way," Thaddeus said and they all teleported together back to the captives.

CHAPTER 19

Garrett led the posse of Orohunters back to the United States while his thoughts remained with Carrie. The venture back seemed like a fog, appearing next to the stolen raft. If anyone saw them they would think it a very strange sight. One person was dressed normally while the others... well, were not. Thaddeus was still wearing his emerald green uniform. It reminded Garrett of some sort of bizarre Marine dress uniform. Then there were the other nine Orohunters dressed in purple police like uniforms. They were prancing into the woods holding their wands out as if they were on military maneuvers.

"Nathaniel informed us he broke your wand," Thaddeus said, holding Garrett back, allowing the Orohunters to take the lead. Garrett did not bother to correct him. "You'd better wait here."

"Yeah, I'm sure your men can talk to animals, too." Garrett said, pushing his way ahead of the commander and the group.

"I didn't think about that," the commander said, following right behind Garrett.

It did not take long to find the prisoners. Llewellyn's voice was a beacon calling out to them; actually, it was more she was begging for rescue. The Orohunters stopped abruptly as the circling animals came into view.

"Should we curse them?" one of the men asked.

"Not unless you want to be attacked," another warned.

Garrett stepped closer to the area where the animals were holding the Goblin and her enchanted slaves. The three captives were standing in a circle with their backs to each other as their heads darted back and forth watching the animals circle them over and over. Five grey wolves stalked clockwise around the captives. Forming another ring, the bear Garrett had talked to earlier was pacing around the wolves in a counter clockwise fashion. Behind them all the other animals stood in a circle watching the three humans fiercely.

Garrett laughed as a brave little chipmunk broke through ranks of bears and wolves to chatter at Llewellyn's.

"Get away!" she screamed, dancing back as if afraid it would run up her leg.

"What did it say?" Thaddeus asked, biting back his own laugh while standing beside Garrett.

"How do you like me now?" Garrett watched as the little fellow scampered back, being very careful not to get stepped on. "Really, he's laughing at her for being so scared."

"I think I'd be scared, too." one of the Orohunters still standing behind them said.

"Lower your wands. It appears that Garrett's friends have everything under control," Thaddeus ordered, tucking his wand away.

The bears stopped circling as the biggest sauntered over to Garrett and stood on its hind legs, towering over him. It growled deeply at Garrett who in turn lifted his chin, exposing his throat. Thaddeus watched, expecting the beast to swipe at the easy kill. The bear only howled with what seemed like rage. Garrett's eye squinted as he breathed deeply, not backing down. The bear finally collapsed back to all fours.

Garrett growled, reaching out behind the bear's ears and scratching its rough fur.

"What..." Thaddeus began, keeping the bear in sight. "What did it say?"

"She asked if I'm the one who talks to the animals."

"Is that all?"

"No, but some things are private." The bear nodded as if understanding and lumbered over to the edge of the woods. The other bears followed their leader's example, coming up to Garrett for a quick pat before disappearing into the woods. Next came the wolves, growling as they passed the Orohunters who were replacing them as guards over the prisoners. Garrett petted each wolf in gratitude as they in turn gave him a lick of respect before following the bears into the woods. The other animals all chattered to Garrett. In response, he called back his thanks to each of them for all their help as they vanished into the darkness of the forest.

"You have ten minutes before the forest is theirs again," Garrett said, watching the brave chipmunk clamber up an old oak tree to watch them.

"We'll be gone in five," said Thaddeus as an Orohunter pulled Llewellyn over to them. Thaddeus pulled off her mask, dropping the bones on the ground in disgust. "You sicken me," he said to the woman.

"As you do to me," she retorted, spitting at him. The Orohunter brandished his wand, effectively gagging her.

"Take her back to the embassy with her husband," he commanded as two Orohunters led the two civilians passed them.

"What will happen to them?" Garrett asked

"We'll investigate to what extent the magic was used on them and how much of their activities where done by their own volition then modify their memories and return them to their previous lives."

"I think you'd better make sure that the other guy is in the cop's custody when you do return them." Garrett turned as the last of the Orohunters headed back to the river. "I bet that guy is in some kind of trouble with the law."

Thaddeus nodded. "I'll need to get your statement."

"I *need* to get back to my wife and find my daughter." Garrett lifted his jaw but not quite as high as he had to the bear.

"I understand." Thaddeus patted Garrett on the back. "You know, most people cower to me."

"I don't mean any disrespect but I don't know you." Garrett replied, standing his ground.

"I like you Garrett. Go take care of your family and we'll talk later."

Garrett nodded and disappeared.

When Garrett returned to the healing center he was careful to appear outside of the building. He did not want a repeat performance of his earlier visit. He slipped through the lobby without anyone taking notice of him. Unsure where to go, he followed the way he had seen them take Carrie earlier. He planned on asking the first nurse, or whatever they were called here, that he ran into. Unfortunately, the hall was eerily empty. He peered into open doors hoping to find Carrie or even someone that would show him the correct way. In which case, he would beg the person's pardon and ask directions. Again, luck was against him. All the open doors led to empty rooms.

Panic began to swell in his throat as he turned a corner and came to another hallway; this one with closed doors. He wondered if he was stuck in some sort of nightmare.

"Garrett," a voice called, startling him from behind.

He turned, thankfully it was Susan. "Oh thank God, Susan, where is she?"

"You can't be wandering the corridors unsupervised," Susan began lecturing, reminding him of the healer from before.

"I wouldn't have to wander if someone would just take me to Carrie," he countered his temper getting the best of him.

"You are so lucky. If Tabatha had found you..." she warned, motioning for him to follow.

"I don't feel lucky." Garrett hurried to catch up to her. "How's Carrie?"

"Resting," Susan answered in a matter of fact tone.

"What does that mean?" He grabbed her arm, stopping her and making her look directly at him. "I want to know how my wife is!" he demanded.

"She's better than when you brought her in, but she needs her rest. She's lost a lot of blood. If you had brought her here just a minute longer or hadn't frozen her to the degree you did... Well, I don't want to think about it." She looked down at his hand on her arm.

"Sorry," he released her. "It's just that I *have* got to see her."

"I understand but Tabatha is ranting and raving about you bringing so many Orohunters into the facility earlier and add to that you practiced healing."

"I saved her life; you said so yourself." They began walking again.

"That doesn't matter to her. She's a boglettor and you broke her rules." They turned into a hallway that he had overlooked before.

"A what?"

"Oh yeah, sorry, a boglettor is a type of sorceress that thrives on rules, taking them to extremes, unable to bend a rule or let a rule get broken without some sort of disciplinary action, unless it serves their purpose." They stopped in front of a door. "You broke a rule in front of a boglettor. Now, all the rules that are broken for the rest of today will be, in her eyes, because of you."

"I don't understand, but that doesn't matter. I'll just apologize to her."

"That will only make it worse. She'll see you as weak and want to punish you more. Besides, boglettors hold grudges, for a long time, too."

"But..," he began. He could think of no response to what she had told him.

"Go in, see Carrie and stay out of Tabatha's sight." She nodded to the door.

He looked at the door as his body became very cold. Shivering, he pushed the door open. The room was dark. Carrie was not alone in the room. There was a healer beside the bed checking over Carrie. He tried to swallow but his mouth had gone dry. He tried clearing his throat but it sounded like a croak.

The young sorceress looked up and saw him standing there. "She'll be fine," she said, pointing her wand at the lights overhead. Garrett walked up to the bed as the lights brightened. "She just needs to rest here for the night."

Garrett let out a sigh of relief noticing the color that had already returned to Carrie's face. Carefully, he took her hand, comforted by the warmth he felt there. His heart finally slowed from the racing pace it had sustained for so long that had swollen his throat. The lump there slid back into his chest allowing him to breathe properly. Carrie had been so cold even before he had cast his charm. He kissed the back of her hand, collapsing to his knees. He closed his eyes, laying his head on their entwined hands as a tear slipped down his cheek. He felt so tired.

"Should I contact anyone sir?" the healer asked from behind him. She conjured a chair and guided him to it.

He raised his head just a fraction, wanting to remain as close to Carrie as possible, to hear her heart and watch her breathing. "No, thank you. I'll do it as soon as she comes around. I need to be here when she does."

"Very good," she commented as she left the room, pulling the door closed on her way out.

Garrett lowered his head back to their joined hands, closing his eyes once more. He wondered if it was really over. He inhaled then giving into exhaustion fell asleep. Later he was awakened by a tickling on the back of his neck. Carrie's smiling eyes welcomed him back to life. She was brushing the back of his hair with her hand. Relief crept into his eyes.

"How do you feel?" he whispered worried his words would somehow cause her pain.

"Et- hem- better," she coughed, shifting to raise her head a little further. "How did you...?"

"With a little help from some friends." He smiled watching her puzzled eyes. He wanted to shout with relief; she was going to be all right. The healer had said that she would be but he had not truly believed it until he saw it for himself. "I went with some dude named Thaddeus to collect Llewellyn. Right now, I should go talk to your parents."

"Thaddeus?" she questioned, shifting further to sit up higher against the pillows.

"Yeah, he and some of his cronies jumped all over me right after we arrived here. He seemed upset that I didn't shudder in fear of him." Garrett flashed a smile.

"I don't understand." She crinkled her nose. He went on to tell her about all that had happened since she had passed out on the river, the freezing charm, the animals, his encounter with the boglettor healer and taking Thaddeus and the nine Orohunters to Llewellyn and her henchman. He smiled at realizing that she really was alright.

"What's her name?"

"Carrie Ellen," she answered. He looked at her, puzzled. "When I found the necklace I decided that she should have it. I figured that whatever protection it was to provide to me would be the same for her if we shared the same first name."

"Very wise," he smiled.

"You look so tired," she said, brushing at hair again.

"Hey, I'm fine." He claimed just before he yawned.

"Liar," she laughed. It was the sweetest laugh he had ever heard.

"Just worried about you," he added.

"But who is Thaddeus?" she asked

"Don't know," he shook his head. "He said he was the Commander of the United Magic something or something like that."

"You mean Thaddeus Louganis, Commander of the United Magical World Federation." There was a spark of recognition in her eyes as she pushed herself up.

"Yeah, that's it Thaddeus Lingos." Garrett did not notice the tension in her eyes.

"Thaddeus Louganis. Honey Señor Louganis holds the position like if all people in all the countries in the world electing a leader. He's that leader. He's just the most powerful sorcerer in the world."

"Why Señor?"

"Because he wants to be addressed that way, he's from Spain and so, prefers the señor title."

"Well, he's Thaddeus to me," Garrett said, standing up he was greeted by an aching in his knees. "I have to go see our daughter."

He thought of the house he had seen in the Chronicler Recital, the one where they met with Belarus and Carrie's parents. It was his daughter's house now. Instantaneously, he was standing just outside a small redbrick house, 19 Rosewill Drive. He walked up to the door and knocked.

"I'll get it," a ladies voice answered from inside. The door opened revealing Carrie's mother. She now had short red hair that framed her face. It was obvious Carrie got her beautiful looks from her. She was wearing an apron; Garrett concluded that it must be close dinner time. He had lost all track of time. "Oh, my Gosh!" she screamed, signaling Carrie's father to hurry over. His wand out prepared for anything, Marcus ran to the doorway to see what had caused his wife to scream. He stood about six inches shorter than Garrett.

"Thank the God's. I don't believe my eyes," Carrie's dad said in a thick Irish accent Garrett had missed before. Garrett was immediately pulled into a fierce embrace by both parents. Garrett was overwhelmed with the soaring emotion of joy they were feeling at his return. It was a sign of just how much he had been missed. He swallowed the very heavy lump in his throat as he shook his father in-laws hand, thinking their relationship must have improved greatly since that meeting around the dining room table.

"I'm sorry for coming like this," Garrett began.

"Don't be silly. Come in boy." Garrett found himself being drug farther into their home. "The stoop is no place for family to talk. Carrie told us she had found you but we didn't expect you show up like this."

"Where is she anyway?" Carrie's mother asked.

"That's why I'm here." This was even more difficult than he had expected. Actually, he had not thought about talking to them. He had just wanted to meet his daughter. Now he stood here before the man and woman he knew had been against him even dating Carrie and he was the reason she had been hurt.

"What do you mean?" Carrie's mother asked a wave of fear coursing through her. "What's happened to my baby?" She reached out for Marcus.

There was no better way to tell them so he just blurted it out. "She's at St. Luke's Medical Center. She was shot with a non-magical weapon. She's fine now. She'll be alright." He tried to reassure them even knowing they would not really believe him until they saw her for themselves. ""

"How did this happen?" Mark asked, looking like he was about to collapse.

"She'll be fine, go ahead and see for yourselves. Before you go, where is Carrie Ellen?"

"She's in her bedroom. You should be able to hear the singing," Mark answered, reaching for his wife's hand.

"I'll bring her along. You two go on and see Carrie. You won't be satisfied until you do." They nodded leaving Garrett alone. He followed the singing that was coming from the end of the hall. Behind one of the doors he could hear two voices sing. Anxiety swept through him as he fought for the right words to say. He took a moment to listen to the little voice on the other side of the door. A little laugh escaped him as he heard his own voice singing along with the little girl. There was a piano playing and the faint echoes of bells ringing could be heard in the background.

> *When the sun goes down, I see no reason for you to cry, we've been through this before. In every time, in every season, God knows I tried. So please don't cry any more. Can't you see it in my eyes, I don't want to have to say good bye. But night calls for us to part. Carrrrrrrieeeee, morning will bring a new day. Ohhhhh, ohhh, Carrrrrieeee, Carrrrrrieeeee maybe we'll dream together somewhere out there. I can read your mind; my heart answers with no ill intention. I wish I could explain. It takes some time. It takes a lot of patience. Well be together again, so dream and you'll find me there. I don't want this to be good bye. Carrrrriiee, Carrrri-ieee, ohhhh we'll be together soon my love. Ohhhhh, Carrrrrieee, Carrrriieeee, maybe tomorrow you'll seeeeee.*

His voice faded, giving way to a guitar solo. However, Garrett listened as his little girl sang her own words to the music behind the closed door. His voice once again joined in with the music

> *Can't you see it in my eyes that it's never good-bye? Ohhhh, ohh, Carrriee, Carriieee, Ohhh, Ohhh, things will change.*

Carrrrriiieee, Carrrriieeee we will be together again somewhere out there, when we dream.

Garrett knocked on the door as the song ended. "Yes," a small voice with a heavy English accent answered. He could hear her scrambling to the door. He should have had one of her grandparents break the news to her. She was going to be in for a shock. He was a strange man standing in the doorway of her bedroom. This was wrong.

"What is it?" she asked, opening the door. She screamed at seeing him standing there before her. To Garrett's surprise it was not a scream of panic but a scream of delight. It was the scream of a young girl at a rock-and-roll concert. She ran to him, throwing her arms around neck. He hugged her back. "Tell me I'm not dreaming," she pleaded as she clung to him.

"It's not a dream, honey," he answered, tears streaming down both their cheeks. He did not know what to expect and was not prepared to be accepted this quickly. Three years of deep loneliness erupted in him, silent tears gushing down his face, tears of love; the love of a two-year-old girl finally meeting her father.

"I was just watching you and listening to you," she told him, leading him into her room. He saw a miniature him being projected from a disk that reminded him of a DVD was singing in the room. It was a transparent, interactive, three dimensional recording "Where's mommy, she told me she was going to bring you home?"

"She wanted to, but she's been hurt. She's going to be fine though. She's at St. Luke's." Garrett's heart began to break, spotting the pain in his little girl's eyes. He could see tears begin to swell in Carrie Ellen's eyes. He was afraid he would start crying again himself. "I'm taking you to go see her right now. Grandma and grandpa are already there. Have you teleported before?"

She shook her head, fighting back the tears. She was so brave, his little girl. Pride swelled inside of him at. He knew she was scared because her mommy was hurt, but she was pretending to be so strong. She did not trust her little voice though and she felt as if she was to take a deep breath she would cry again.

"Well, I have and it's a bit scary. I could really use your help getting back to mommy." She nodded, offering a little smile. "Okay, I need you to take hold of my arm and hold on tight. That'll help me not be so scared. Okay?"

"Okay," she whispered softly, no trace of tears.

"I know you will, honey. Now, it's important you keep a tight grip on me especially if you feel like you're being pulled away." She nodded again. "Excellent, now please go ahead and take a real strong hold on my arm. Wow, that's strong."

She grasped his arm even tighter with both of hers and squeezed her eyes shut. "That's great, honey." He got the impression that once she seized hold of him he was going to have a difficult time getting her to release him. "We're going to go on the count of three. Ready?"

"Yes, daddy," she answered, still holding him tightly with all her might.

"One- two-three..." They were hurled away from the house.

Garrett led Carrie Ellen to her mother's room, amazed at finding her parents standing outside the room rather than inside with Carrie Anne. "What's going on?" Garrett asked while his heart started to race. Carrie Ellen still had her arms wrapped around his neck. Was there something wrong? He pushed through his in-laws and into his wife's room.

"What's going on?" Garrett asked, bursting into the room and finding Thaddeus Louganis and two of his shadows standing at Carrie's bed.

"Garrett," Thaddeus answered, turning with a smile. "We were just finishing up with your wife."

"I don't care what you were doing. You have no right being in here and bothering her," Garrett roared. "Get out now!"

Carrie Ellen tightened her hold on Garrett feeling his rage.

"There is no need for you to raise your voice," one of Thaddeus companions lectured, positioning himself between Garrett and Thaddeus. "You are scaring the little girl."

"This little girl is none of your concern and I don't need a lecture from a crony," Garrett roared, raising his voice even further. Carrie Anne flinched in her bed stunned by Garrett's protectiveness. She struggled to sit up. "You need to leave now!"

"If you won't think about your wife's health, maybe you'll think of your daughter," the other crony retorted.

"I warned your buddy not to..." Garrett began to advance on the sorcerers as the door burst open.

"What's going on in here?" a voice called, roaring even louder than Garrett. He turned, expecting to see his mother-in-law. Instead, he saw the healer who had chewed him out when he had first arrived with Carrie in tow. "I should have known it was you."

"There are too many people in here," she barked, glaring at Garrett before turning her regard to the others in the room including Carrie's parents. They had followed her into the room.

"We had just finished up here," Thaddeus repeated, giving Tabatha a nod. She responded back with respect, knowing who Thaddeus and the cronies were. "Garrett, could I have a word with you outside, please?"

"Yes, I think you should step out of the room for a moment," the angry healer bellowed.

Carrie nodded, her eyes smiling at him. Carrie Ellen climbed out of her father's arms and climbed in bed with her mother, watching the men leave. Garrett followed Thaddeus out the door with the two Orohunters following closely on their heels. Garrett was surprised that Carrie's father Marcus had also followed them.

Once they were all outside the room and the door was shut, Thaddeus turned to face Garrett. "All right then, I just wanted to say that I really admire you Garrett." The anger Garrett was feeling quickly vanished. He had been unprepared for the compliment. Thaddeus really was not used to people standing up to him.

Garrett nodded not knowing what to say.

"Your wife has explained all of what has happened to you and I am impressed." He paused, realizing that what he thought of Garrett had little meaning to Garrett. He let out a slight laugh as he began to explain further. "I do like you Garrett as I said before. You are not intimidated by me and you treat me like a normal human."

"You are," he retorted, looking the man square in the eye, thinking it was a stupid statement.

"Thank you," Thaddeus actually began to blush as if this was the greatest compliment he had ever been given. "I would just like to shake your hand and ask if it would be all right to visit you after the trial."

"The trial?" Garrett seemed puzzled, not thinking there would be something as civilized as a trial.

"Why yes, you captured Llewellyn." Thaddeus shook his head still not believing the turn of events.

"Pretty weird, the entire thing, if you ask me," Garrett said, thinking he ought to say something.

"I guess it would seem that way to you." He raised an eyebrow as he looked at Garrett. "It is a shame that there are Rubes and sorcerers out there who seem to have a need to take others' lives."

The healer came out of the room glaring at Garrett. Garrett noticed her politely nodding to the embassy officials. Well, he wasn't there to win a popularity contest.

"Well, it looks as if you're free to return to your family. I would just like to shake your hand before we leave." He put his hand out for Garrett to shake.

Garrett looked at it for a moment, thinking the man had a habit of telling people what to do. "Yes," he said as he took the man's hand and shook it.

"I'm sorry?" Thaddeus asked as they shook hands.

"I would enjoy speaking with you after the trail." Garrett smiled, wondering if he could be friends with the man.

"Excellent, we have trespassed upon you long enough; you should be with your family. However, I would like you to think about your assignment now that you have returned." He nodded at his two shadows. Garrett and Marcus watched them vanish around the corner.

"My assignment?" Garrett asked, looking to Marcus for clarification.

"Once an Orohunter, always an Orohunter."

Garrett walked into the room smiling. Carrie Ellen squirmed free from the bed and jumped back into his arms. Carrie's parents beamed at Garrett as if he were the head of the United Magical World Federation. "Well, the nurse sure doesn't like me," Garrett said, trying to break the tension.

The group exploded with laughter, leaving Garrett looking around confused. Then just shook his head and walked over to the bed wanting to be closer to his family. "Honey, they're not called nurses. We call them healers." Carrie Anne took his hand, giving it a squeeze. "Besides, that healer does not like me much either. She is Tabatha Lovegrove, a boglettor. She went to school with us and had a huge crush on you. She even slipped you a love potion once but you were too enticed by me." She was gloating now.

"Perhaps it was you who gave me the love potion," he teased, resting a leg on the bed and smiling at his in-laws.

"Watch it mister." She gave him a playful swat. "Remember the chest hair." He clutched his hand to his shirt as if trying to keep anything from being put down it.

"I can't believe you talked to Thaddeus that way," Cassidy said.

"He admires daddy," Carrie Ellen stated, beaming up at him, still clinging to his arm.

"What?" Marcus asked.

"He just appreciates being treated like a normal person. Too many people follow him around, kissing the ground at his feet," she answered as if she had been part of the conversation.

CHAPTER 20

Garrett stood in the middle of a large rectangle room surrounded by women and men peering down on him from their seats. His stomach tightened as the urge to be sick seized him. He felt like he was in a play and had forgotten his lines, the audience gazing down at him examining his every word his every gesture as if he were a new species of animal in the zoo. Next to him were two large wooden chairs with steel restraints. At the north end of the room sat the practitioner. Carrie Anne had explained the night before that was the one who would marshal the proceedings until Thaddeus took over the duties. He had been the one to introduce Garrett and had him walk down the stairs to the stage. To one side of the room, sitting next to the ambassador was Carrie's father Marcus and Carrie Ellen. He realized that this was the furthest he had been separated from her since their reunion.

Garrett had believed her to be too young for this but her mother had disagreed, arguing that Carrie Ellen needed to see for herself that the people who had kept her father from her were going to be punished. She would have no doubt that her family was safe. He smiled up to his little girl, watching her smile and wave back at him. He felt reassured with her there. A warm feeling spilled over him, telling him his wife was right. His wife; it was still strange thinking of Carrie Anne that way.

The double oak door on the south end of the room banged open causing him to jump. Carrie Anne had warned him this would happen. It still caught him off guard. Llewellyn and Nathaniel Skopector were ushered into the room by six Orohunters. Garrett's mouth went dry noticing the determined expressions on the prisoner's hollow faces, their hands shackled in front of them.

Jeers rang down from the crowd. Garrett glanced about surprised that there was not an empty seat to be found. While looking around, he noticed there were people actually sitting on the stairs and others standing all along an upper balcony. How long had it been since there was a hearing like this? He wondered to himself. The crowd hissed as the prisoners continued their journey to the wooden seats. Garrett chuckled as he heard chants of condemnation ringing through the crowd.

Garrett swallowed hard as the two villains were forced into the seats beside him. He hated being this close to them, even hearing the steel restraints echo over the crowd's jeers securing the Skopectors grated along his already tense nerves. Garrett shivered as a steel cage came out of the floor surrounding the Goblins. He felt their rage burn for him as strong as the odor of fear that also assaulted him. He looked to his wife for support. Her eyes met his and in them he found a strength he never knew he had. He would never be able to explain to her the power she gave him.

Another bang of the doors caused him to jump and look back again. Garrett turned, watching three men walk in. The first was Thaddeus Louganis with his emerald green uniform and brown fedora hat. He looked very distinguished marching with such a firm look on his face. The audience saluted him, standing and rapping their wands against the seat in front of them.

The other sorcerers marched precisely two paces behind him, forming a perfect triangle. Garrett wondered how many times they had rehearsed it before getting it right. He briefly wondered who the other two men were. They were wearing brilliant red uniforms and funny green berets. The gentlemen's faces were also stern and their eyes were staring straight ahead. Together the three men marched to the other end of the room to the exact center.

Thaddeus took his wand out from somewhere inside of his uniform, waving it extravagantly in the air. There was a sound as if someone was trying to skip large pieces of concrete along a sidewalk. Garrett watched in amazement as an arched stairway appeared out of nowhere, three chairs sitting along the top. He would never get used to having magical abilities, he thought to himself. Thaddeus climbed up the stairs followed by the other two men. The three seats at the top were setup so that once the trio was settled they again formed the odd looking red and green triangle.

Thaddeus raised his hands signaling for the chorus of wand tapping to cease. "Since the criminal activities performed by these two occurred across two continents, it is the responsibility of the United Magical World Federation to preside over this hearing rather than any specific Charter." He stopped to clear his throat before continuing. "We are here to determine the guilt or innocence of Nathaniel Skopector and Llewellyn Skopector; husband and wife." There was another round of jeers as the names were spoken followed by more rants of condemnation. Garrett appreciated their display of displeasure. Thaddeus waited for the crowd to calm down before continuing.

"We have already witnessed testimony of their crimes from Orohunters Garrett and Carrie Montgomery. The crowd began tapping their wands again. Garrett blushed looking up. He shook his head, spotting his father-in-law making rude faces at the Goblins while his daughter joined in blasting raspberries at them. He could not help but smile and nod; grateful for the salute he was being given. A lump grew in his throat making it difficult to swallow as his eyes watered. He stood at attention before giving a slight nod to acknowledge their warm welcome. He looked toward the sorcerer in charge of the hearing who was once again waiting for the crowd to quiet.

"Orohunter Garrett Montgomery had to endure three years of a life without magic because of these foul creatures." The crowd resumed their chorus of hisses, boos and his daughter's raspberries. Garrett noticed her grandfather copying her along with a couple of other sorcerers now and laughed. This time Thaddeus did not wait for the noise to end. "These animals murdered Rodney Burton a faithful wizard who served the embassy with honor. His record will be expunged of any wrong doing."

Garrett gave a slight bow of respect and closed his eyes to hide the tears forming in his eyes. He could still only recall a few moments of the time he had spent with Rodney but in his heart there was the connection of shared experiences resulting in the love for a friend, truly a man who was part of the family. The pain in his gut over his death made it difficult to stay composed. He felt his heart swell in his throat as he thought of the man whose last act of service was fetching bandages. To get it together, he swallowed hard, took a deep breath and once more looked deep into Carrie Anne's eyes. Once again, he was ready to face whatever came next.

"Furthermore, this detestable pair is responsible for the murders of two non-magical individuals in the United States. They pursued Mr. and Mrs. Montgomery causing harm to them both and abusing magic along the way to include using it to control non-magical people for their evil purposes."

More hisses of loathing for the prisoners rang down but Thaddeus again did not wait for quiet. He continued on, saying, "The injuries sustained by Orohunters Carrie and Garrett Montgomery nearly resulted in their deaths."

Garrett looked up to see Carrie Anne still standing there eyes glued to him. She testified earlier and now waited for him to finish. He knew her eyes had never left him. She was prepared for another Goblin attack, keeping a watchful guard over him. There were no more secrets for either of them. Standing beside her was Sheba and Reginald. Garrett nodded to them knowing that their contribution had been ignored but he still acknowledged that their service had been just as vital. He was in their debt for all they had done to keep Carrie safe and bring them back together.

"What say you members of this high inquisition?" Thaddeus asked.

There was a calamity of noise as the crowd erupted with loud verdicts of guilt. They proclaimed their decision so strongly that Garrett nearly stumbled into the cages from the resounding echoes. He was sure they roared loud enough for all of Brussels to hear.

The two prisoners glared through their cage at him. He could feel their hatred in their eyes, finally realizing the depth of their desire to harm him. It was as if they were pressure cookers and only he could hear their steaming cries of hatred. He glared at them wanting to invoke his own punishment.

"Prisoners, do you have anything to say before sentencing?" Thaddeus asked, looking down at the prisoners for the first time.

Llewellyn said nothing. She sat there, cursing the courtroom dignitaries and audience members alike with her eyes. Garrett thought, if she could cast a spell with those eyes, he and the three court members would surely be dead and the others in the room severely maimed.

Nathaniel was another story. His jaw tightened into a stern expression. Garrett imagined his glare sending waves of shivers down the spines of all his former students. He vocally cursed the panel claiming they would have dire misfortune for dare judging great warlocks the likes of him and his wife. He continued on, proclaiming that he and his wife were above any court and cursing all the witnesses and anyone and everyone who dared to hiss and/or boo at them. He pledged retribution for the humiliation leveled against him and his wife, claiming they should all live in fear for when the Goblins rise again.

"The prisoners have earned themselves a life long ban to Smag Bluc Prison," Declared Thaddeus. Garrett had learned that Smag Bluc Prison was a prison somewhere near the South Pole buried deep beneath one of its glaciers. The panel was disappointed that they could not sentence them to a harsher punishment.

"Who gave you your orders?" Garrett barked at the Skopectors as the crowd began to resume its jeering of the criminals.

"You will suffer the most," Nathaniel threatened. "Your pain will be unfathomable."

"Perhaps if you took responsibility…" Garrett suggested, all but pleading for Llewellyn to give up the name and confess to being just a lackey to someone else's evil machinations.

"Responsibility, don't you preach responsibility to us you half-breed," Llewellyn cackled as their cages began to shake. "You have only begun to learn what misery life has in store for you. You will have your reckoning. You will be forced to take responsibility for all of your crimes against the magical world."

There was a loud crack as both cages vanished.

Thaddeus and the other two officials sat down. Carrie Anne had explained that this would signal the conclusion of the proceedings and those in attendance would begin to leave. Garrett was to wait for her. Therefore, he remained standing in the center of the room as his family rushed down to him. Carrie Ellen led the group, hopping down the stairs two at a time, only as a nearly three year old girl could do.

Once the room emptied of all but Garrett, his family and the colorful trio of officials, the trio stood up and walked down to the others. "We would like to commend you on the capture of these Goblins." One of the red uniformed officials congratulated, extending a hand.

"Thaddeus, I was curious, what are you going to do concerning the leader?" Garrett asked, adjusting his hold on Carrie Ellen as she squirmed in his arms.

"Leader?" the other red uniformed official asked. "You have captured the leader, I dare say boy."

"I'm referring to the Goblin in bright orange robes I saw while using *leer poma* on Nathaniel." The three men looked at each other as if they did not want to have this conversation. Finally, Thaddeus extended his hand to Garrett.

"I'm sorry Garrett," he claimed as they shook hands. "We have found no evidence supporting there being anyone else involved."

"I know they were taking orders from someone else," Garrett protested, shaking his head, dissatisfied with their conclusion and lack of action.

"You are entitled to your opinion but the evidence does not support that." The first red uniformed man argued. "And we ask that you, please, not vocalize your opinion on the matter, spreading panic throughout the magical community."

"You've got to be kidding?" Garrett could not believe it. "You're not really this thick are you?"

Thaddeus separated himself from the other two, signaling for Garrett to walk with him. Garrett set Carrie Ellen down as she glared at Thaddeus in disgust. "I know you have your own theory and that you have been through a tremendous ordeal. However, there is no proof either way. What is important right now is your readjustment to life as an Orohunter."

Garrett took a deep breath, closing his eyes. He wanted to argue about there being a ring leader but realized that it would be pointless. The authorities had come to their own conclusion and would not be swayed to change it. Therefore, when he opened his eyes he elected to follow the change in subject. "Upon my return one of the things I found most alarming was the way my family was treated."

"How is that?"

"You see," Garrett paused, choosing his words carefully. "They were unable to prove I was dead. Therefore, no support was provided."

"I don't seem to understand." He looked questioningly at Garrett. "You were not dead. You stand before me right now as living proof of that fact."

"Well, my family would have been financially provided for if I would have died while working at the embassy, in the line of duty so to speak."

"That is correct. However, as I just said, there is proof that you were not dead. You are standing right in front of me. Therefore, there is nothing to be received. You were an embassy official, classified as missing in action if I am not mistaken."

"I'm sorry, sir but if I was not dead, than I was still working for the embassy?" Garrett asked.

"I thought I just explained that." Thaddeus looked back at Garrett's family in confusion, began to shuffle his feet, realizing where Garrett was leading.

"Thus, I am due three years back pay," Garrett asserted.

"I don't see..." one of the red uniformed men began. Thaddeus raised a hand, halting the man's protest.

"Yes, I understand your view and may I add that you and Carrie are due a sizable reward for the capture of the Goblins responsible for these attacks." He nodded to Garrett. "I'll make sure you are adequately compensated immediately."

Garrett nodded back, wondering if the friendship he had begun with Thaddeus had changed. "Thank you."

"With that out of the way, I have considered the problem of how best to have you re-enter your service to the embassy." Thaddeus' eyes narrowed as he watched Garrett carefully.

"There is still a lot of magic I need to relearn," he replied, glancing back to Carrie Anne for any kind of clue as to where this conversation was leading.

"I think he deserves some time to get reacquainted with his family," Carrie stated, seizing Garrett's arm.

"If we are going to honor his three year *paid* vacation," one of the red uniformed men interrupted, "I can't see how we can honor any more time off."

Again Thaddeus raised his hand, ceasing Carrie's objection before it began. "As I understand it, Garrett is no longer in possession of a wand."

Carrie began to answer but she caught Garrett's eye, warning her not to contradict Thaddeus. "Umm, Nathaniel did snap a wand while we were being held captive."

"I see," he paused, carefully considering the possibilities. "Garrett, however, you were still able to teleport without the service of a wand?"

"I was able to bring Carrie to St. Luke's, yes," he answered, not completely untruthfully.

"Very powerful for a sorcerer to accomplish such a thing," one of the red uniformed officials said.

Garrett began to wonder if Thaddeus did suspect that the wand had not actually been destroyed after all.

"Are you comfortable being in America?" Thaddeus asked casually.

"Yeah," Garrett answered, not making a connection.

"Excellent, you'll have one week to get your affairs in order, then you shall enter the FBI field training program." Thaddeus nodded indicating that he was very happy with the way things were turning out.

"But...," Garrett began to plead but Thaddeus raised his hand, silencing him as if the act was magic.

"In the evenings, you'll be allowed to teleport home. And, let me see... Ah yes, we'll have Reginald here join you for the training."

Sheba and Reginald had just made their way over to the group.

"Join who, where?" Reginald asked.

"You'll be assigned to the American's FBI field training program along with Mr. Montgomery here." one of the red uniformed men informed him.

"You'll have to be assigned different rooms to prevent any chance of the American's noticing anything out of the ordinary," the other red uniformed man added.

"The Americans will probably separate them due to their different nationalities anyway." Thaddeus commented.

"When do we leave?" Reginald asked eagerly, ready to begin.

"Next week," Carrie answered obviously uncomfortable with the development.

"Well, it seems as if everything has been covered. It is time for us to take our leave," Thaddeus said to his two companions.

Carrie Ellen could no longer wait to hug her Daddy again, running over and jumping into Garrett's arms. "Daddy what are we going to do with all that money?"

Garrett glanced over at his in-laws before smiling at his wife. "Well first all, I think we should buy our own home somewhere near Canterbury. That way we can get a dog and a cat for a very special little person."

"Oh, Daddy," she squealed, hugging him.

"I also think it would be nice to purchase some land in West Virginia and use it as a wild life refuge." Garrett looked to Carrie, silently asking her opinion. She nodded her approval. "I think we owe some friends there at least that much."

"What else, Daddy?"

"Well, I think we should take Reginald here to the barber and have his hair done properly before he goes to the FBI."

They began walking down the hall. "You know what else I want Daddy?" she asked as they stopped to wait for the lift.

"No sweetie, what?" he asked, looking down into her large brown eyes, holding her hand.

"I want to hear you sing that song."

"I tell you what," he began, "when we get home, I'll sing you any song you want and then I'll write one just for you."

"Really, Daddy?" The doors to the lift opened and they stepped inside.

"Absolutely," he promised as the lift doors slid quietly shut. "I think with you and mommy there isn't anything I can't do." The elevator doors jangled close.

EPILOGUE

Back in the United States, somewhere near the Georgia and Florida border an elderly couple was driving home from the bingo hall. A young man wearing black jeans and a black t-shirt stood beside the road watching them drive by. He gave a sinister smile.

"Why the devil is that fool wearing dark clothes at twilight, standing beside the road?" the old man cursed. "He's just begging to get hit."

"Easy now Delbert, it's not like it's pitch black out here." She was the one driving the gray Mercedes, glancing out the rearview mirror at the boy. "Was he wearing black lipstick and pink eye shadow?"

"The devil is in these kids, I tell you Rose," the man complained, wrinkling his mouth as if finding something disgusting on the bottom of his shoe.

"The Devil is not in me yet, old Del." The boy laughed, watching the car pass over a hill and slipping out of sight. "But you and wrinkly old Rose can ask him when he will be coming for me."

About two miles further down the road Delbert was still telling himself to put the boy out of his mind. However, a hundred yards later, in the opposite lane, the boy stood waving his arms as if trying to flag them down. Rose eased off the accelerator preparing to stop.

"I told you he was wearing lipstick. Isn't that interesting?" Rose thought nothing about how the boy had managed to get ahead of them.

"Woman, what the hell is wrong with you? Don't you dare stop this car!" he hollered at Rose who added pressure to the gas, obeying his order. She looked offended by Delbert's tone but continued to speed away.

"What has gotten into you Del? That boy could be in trouble." She looked back in the rearview mirror but she did not see him. The last bit of sunlight vanished engulfed by the dark, too quickly she thought.

"That boy is trouble," Delbert protested.

"Now Delbert," Rose began but was interrupted.

"Are you telling me, it doesn't strike you as odd that this fella is two miles ahead of where we last saw him?"

The realization of the impossibility struck her like a snake attack. "How?" she muttered.

"How the hell should I know you old wart-hog?"

"Easy Delbert," a calm voice that was neither his nor Roses warned from inside the car. The blood drained from their faces as they saw the same boy in front of them but closer to the median this time. There would not be enough time for Rose to stop. They were either going to hit him or miss by mere inches.

The young man stood, boldly waving a finger as if scolding them. He smiled and laughed, waiting.

Delbert felt the urge to snatch the wheel and make sure they hit the man but he could not move. This was not natural. He squeezed his eyes shut, tensing up, expecting to hear the car clip the fool. He counted because that was all he could think of to do. Count the seconds until they hit the thing, count the seconds in a kiss, a lifetime, he grunted and prayed for the car to hit him.

"One, two, three… eight," he opened his eyes, seeing nothing but the road. "Where'd he go?" he asked, swiveling to look back. He expected Rose to say "who", hoping he had been dreaming. There was no way a crazy boy could have been standing in three different spots as they drove past.

"I don't know," She answered in a shaky, uncertain voice.

Her answer confirmed that this was not a dream. She had seen him, too. He closed his eyes not wanting to see him again.

Rose must not have seen the man in black again. She hadn't made a sound. The only thing he heard was his heart beating and the whining of the Mercedes engine. He let out a deep breath, finally feeling it was safe to open his eyes when a voice deep inside warned not to after all.

The boy suddenly appeared on the hood of the car as if it were a proper place for a person to travel on. He knelt on his knees resting his face against the windshield as if trying to get a better look at their fear, as if they were animals on exhibit at the zoo.

Rose screamed, jerking the wheel, sending the car into a swerve as if they were on an icy road rather than a dry summer night in northern Florida. Delbert thought she was trying to throw the man off the car. It should have been easy, but this was not a normal boy. There was nothing for him to hold onto; yet, he did not fall off. He just smiled, showing his teeth, enjoying the ride.

She jerked the wheel the other way but the boy just threw his head back roaring with laughter. She kept tugging at the wheel as if riding a mechanical bull, attempting to dislodge its rider. With hands sweaty with fear, Rose lost her grip of the steering wheel. It began spinning on its own as if the tires could turn 360 degrees. Smoke rose from the steering wheel as it spun around and around.

The car would not obey. The steering wheel just rocked back and forth as if a four-year-old was playing with it.

The passenger's side tires hit loose gravel, sending the car into a turn, sliding off the road. The car tumbled down an embankment into a drainage channel running parallel to the road. The Mercedes swiftly began sinking into the muck. It was just deep enough. The car was at an odd angle, with the passenger side sinking first. The driver side stayed afloat for just a moment longer before gravity began sucking it into the muddy waters, too.

From the embankment, the young man sat on his hunches, watching the sinking vehicle as another wider man magically appeared next to him. "There you are. Who were they?"

"Quiet Chirper," the first boy commanded. "I don't want to miss any of this." Casting a spell, allowing them to see inside the car, he and his companion continued to watch the gruesome scene. The Mercedes was now completely submerged beneath the water and muck; the headlights giving the water an eerie glow. Lights magically came on inside the vehicle. The windows were closed; none had shattered as it had crashed down the embankment.

The old woman was already dead. A blood vessel had burst in her head when the steering wheel had begun to spin out of control. Her limp body pressed against the seat by the seat belt.

"Shame she died already," the boy in black said to the new arrival.

"What'd they do to you, Joe?"

"They didn't stop. Now, shhh.... The best is yet to come."

The old man freed himself from his seat belt. Water had filled the car quickly but an air bubble was hanging over Rose. Like a fish the old man attacked the air bubble with his mouth, puckering his lips, inhaling air. He squeezed his lips together as the last of the air surrendered to the water. The old man could see outlines of the two thugs sitting on the embankment.

Joe's eyes met Delbert's. There were no pleas for help. The old man accepted the fact that he was going to die and he was ready to join his wife in the hereafter. Joe snapped his fingers, shattering the windows, spilling more water and glass on to Delbert.

"That was cool," Chirper said with a cheery voice.

"Okay, what do you want?" Joe looked annoyed at having to share his fun.

"I was told to tell you that *he* is back."

"Who's back?" They began walking away from the canal.

"Garrett," Chirper said almost as a sigh. "Now it's our turn."

"Excellent, let the games begin."

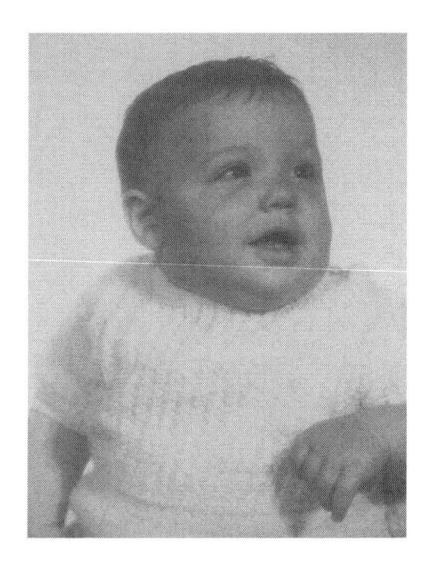

About the Author

Christopher Andrew Burton shares time raising his only child in Michigan while also enjoying sports, reading and playing poker. When his son was born in 1998, Chris gave up his dream to be a writer to get a "real job". However, his son's passion for reading books led Chris to return to his love of writing books.

Chris attended college at Saginaw Valley State University in Michigan where he majored in Psychology and Creative Writing. During his time at college, he spent a semester studying abroad in England, Scotland, France, and Belgium.

Chris is a descendent of the Iroquois on his mother's side and Blackhawk on his father's. This is a large part why Chris aspires to continue writing the Orohunter series evolving the magic in the books, and always including Native American history. *Orohunter: 5th Pentacle of the Sun* is his first work to be published. He is currently working on *Orohunter: A Year to be Remembered*, *Mind Crimes: Birth of Betrayal* and *This Side of a Dream* a book of poetry.

Made in the USA
Charleston, SC
13 November 2011